THE GIRL DOWNSTAIRS

IAIN MAITLAND

INKUBATOR
BOOKS

Published by Inkubator Books
www.inkubatorbooks.com

Copyright © 2021 by Iain Maitland

ISBN (eBook) 978-1-7398132-3-9
ISBN (Paperback) 978-1-7398132-2-2

Iain Maitland has asserted his right to be identified as the
author of this work.

THE GIRL DOWNSTAIRS is a work of fiction. People, places,
events, and situations are the product of the author's
imagination. Any resemblance to actual persons, living or
dead is entirely coincidental.

PRAISE FOR IAIN MAITLAND'S BOOKS

The Girl Downstairs

"No-one does uncanny like Iain Maitland. *The Girl Downstairs*, a tale of poignant grief, explodes into unimaginable horror." -Barbara Nadel

The Scribbler

"One seriously weird killer and an engaging cop-partnership dynamic. Exciting." -Sunday Times

"*The Scribbler* is well-paced, engaging and punctuated by ... unexpected humour, leading to a compelling and incredibly satisfying crime read. Highly recommended." -Raven Crime Reads

"I feel like I have just made one of the greatest discoveries on earth ... What a mind this author has ... a fantastic ... dark, gripping, creepy and tense read." -A Lover of Books Blog

"The Scribbler is a slow burning, tense and downright creepy thriller." -Suze Reviews

"A creepy read with an explosive ending, I was engrossed from start to finish." -Jera's Jamboree

"Brilliantly creepy." -Scots Magazine

"A brilliant read [on] LGBTQ+ crimes that traditionally were underreported. Thankfully, times have changed." - Neil Boast MBE, former LGBT Liaison Officer, Suffolk Constabulary, and former head of task force on sexual exploitation and trafficking

"Iain Maitland has a delicious and dark style of writing, he tricks you into thinking you are just meandering along nicely ... then he jumps out behind you and knocks you sideways as he delivers some dark and deadly punches, then lets you breathe before he does it all over again." - Chapter In My Life Blog

Mr Todd's Reckoning

"Splendidly creepy." -Geoffrey Wansell, Daily Mail

"Iain Maitland has pulled off a masterstroke. Combining the ingenuity of an Agatha Christie, the horror of Rillington Place and the wit of the best of British, the story keeps you on your toes, fills you with dread and makes you laugh out loud." -Martin Carr, Abbottvision

"Maitland conjures madness from the inside, looking out ... a brave book." -Jeff Noon, Spectator

"Truly scary ... a fabulous dive into the mind of a classic, self-justifying psychopath ... A fantastic book." -Barbara Nadel

"Iain Maitland's Mr Todd lures us into his moral abyss. The banality of evil ... drip feeds us its shockingly tense story of unending horror ... Riveting, terrifying." -Paul Ritter

"Superbly crafted ... spellbinding and gripping ... brilliantly observed ... The setting of an ordinary two-bedroomed bungalow in suburbia is genius ...." -Linda Hill, Linda's Book Blog

"From page one Iain Maitland hurls you through the secret underground tunnels of an insane mind bent on destruction. Cleverly conceived, what begins as quite touching drives relentlessly onwards into furious criminality. Mr Todd's Reckoning is phenomenally dark and utterly compelling." - Chris Dolan

'This novel grabbed me from the very first page and refused to let go ... wonderfully quirky yet frightening ... The atmosphere that Iain Maitland creates with his writing is incredible ... he is a master of suspense." Bookaholic Confessions

Sweet William

"A breathless journey through fear and love that explores how interdependent those two extreme emotions are." -Ewan Morrison

"A dark, rocket-paced thriller." -Jon Wise, Sunday Sport

"Taut, darkly humorous and heartbreaking, with an unforgettable narrator, *Sweet William* packs a real emotional punch." -Lisa Gray, Daily Record

"A compassionate novel imbued with a deep knowledge of mental health issues ... Tense and insightful ... A heart-stopping thriller with a powerful denouement." -Paul Burke, Nudge Books

Out of the Madhouse

"An excellent exploration of the phenomenology of mental illness and its wider impact." -Joshua Fletcher, psychotherapist

"I love this book; profoundly moving, beautifully written ... incredibly important ... wonderfully hopeful." -James Withey, Founder, The Recovery Letters project

"Confronts the shocking bleakness of mental illness head on." -Charlie Mortimer, author, Dear Lupin

"The overriding ingredients ... are the warmth of his connections, ... and the power of communication." -Dr Nihara Krause, Stem4 Founder & CEO

Dear Michael, Love Dad

"A wonderfully entertaining and moving book, with lessons for every parent." -Daily Mail

"A moving read - honest, funny and sad." -Woman and Home

"Raising the issue of men's mental health is important and *Dear Michael, Love Dad* is to be praised for that ... [a] loving and well-meant mix of letters and commentary." -Daily Express

"By turns acidly funny, exasperating and poignant, painting a moving portrait both of mental illness and of a father in denial. But paternal love ... shines through." -Caroline Sanderson, Sunday Express

For my family – Tracey, Michael, Georgia and Jonah, Sophie, Glyn, Halley and Zack, Adam and Sophie and Dolly.

PROLOGUE

Dusk is falling as I walk towards the pier. The BBC weatherman says snow is coming soon, and it certainly feels like it.

I stop as I see her. And catch my breath. It's my daughter.

She is huddled by a beach hut, sheltering from the wind.

But, of course, it is not my daughter. It cannot be. My family, such as it was, has gone. Wife. Daughter. Both dead. And I am all alone.

Other than my dog, Fluffy. I call him Fluffy because he is a smooth-coated Jack Russell. This means he is not fluffy at all. The name is just my little joke.

Today, my family has been on my mind. The eighteenth of November is – was – my wife's birthday. We had birthdays in October, November and December. Mine is in October. My wife's November. My daughter's was in December.

I am standing still. Staring into space.

The sight of the young girl. My mind full of terrible memories.

Fluffy pulls on his lead. He wants to walk on.

She reaches out her hand towards Fluffy as we pass by. He

stops and sniffs. She puts her hand inside her hooded fleece, a threadbare thing, more of a cardigan really. Too thin for this weather. Fluffy moves forward to eat whatever it is she's offering to him. Her last scrap of food.

She then looks up at me and smiles. Although she is dirty and down on her luck, she has the prettiest eyes I have ever seen. The kindest, friendliest face. She does look a little like my daughter. At first glance, anyway.

I know I should keep walking. Be ruled by my head, not by my heart.

But I do not. It has always been my weakness. Instead, I rummage in my pocket and drop a few coins into her third-full paper cup.

She smiles at me again as she takes them and says, "Thank you," in a soft and gentle lilt of a voice. I can't place the accent. Northern, I think. Or Welsh. I am not sure. I am not good at that sort of thing.

I hesitate. I wonder if I should say something encouraging to her. "Good luck" perhaps. Maybe "all the best". But these phrases have a finality about them, as if I am saying I will never see her again.

I know that will not be so.

That I will be drawn back.

As I have been before.

I will walk this way tomorrow evening, give her more change, perhaps a five-pound note. And the next time, the night after, with the snow almost upon us, a blanket to keep warm. The wind is always strong on the seafront, and now temperatures are falling fast. I may give the girl one of my daughter's coats still hanging up in the wardrobe. There is a nice one left there. From Topshop in Oxford Street.

Fluffy is away and pulling on his lead towards the pier. To the smells and the cast-away fast food. As I reach the slow incline up to the pier, I look back, expecting to see her head bowed, crushed by her homeless life. But she is sitting up and smiling at me, one more time. It is that smile that does for me.

Yes, that is the one that strikes at my heart.

I should not have looked back. Just kept on walking.

I wonder where this will now take me. And her. To heaven. Or to hell, most probably.

PART I

THE PIER

1

MONDAY, 18 NOVEMBER, 8.42 PM

She is on my mind all evening. The girl. As I make my tea. Eating it on a tray in front of the television in the living room with Fluffy by my feet. Watching some soap or other full of identical, angry young people. "Yeah?" "Yeah!" is all they shout back and forth into each other's gormless faces.

As I finish, giving Fluffy the last piece of sausage and putting the tray to one side, I lean back and shut my eyes. I go back over everything that has happened to bring me to this point in my life. I relive it all, moment by moment. Every little thing.

It does me no good. I know that. I'm driving myself mad. To the edge of insanity. If not beyond. But what else do I have to do, other than to sit here alone, night after night?

I live in Felixstowe. It's in Suffolk, on the east coast of England, some seventy miles north-east of London. It's an odd kind of place. An old Victorian town centre that has seen better days. A seafront with a promenade and a shingle beach. A theatre at one end and a pier at the other. A funfair and amusements further along. The port, of course. Huge

container ships coming in and going out endlessly. The usual
sprawl of housing estates all around. Felixstowe has been
described as a "charming seaside town" by the local tourist
body.

I suppose it is. In a way.

If you just see what's in front of you.

And don't look behind it.

I know different, of course. I used to have a job, in marketing, in local government up the road. But I lost that. I was
made redundant, as they called it.

Afterwards, I went away for a while. Locked up. When I
came out, I took a series of jobs to help make ends meet. The
redundancy money, such as it was, does not go far. Not far
enough, anyway. And my meagre pension is some years off.

I worked in a supermarket in town during the day.
Stacking shelves, mainly. Some till work. I stuck out like the
proverbial sore thumb. A man of my age, amongst teenagers,
mostly. And plump middle-aged women called Sharon and
Cathy. There was a nice young girl there, Frances. "Little
Fran" I called her, but she left for university, and I never saw
or heard from her again. I tried to stay in touch, but without
success.

I also worked evenings and weekends for a while as a cab
driver. It got me out and about. Kept me busy. Took my mind
off things. Bad things. And the downside of my existence,
sitting at home, night after night, stewing over the past. That
was an eye-opener, that was. Cab driving. To the seedier side
of life.

Not just the gangs of young men and women piling into
the cab on Friday and Saturday nights.

And the sex on the back seats. The threats of violence.
The vomit. The piss. Blood once, from one of a group of girls.

But the proper, seamier underbelly of the town. They all

have it, every town everywhere, and you don't have to look that hard. Not really.

The drugs, a thriving business, with the constant back and forth from the nearby housing estates in Trimley St Martin and Trimley St Mary to the seafront. The county lines that had infected Ipswich, Bury St Edmunds and other Suffolk towns seemed to have bypassed Felixstowe, stuck out as it is by the sea at the end of the long A14 road. Some of the locals stepped up enthusiastically to fill the gap.

I remember the first young girl who offered to show me her breasts rather than pay the fare. Some young girls offered more than just a look. Whatever I wanted, from a few of them. My pick-and-mix choice.

Then there was the rat-faced man – not much more than a teenager, really – who paid me to drive him and his two holdalls to Manchester late one night. A fistful of cash. Far beyond what I'd normally get for a week of taking old ladies to and from the Marks and Spencer Food Hall over at Martlesham. I did not ask what was in the holdalls. I guessed at drugs or guns. He handed over the money as he got into the cab. A near-silent journey. His head down over his mobile phone. He left near a parade of shops on the outskirts of Manchester, with little more than a nod towards me.

There was an incident at work. The supermarket. I felt I had to leave.

And I stopped the cab work. It got too much for me, what with one thing and another.

I got beaten up one night. Quite badly. Enough to make it hard to work for a while.

And so I retreated to my house in Bluebell Lane, near the woods and fields and the farmland on the outskirts of town. Eking out my redundancy payout and most of my savings before going on benefits. I'm close to that now. The benefits. I got Fluffy, formerly known as Harold, from the Blue Cross. And settled back to live out my days as best I could.

Without much money. And little peace of mind.

No life at all, really. A wretched existence. Half-played games of solitaire and chess on the living room coffee table. Playing against myself. To pass the time. To keep me sane.

Preferable to death, I suppose. But not by much.

<hr />

THE MADNESS IS upon me again.

It is close to midnight.

And I am searching for the girl.

I start at the hut by the pier where I saw her late this afternoon. I think she might be sheltering here. I walk around it. I try the padlock on the door. I shake it hard. To see if she might somehow have got inside the hut. But she has not.

I am wrapped up well. It is a crisp, cold night.

A full moon.

I move quickly along the promenade.

One beach hut after another. I am locked into a rhythm. I look front, sides, back. Check the padlock. Nothing. I move to the next one. Front, sides, back. Check the padlock. Nothing. Move on. Again, again, again.

She is nowhere to be seen.

I fear for her. As a girl.

I worry what might happen.

I have seen more and more beggars lately in the town. Young men, mostly. Eastern Europeans, I think. I have no sympathy for them. They have youth and strength and vigour. There is work for them, if they wanted it. They choose a life of benefits and begging. I guess it pays more.

If I were a young homeless man, I would go to pubs and restaurants late each evening. Offer to wash up, clean the yard, clear rubbish – anything in exchange for hot food and drink. I would keep my self-respect.

It's different for girls – young women, really. On the streets. They are weaker physically, and when they are wet and cold and hungry, they are vulnerable to offers of money and the inevitable descent into sex work.

I hurry on. As fast as I can.

I think I know where she might be.

There is an old Victorian shelter down by the theatre.

There is noise. Shouts and jeers and whistles towards me from the other side of the road. A group of young men, tipped out of a club, full of testosterone and alcohol, and looking for trouble.

I slow to a hurried walk so I do not attract further braying attention. After one or two more yells in my general direction, they go on their way to break off car wing mirrors, pull up flowers and vomit in front gardens. A typical night out in Felixstowe.

And I am now by the theatre and to the shelter. This ornate relic from a bygone age, looking out across the beach towards the dark, black sea.

She is not at the side of it as I approach. Nor at the front.

There is just one large, huddled-up shape.

Curled up beneath the bench at the back.

I shake the shoulder closest to me with a sense of urgency, to describe, to ask, to say *Have you seen this young girl? She is homeless, she is young, she is hungry, she has nothing to eat, nowhere to go, this pretty little thing.*

And I realise suddenly I have nothing with me for the girl to eat or drink. I had worked myself into such a lather as I lay in my bed that, other than getting dressed and checking Fluffy was settled in his bed, I rushed out without thought or preparation.

The huddled-up mass, after two or three increasingly

firm shakes from me, groans and rolls over slowly. An old drunken woman, with sleep-stuck eyes and dribbling lips. She is repulsive. But in my madness, I have to press on.

"Have you seen her?" I say.

"The girl!" I shout. "The girl by the pier!"

The woman looks at me through hazy eyes, unable to focus. Sleep or drink or drugs, I cannot tell. She is covered with layers of old clothes, jumpers, cardigans, and some sort of dirt-stained blanket. Incongruous, light-grey jogging bottoms cover her bottom half, other than a roll of vein-marked white flesh exposed and hanging over the top of the waistband. She wears blue, slip-on plimsolls.

Whether she has wet or soiled herself, I cannot say. There is a smell that suggests a combination of both. Judging by the dark stain to the front of her jogging bottoms and down her legs, she has certainly wet herself.

I shake her again, to rouse her from sleep. I ask her repeatedly, "Have you seen the girl?" The jumbled, incoherent nonsense of her mumbled reply suggests that, whether she has or not, she cannot tell me.

I stop, think, wonder whether to carry on along the prom out of town towards Old Felixstowe.

Or turn back towards the pier and to my car beyond and home.

I see a police car patrolling the seafront, coming towards me from the pier. I drop my head, wrap my scarf around my face and hurry away to my bed and my sleep and my dreams. My nightmares, really.

IT IS PITCH BLACK.

At night.

I am drowning in a canal.

The sides stretch up smooth and high.
And the water is cold and deep.
I cannot swim.
I am searching for something. And trying to escape.
I cannot find what it is I want.
And my hands slip away from the sides.
I am thrashing about.
Ever more desperate.
And my head sinks beneath the water.
I awake, drenched in sweat.

2

TUESDAY, 19 NOVEMBER, 4.57 AM

I have not slept well. It's been a restless, troubled night. Reliving one of my nightmares over and again.

And thinking about the girl. When I have been awake. I know what I am going to do.

And I know why. In my moments of clarity, I understand how I have come to this.

I got myself into a routine once I had retreated to my little home in Bluebell Lane to eke out my existence. I walk Fluffy across the fields before breakfast. I then have my breakfast. Porridge with fruit, usually. A banana. Or raspberries. I alternate them. I have a little chart on the wall to remind me which is which for each day. My memory is not always so good these days.

In the mornings, I do the housework. The hoovering. Cleaning. Any odd bits of DIY that need attending to. I work to a list. I have my lunch with the news at one o'clock on BBC One. A sandwich, crisps and a yoghurt. In the afternoon, I take the long walk into town, for milk and bread and suchlike, to go to the library, to pick up a little something for

Fluffy, get a local newspaper to keep abreast of what's happening hereabouts. I like a schedule to my day.

Teatime and the long dark evenings of winter are especially tricky for me. I try to keep my mind busy. I have a nice evening meal, a ready-made lasagne from the Tesco Exclusive Range with some salad and a glass of fruit juice; orange mixed with pineapple is a favourite of mine. (I mix them myself.) I listen to the radio, mostly Radio 4. And I read long into the night until I fall into sleep.

Not much of a life. I have yearned for something better.

Love. That's what. To love and be loved.

It's what drives me on. Into madness. To do what I have done before. And am about to do again.

When I cannot sleep, I read. As I am doing now. I am an avid reader of crime novels, Agatha Christie's in particular, and adventure stories – Alistair MacLean is an old favourite; Dan Brown a more recent one. I am currently reading *10 Rillington Place* by Ludovic Kennedy. It is about the serial killer John Christie. I picked it up from a second-hand bookshop in town. I don't know why. It's not a very pleasant book, but something about it caught my eye.

John Reginald Halliday Christie, to give him his full name, killed his wife and other women back in the 1940s and 1950s. He then buried the bodies around his rented ground-floor flat. His own home! A silly thing to do. One of the other tenants later tried to put up a shelf in a kitchen alcove, peeled back the wallpaper and saw a stack of bodies piled there. You would think someone would have noticed the smell.

You would expect that, after the bodies were discovered, Christie would go on the run. I would be prepared. And I would leave and start over somewhere, somehow. Cash in a holdall. Instead, he wandered about London, having a cup of tea at one café and an iced bun at another. Almost as if he were on a day trip to see the sights. One day, up by Putney

Bridge, he was challenged by a police officer, and there it all ended; the game was up. If you've buried bodies in your home, you need to have an escape plan. A "plan B" as it were. At the very least, you need to disappear. And not get caught.

But I digress. My mind wanders all over the place at times like these. And I have just stopped taking my medication. I do not think I really need it. I want to be happy and live well without it.

I sit up and look out of the bedroom window, waiting for daybreak.

Then I am up and getting ready to walk Fluffy. And on we go, into another day. But today, I have something to live for. A brighter future. Or at least a chance of it. If I can just find the girl by the pier.

———

JUST GONE 11 a.m. There is knocking at the front door. Firm but insistent.

I ignore it.

I know who it is. And what she wants. She will go away. Eventually.

Mid to late morning is a difficult time for me. I have done my chores and ticked them off the list. It is too early to start preparing lunch. And I always struggle with free time. I need to be occupied. I know that. I try to timetable my day and keep busy, busy, busy. When I am not doing something, my mind clouds over and I think my ever-darkening thoughts. And I know where they will take me.

I now sit still, as calmly as I can, in a chair at the kitchen table overlooking the garden. I have my trusty old binoculars. I often get out and about with them both day and night. Today, I want to watch for the robin. I like robins. There is one that has been coming into my garden in this colder weather. I have a little half-coconut shell nailed to the fence, and I fill the bottom of it with bird seed. I see the robin eating there some days. But all I see today is the Lump staring across the fence from his garden on the other side of the alleyway between the two properties.

Knock. Knock.

I blank it out.

No matter how many times.

3 Bluebell Lane probably sounds an idyllic address. It is a handsome enough house, although I have always thought of it as a cottage – the "chocolate box cottage" of my dreams. The word *cottage* has a nice sound to it. There is a small and tasteful extension – a nookery, actually.

Everything about it is perfect. Other than the neighbours. The Lumbs – the Lumps as I call them – live next door at 1 Bluebell Lane, the last property before endless, open fields. Or they did. There is only one Lump left these days.

The father was a rough-and-ready fellow who worked at the docks, most likely shifting things about and stealing them (as most dockers do). He spent much of his free time – day, evenings, weekends – in his workshop to the side of his house, and closest to mine, drilling and hammering and singing along to Meat Loaf CDs and driving me mad.

He fell off a crane, or something high up, at the docks two or three summers ago and broke his back and died. Some sort of complications, I imagine. It's been much quieter, rather peaceful in fact, ever since. But the Lumps are – *the* Lump is – still a thorn in my side.

Knock. Knock. Bloody *knock.*

Louder this time.

It makes no difference to me.

Mrs Lump was a nasty piece of work. A tall, solid woman, looking more like a beast than a man, she worked as a receptionist at my local doctors' surgery. I think she was behind me getting struck off the list there early last year. So I have since had to go into Ipswich instead. It is an educated guess. She looked down her nose at me whenever we saw each other, and she never spoke. Not a single word. She always thought she was better than me. But then she got COVID-19, just when everyone thought the worst of it was over. She died quite quickly. I cannot say I mourned for her. She was a horrible woman.

The son, the Lump, all six feet four of him, is a simpleton. There is no other word for him. He lives there alone now. I don't know how. I think perhaps there were life insurance payouts for the father and mother. Even so, I do not know how he manages on his own. Bumbling and fumbling about. It can only be a matter of time before he burns the place down and they take him away to assisted living. I do not know what he does all day. He must be in his mid-twenties. But he does not work. Just stands there. Staring.

The knocking has stopped.

I knew it would.

She has gone away. For now, anyway.

I see the Lump, as I do most days at this time, by the fence on the other side of the alleyway that separates the two build-ings. He is staring over, from his garden, watching me. It is as if he is in some sort of trance. I imagine he is standing against the fence urinating. That is how he looks to me. I will not be intimidated. I gaze out as if relaxed and at ease. I will not let him see how irritated I feel by his presence.

Being struck off by the GP was unfair. Mrs Lump was involved, without doubt. According to the NHS website, a GP can only remove you from their list immediately without warning if a patient has been violent or abusive, or has behaved in a threatening way and the police have been called. Well, that is not me. I have a temper, as most normal men do, and it has been an issue at times in the past. But I am certainly not violent or abusive, and I do not behave in a threatening way!

If I were like that, I would be picking up a knife from the block beside me.

And I would be striding into the garden. Through the gate. To the alleyway. Into his garden.

And sinking it slap-bang into the middle of the Lump's stupid fat forehead. And I'd bloody well laugh when I did it.

IT IS MID-AFTERNOON. The schools are out. It is not yet dusk.

I am back at the pier. On my own. With my hat, scarf and gloves. It is colder now.

Looking for the girl. Before she settles down somewhere for the night.

The pier, at least the length of it stretching out into the sea, is rotten and decomposing. Much like Felixstowe itself. I think it must be dangerous to walk on. It has been closed off for years. It can only be a matter of time before it collapses into the sea. Good riddance to it, I'd say.

It would be better off gone. But it would be a major expense to remove it, and I believe the council bigwigs would rather spend money on schemes that only benefit their own back pockets. These people do very nicely out of us ordinary folk, what with their allowances and expenses and backhanders. And "jobs for the boys", of course.

The front of the pier is new and busy. A few years ago it was renovated, and there is now a pleasant enough restaurant and fast-food places where you can buy fish and chips and multicoloured fizzy drinks and 101 flavours of ice cream.

She is nowhere to be seen outside.

The girl. She is not begging. Nor hidden away, getting ready for another long, cold night.

I know where she will be. Inside the pier.

When the front of the pier was being rebuilt, many in Felixstowe hoped it would be something like the one at Southwold – upmarket, with small cafes and dainty knick-knack shops. An attraction, drawing in people from far and wide.

What Felixstowe got was an amusement arcade. One huge aircraft hangar of a space, packed front to back, side to side, with machines. All you can hear is whirring and ringing and the shouts and yells and screams of teenagers. It makes Clacton look sophisticated.

The cacophony and the menacing and unbridled feral children everywhere repel me. But I force myself to go in. To see if she is here, checking for left-behind change in the trays of the machines.

I hope that is what she is doing. It could be worse. I imagine there are drugs to be had here, as there are where all teenagers gather these days. Or she could be in the toilets, in a clumsy sexual embrace with some young thug for a rolled-up twenty-pound note.

I shake my head free of the image. Stride in, making my way to the change machines, putting in a five-pound note for two-pence pieces. To show I'm just an ordinary fellow having some fun on the machines.

I have been in here before, of course. In recent months. For much the same purpose. I know what to do. And what not to do.

When I was young, and the world was a nicer place, middle-aged men in amusement arcades could interact with children there. Smile at them. Share a joke with Mum and Dad. Maybe hand over a small cuddly toy they'd won. They were happier, more innocent, times back then.

These days, as I know to my cost, you can no longer do anything like that. If a child falls over in front of you and is hurt and crying, you have to walk on by. Ignore the little chap. If a baby in a pushchair looks at you and gurgles, you turn away. You cannot even stand near a small child for fear of being called a pervert. As I have been. And more.

It is easier with teenage girls. I have a kind of bond with them, almost an understanding, as if I were a kindly uncle. Uncle Philip, that's me. They seem to be drawn in my direction. There is something about me. I think I seem much younger than I am to them. A ready-made friend. Of course, I know I cannot usually approach them one-to-one, and that I have to keep my distance on an individual basis. But two or three, in a small group, and I can start up a nice little chat.

She is not in here. The girl. Nowhere to be seen. I've been all over.

I was going to approach a group of teenage girls, but there is only one small group. They are younger, pretty pre-teens, and their mothers are nearby.

There is a bigger group of teenage boys, aimless and aggressive, and they have spotted me.

Teenage boys, yobs and thugs for the most part, scare me, especially when there is a gang of them. "Felixstowe's Finest", I think of them. Another of my little jokes. In reality, they are inbred, half-witted monsters. Most of the families in Felixstowe have lived here for years, and the inbreeding is simply horrific on occasion.

I have to keep moving and not catch their eye and walk away if they turn on me. There are no constraints nowadays; they can simply say and do whatever they want without any fear of comeback. A year or two ago, one young thug accused me of being "a paedo" – his exact words – because I was having a little chat with what must have been his girlfriend.

He threw some sort of liquid at me from a container in his pocket. I assumed it was lighter fuel. I don't know why. Then rummaged in his pockets for what I thought was a box of matches. To light and flick at me. I was too scared to move.

But he could not find what he was looking for. There was a moment as he sneered at me, laughing at my fear. Then he turned and swaggered off. Afterwards, I went into the men's toilets and used sheets of toilet paper to wet and wipe off whatever it was.

I went home and changed my clothes. And I felt so humiliated that I plotted how I was going to get my own back. Which I never did. For a while, I drove round with a full petrol can on the passenger seat, just looking for him. Eventually, I thought better of it. Sometimes though, I wish I had taught him a lesson he'd never forget.

I take one last look around the pier, watched by the gang of youths.

She is not here.

I leave as nonchalantly as I can. Inside, I feel my temper rising. But I can control it these days.

GONE MIDNIGHT, and I am back on the prom, heading to the pier. I am obsessed. I know it. There is nothing I can do. I will pursue this to the end. My own, most likely.

I lay in bed for ages, thoughts of the girl rolling round my mind. My body aching in agony.

And it came to me quite suddenly where she must spend her nights, sheltering from the cold and the strong wind. Beneath the pier. I do not know why I did not think of that last night. Sometimes I don't think straight. I forget things.

It is quiet along the promenade. I can hear the odd shout and the roar of a car up and back and away towards the town centre, up Convalescent Hill. But there is no one around the prom, the pier and the faded leisure centre beyond it. Just rubbish, crisp packets and fish and chip wrappers blown about in the chill night air.

In the distance, the lights and the occasional noise and the tall, alien-like cranes of the docks form an eerie backdrop. It is as if Felixstowe is riven in two, the tired, broken-down town settled for the night and the endless, restless energy of the docks, twenty-four hours around the clock.

I stop where the prom meets the pier and look around me. There is a man, with a big dog – hard to see what it is – an Alsatian maybe, walking away and up the hill to the town itself. There is no one else to be seen.

I crouch and look under the pier as the pebbly beach rolls away and into the sea.

There is a body there, curled up beside one of the huge metal pillars supporting the pier.

It is her, the girl. And she must be wet and cold and frightened.

And I realise then what it is I am going to do. As I was always going to do from the moment I saw her. It's not about giving her a five-pound note or a warm and waterproof coat. It's more than that. I want to bring her back to my cottage in Bluebell Lane.

I look left and right. Then step onto the pebbles. The *crunch-crunch-crunch* of my footsteps sounds deafening in the silence. I wonder if the noise will wake her and she will panic and run off. Or whether she will see my kindly face, recognise me from yesterday, and be reassured by my arrival. That I am here to rescue her from her miserable existence.

I am close now, and she has not moved. I think she must be in a deep sleep. Hard to imagine anyone sleeping below the pier, more exposed to the elements than I thought, the crashing of the waves, the wind whistling through and the ever-present threat of passers-by. I guess you can get used to anything if you have to.

I feel a surge of excitement with the first touch – my hand on her shoulder, her back to me, pulling her slowly over so that she will be lying down on her back in front of me.

It is a man. A young thin man. Unkempt and dirty. He stirs and struggles as he realises what is happening.

I step back, stumble and fall as he lashes out his arm towards me.

He is up on his feet, half standing, half crouched under the pier. I can see his face in the shadows, part scared, part angry. He moves slightly to one side to stand in front of two or three carrier bags packed full of his belongings. To protect them.

"I'm sorry," I say, my breath swirling like smoke in the biting cold.

He looks at me, uncomprehending, still half-asleep. Expecting me to have been just another down-and-out trying to steal his belongings.

"Here," I add, reaching instinctively into my pocket for a five-pound note. But I have no notes, only loose change, which I offer to him.

He looks at the coins in silence, almost with contempt. But he reaches out his hands and takes them anyway.

A stand-off. I am frustrated and furious with myself for my stupidity. He waits for me to say or do something. I'm not sure what he expects. After a moment or two, he smiles at me. A lopsided, wolfish leer. I imagine tobacco-stained teeth, meths on his breath. He disgusts me.

He says nothing. But the way he stands. How he looks at me. The loosening of his body. It all tells me what he thinks I am. Why I am here. What I want. From him. I am looking for sex in return for money. The thought revolts me.

I imagine his hands at my trousers, unzipping me, as I stand there looking back and forth along the prom. Dropping to his knees in front of me. I step back instinctively, and he must see from my face what I am thinking. I flush red and hot, although he cannot see that in the dark. He makes some sort of clicking gesture with his fingers – money, that's what he wants – and some sort of chirping noise with his lips.

He is mocking me.

As I turn to go.

Hurrying away home to my warm safe haven, and then my bed and my ever-tormented sleep.

———————

I AM STANDING in the middle lane of a motorway.

The sun is blinding me.

Cars swerve to avoid me.

Angry faces at the wheels, shouting and screaming at me.

To move.

To do something.

To see whatever it is behind me.

I turn.

A tanker.

On its side, ablaze.

All the cars that swerve to avoid me.

Crashing into it.

I wake up, and I am shaking.

3

WEDNESDAY, 20 NOVEMBER, 2.23 AM

I cannot sleep. I am tortured. My mind and body. My endless nightmares. I am now up.

And I am sitting at my computer, trawling through images. Girl after girl.

Searching for one who looks like the girl by the pier. I want to have a picture that looks something like her.

I have only seen her face. Her sweet, beautiful face. Soft and kind and gentle. And her eyes. Her steady, mesmerising gaze that drew me in and pulls me back again and again to find her. It is the eyes. They truly are the windows to the soul.

Huddled over, I could not see her properly. But the look of her reminded me of my daughter. So much so that I had thought it was her for a split second. My brain a moment or two ahead of my conscious thoughts.

I imagine the girl on the pier being happy. I can see her in my head. On the beach. In summer. It is warm, and the waves crash onto the shore. She is laughing, her head tipped back joyfully. She is in a bright red polka-dot bikini. She's striking, and everyone looks at her. She has been swimming and is now drying herself with a colourful beach towel.

She is young and lithe with long arms and legs, slim but shapely. The epitome of youth. Her whole life ahead of her. This is how I see her in my head. Strong. Vibrant. Young. So much to come. Happiness. Goodness.

I search for "missing girl Felixstowe". And "missing girl Suffolk". That somehow her face will suddenly be there in front of me on the screen. Madness, I know. All there are to see are images of dirty, bedraggled girls, with handwritten signs and knocked-over bottles and used syringes around them. Girls who should not have let themselves be photographed.

Next, I search simply for "young girl", and there are endless pages of sweet, cute little things, mostly five or six, maybe younger. In dresses. And swimsuits. And funny hats. With puppies and kittens. And, slightly older, in bras and knickers and bikinis. I click from one to the other, on and on, faster and faster.

I stop. One photo shows a young girl – preschool, I'd say – running down a grassy slope, her face slightly obscured by the faux fur of her anorak hood. It is my daughter, as near as makes no difference. When she was little. The three of us had gone to Yorkshire for a weekend break. And we visited an old ruined castle near Harrogate. Spofforth Castle. My daughter running up and down whilst I took photographs. Happy days.

And here she is, in front of me and in my head.

I pause, my screen full of pictures of pretty little girls.

And I bow my head for a minute, maybe longer, with my terrible thoughts.

And then I am searching for "teen girl". And here they are now, half-girls, half-women, staring into the screen. Some proud. Others vulnerable. A few make eye contact, staring at me with haughty disdain. They pout their lips, throwing back shoulders, attempting an air of sophistication. Or sexuality, although they should be too young to have such knowing looks.

Through them all I go, searching for the face, the body, the sense of someone who looks something like the girl by the pier. And, page after endless page, changing my search phrases for variations of *young girl* and different ages and what she might be wearing, I finally find a face that matches. Or something close to it.

But the hair, blonde and cascading, is wrong. I did not see the girl by the pier's hair clearly, as it was beneath a hood. But it was different – brown, I think – and streaked maybe, and scraped back and tied in a knot at the back of her neck.

And the body is wrong, too. This girl in the bikini with her curves and shapes and sexual pose is not right. It's just not right at all. The fullness of her figure. Her long legs, slightly apart, her way of standing. The overt sexuality.

And I am searching again. Taking a face. And a body. A bit of this. And a part of that.

And finally, I am creating a composite, Photoshopped lookalike. As I see her in my mind.

There she is. Perfect. Cut and pasted in front of me at last. Just so. The girl by the pier.

———

STILL I CANNOT SLEEP. I walk restlessly about my cottage.

It's not just the endless nightmares. I can live with those. I have to.

My mind is on the photograph in my hand. And the girl.

My cottage, most of it, dates back to the nineteenth century. You walk to it via a little path from Bluebell Lane and knock on the heavy wooden door. Entering, there is a small hallway where I am standing now, and a slightly curved staircase that leads up to two roughly equal-sized bedrooms with beamed ceilings. It had a thatched roof originally, but this was later replaced with tiles. They give it a sturdy look.

They say round here that my cottage is haunted. Ghosts of those who died in torment. Over the years. Lost souls. I pooh-pooh such nonsense. I cannot say I have seen or heard anything other than the odd knock and the whistling of the wind. I am not a believer. When you're dead, you're dead. If it is haunted, the ghosts would come up from the cellar. I keep the door, to the side of the foot of the stairs, locked. But that is for practical rather than superstitious reasons.

To the left of the hallway, there is the living room, with a fireplace that Fluffy sleeps in front of, in his basket, except when he is by my feet, waiting for the leftovers of a meal I've eaten on a tray. I call it a nooks-and-crannies kind of room, with its uneven floor and window bays and its bumpy walls. It is, in truth, a dreary place that forever smells of damp and dust and soot from the fireplace, no matter how often I clean and polish. The walls were painted a bright canary yellow once, although that has faded now, almost to the colour of pale urine.

To the right, as I walk into it now, is a more formal, dark-painted room, with bookshelves to either side and a dining table in the middle of it. Oak, with six battered old leather-seated chairs around it. All too big for the room. Too much for me these days; I never entertain. I am a private person, keeping myself to myself. I can smile and make small talk well enough up the town, about the weather and the Ipswich Town Football Club and new shops opening and closing. But that's about it.

I don't engage with people. Talk about my feelings.

I keep all of that to myself. It's better that way. Safer.

I know, when my emotions are unleashed, where it all

leads. Where it's led before. And will do again. If I am not very careful.

This dining room used to be a kitchen. And there was an outside toilet. And a tap to fill a tin bath, most probably. Sometime in the 1950s or 1960s, the owners added a flat-roof extension right across the back, with a kitchen to one side and a bathroom and toilet to the other. These have been decorated and the appliances upgraded over the years, the toilet and bath and basin changed, too. But there is still a dilapidated feel to the extension, and it always seems to be a few degrees chillier than the original part of the cottage.

The garden is fenced to either side and lined with a mix of bushes, mostly laurels, down to the bottom, so many yards away. Never-ending fields beyond. A farm in the distance. Neighbours to the left and right. The Lump to one side, the alleyway between us, and the perfect family to the other, on the other side of my fence. A shed at the bottom to the side of a small vegetable patch. I dug it over to soil last year, but never got round to relaying turf. I should have done.

Closer to the cottage and extension, there is a patio area that I relaid the summer before last. It was level when I finished, but part of it, most of it really, seems to have sunk down a little since then. It now looks lumpy and uneven. I cannot bring myself to dig it up and start again.

I put the bins, one blue, one green, one grey, over the worst of it. On Wednesday mornings, I wheel one or two of them out through the gate in the fence and into the alleyway and round to the front of the cottage, where they sit at the end of the driveway to be emptied by the dustbin men.

"Driveway" is a rather fancy term for what it is really, a patch of scraggy land by the trees where I park my car, a Nissan Almera. It is old and battered, much like me. But it does its job, taking me out to the big supermarkets at Warren

Heath and Martlesham Heath on alternate weeks for my shopping. And occasionally, further afield.

We've had petty vandalism down here at night. Bins tipped over. A large penis scratched onto the bonnet of my car once. And couples have come down to the far end of the lane to have sex in their cars.

Technology is amazing these days. You can have dash cams in cars and even tiny cameras and listening devices in rooms, seeing and hearing everything. I am good with things like that.

I put up a big, easy-to-see camera and a sign to deter the vandals and the dirty couples. It stopped soon enough.

There is the nookery to the side of the cottage, a garage conversion and extension really, entered by a door in the corner of the living room. It is a self-contained unit, a room with a bed that rather cleverly folds up and folds down from the wall as needed, an armchair and a coffee table at the front and a tiny kitchenette and a toilet and shower at the back. What some might call a granny annex. It is the nicest place of all. It is warm. It has proper double-glazing, and the windows don't rattle in the wind. And it has its own heating rather than relying on the fire and the heavy gas cylinders all around the rest of the cottage.

It is dark in here, in the little bedroom in the nookery, although the light of the moon shining through the window allows me to move around easily enough. The bed is against the far wall, flipped up on its side, legs folded down, beneath a shelf when it is not in use. Curtains are pulled round it. I put the photo of the girl by the pier on the shelf and look at it for a minute or two, just thinking about things. What I'd like to do. What I hope happens.

I pull the curtains back from around the bed, deciding that I should clean them in the morning. That they have never been washed in the years they have been there. They must smell by now, no matter how fresh the room otherwise is. I start to unhook the curtains, one hook at a time. I realise I should leave this to the morning, but know I will not rest until I have at least taken them down and put them in the washing basket.

And then I stop. There is a glimpse of white material sticking out from the edge of the upturned bed. I wonder what it is, a dusting cloth maybe, from when I last polished and cleaned this room. I pull at the material, and it comes out easily enough, and I look down at a pair of little white panties in my hand. I turn them over, in the moonlight, feeling them with my fingers. They have been worn. They should not be here. I overlooked them. They should have been burned. Thrown on the fire.

I look up and glance out of the window and across into the lane.

I jump, startled by what I see.

There is someone standing there, a hand on the gate, looking straight at me.

I KNOW WHO IT IS. My admirer from the top of the lane. The knock-knock-knocker.

A middle-aged woman, a granny. Angela. Widow Woman, I call her. We met last year when her dog, a big fat Labrador, did its business by my gate. I happened to be coming out with Fluffy at the time, and she asked me for a poo bag, which I gave her so she could pick up the mess. She took something of a shine to me as I smiled and nodded and listened to her endless twaddle. She soon started bumping into me whenever I walked Fluffy. I soon got wise to what she was doing and changed my routine. I also took a dislike to the Labrador, who would always stick his nose into my crotch at every opportunity.

She stalks me by day, knocking on my door. And now by night. She is an obsessive.

I do not step away from the window, as others might instinctively do. The net curtains are heavily patterned and thick textured. She should see me, but with the moon where it is, I am not sure that she can. I may just be a shadow. A dark blur. A piece of furniture, even. If I stand still, she may not realise I am here. Watching her.

She remains there, just staring. I gaze back impassively. If I move, she will see me. So I wait. And she waits too. Whoever blinks first. It will not be me. I wonder if she stands there every night, and if so, how long she has been doing it. And how long she is there each time, just looking and waiting.

Whether she sometimes opens the gate. Comes up the path.

Walking around, peering through windows, trying door handles. Tapping on windowpanes.

What she would do if I forgot to lock a door one night and she came in whilst I was asleep.

She told me her life story, of course, which she repeats, near enough word for word, every chance she gets. An endless spew of trivia. How her sainted husband, Barry, who did a desk job at the docks, had died nine months earlier. How she has since kept busy (she was always a housewife, devoted to her husband's every need).

How she has two grandchildren, a little boy and a small girl, who stay with her as often as not, because her daughter is bipolar. And divorced. And has to go in and out of places. And how the children, lovely though they are, run her ragged with their games and hide-and-seek and this, that and the other. I smiled – winced – my way through it all. I don't do idle talk. No, not me.

I think suddenly that I should step back, open the front door and stride down the path towards her.

Asking her what the hell she is doing. Tell her to go away and leave me alone. But the truth is I am scared of her and what she might do.

I am worried there will be shouts and screams and a scuffle, and the police might be called. I cannot have that.

And so I wait, full of doubts in my mind and agony in my body. I cannot stand like this, my weight somehow all on my right side, for much longer. Standing as still as a statue was a game I used to play as a child. I was not good at it then. I cannot do it now. I am too old. My body wants to move. To shift its position. But I deny it. I have to wait until she turns and goes, unsure whether I was ever there or not. Her imagination working overtime.

If I shift my position to balance my weight equally on both feet, she will see me. A slight movement, even an inch or so to my left, will give the game away. To her, what might have been a wardrobe or a chest of drawers will suddenly come to life and move. And she will know it is me. And I wonder what she will do. But still she waits there, on and on. Unmoving. Her hand on the gate, as if she is about to open it and enter.

And she sinks down, obscured by the gate, onto her haunches.

I look down and away, the slight movement of my head unnoticed by her.

When I eventually look up, she has disappeared. And I wonder what she will do next.

I AM WOKEN by the sound of a helicopter overhead. Lying in my bed. Trying to sleep. Fluffy by my feet.

This is the third time I have heard a helicopter in recent days. Daytime before. Now in the middle of the night.

Circling, searching, looking for something. Or someone.

I sit up and put on my slippers and wrap my dressing gown around me. Move to the front window of my bedroom. Look out and up.

I am not sure what I expect to see from underneath a helicopter high above. There must be some lights, surely. And it would hover, I think. So there should be near-stationary lights within sight.

But I cannot see anything but dark sky. Lights far and away. Maybe planes. The ever-present shimmer of the docks. But no helicopter.

I push open the window to hear the sound more clearly. It is there. Strong and clear and repeating. The whirr of the blades. But nowhere to be seen.

I wonder suddenly if the noise is inside my mind.

My imagination working too hard.

It would not be the first time. *I can never believe a word you say,* someone once said to me. *It's all in your head.*

I move quickly to the back window of my bedroom, standing next to an old-fashioned bureau and looking out and up. Once more, I just see the black sky, odd lights in the distance, but nothing close, nothing above the cottage nor circling the lane or fields.

I open the window, listening again for the sound of the helicopter. I hear it. Yes. For certain. But I do not see it. Reality, or my imagination at work? I think it is my mind. That it is somehow failing me again.

The noise of the helicopter gets louder, as if it is coming in lower to see what is happening. I look up again, but still I cannot see anything. It is like that for a few minutes. And then it becomes less noisy, more distant.

All that is left is the sound of the helicopter going round and round in my mind.

It is still there as I get back into bed and wrap everything around me. Fluffy lies there still, unmoving, breathing noisily through his blocked nose.

I think this is it. I am starting to go insane. I cannot trust the workings of my own mind any more.

4

WEDNESDAY, 20 NOVEMBER, 11.17 AM

I am hurrying down the prom from the theatre at one end to the pier at the other, the composite photo of the girl tucked safely in my coat pocket.

The wind is as strong as ever, and it's now cold enough to snow. I am well wrapped up, with scarf and gloves. A thick woolly cap, too. I have my winter coat on, although it is a thin old thing, really. I need to buy a new, thicker one.

I feel sick and nervous inside. I know I should not be doing this, drawing attention to myself in this way. This must be the last time. It has to be.

The mornings are quieter along the prom and on the pier, especially when it's turning wintery. A few hardy souls walking dogs and little groups of white-haired old women coming in and out of the leisure centre for keep-fit. That's all. There are no slutty girls and slab-headed boys spoiling for an argument.

I stop and show the photograph to everyone I pass by on the promenade. "My niece," I say in a worried voice. Most stop and take a cursory look. One or two turn away in the wind and push on by with muttered comments about the

weather and being in a hurry and having things to do. Most
of those who stop and look shake their heads and move on
quickly. No one bloody cares, that's for certain. It makes me
angry, the indifference. But I do not show it. I can control my
temper, even now I am off my medication.

Some old women, sheltering by the leisure centre
entrance, cluck and fuss and bicker whether it looks like
Lorraine's daughter, whoever she may be, and they wonder
whatever happened to her. Didn't she move to Fakenham? Or
Hunstanton? The minibus then arrives, and they are on their
way, too, without a backwards glance.

I stand by a lamp post and wonder whether I should go
home and print off copies of the photograph. Attach them to
lamp posts all over town. *Missing! Call This Number. A Reward!*

But I imagine a policeman looking at it, checking the
contact details. And I decide not.

And then I am on the pier and inside the amusements
again. A slobby middle-aged woman sits in a kiosk, bored
and playing with her phone. An old man – in his eighties,
I'd guess – pushing coins into an old-fashioned fruit
machine. Two teenagers, maybe fifteen or sixteen, one
male, the other female, closest to me. He's at a machine,
trying to manoeuvre a metal claw to pick up a soft toy for
the girl.

I wait for him to finish as he swears aggressively at his
second or third failure. He seems aggrieved, somehow diminished in front of the girl. She seems disinterested, barely able
to keep the look off her face. She is a fat girl; I think she
might just prefer an ice cream. They turn to go, and I step
forward.

"Hello," I say simply, polite and friendly. I look at him, not
her. Looking at the girl could make him feel less important,
threatened even. "I'm searching for my niece." I show them
the photograph.

They look at each other, and both laugh at the same time. A sneering, abusive sound.

"Fuck off," he says, pulling her arm and pushing by me. "Wanker."

She looks at me, a pitying look, and smirks to herself.

I am outraged, but do my best not to show it. I just turn away, slip the photograph in my pocket and move towards the old man by the fruit machines. He is humming to himself, in a world of his own, and is jigging slightly side to side in some sort of rhythm. It might be Parkinson's. He takes a coin from a plastic container with his left hand, slips it into the machine, pulls the handle with his right and makes grunting noises as the fruits spin round.

I touch his arm. He does not notice me at first, absorbed in his game. I wait as he takes another twenty-pence piece, inserts it, pulls the handle, jigs a bit. As the fruits stop spinning and he shakes his head in frustration, I touch his arm more firmly. He turns towards me, and I show him the photo. "My niece," I say, "Shannon, I am looking for her." *Shannon* is the sort of name young girls have now.

He *ums* and *ahs*, peering at the photograph and rummaging in his coat pocket. He takes out a case and puts on glasses, closing the case and pulling the photograph out of my hand to take a closer look with his faded eyes. He is trying to be helpful, but I could scream with frustration. I really could.

He asks her name. And how old she is. And why she is missing. I come up with the answers: Shannon. Twenty-two. She had an argument with her mother, my sister. And finally, another long agonising wait, he says *no* and turns away with a final shake and a judder. I could punch him.

I take deep breaths and move across to the middle-aged woman sitting in the kiosk, fiddling with her phone. Like she has nothing better to do. Like working.

I put the photograph on the shelf of the kiosk, ask if she has seen my niece. She pulls it through the window, studying it with a bored expression.

She then stares at me with a look I cannot read.

"This is your niece?" she asks sceptically. She's almost scornful, doubting that such a pretty girl could be my niece.

I nod. "Shannon." Then add in a low voice, "She's twenty-two, had a bit of an argument with her mum. Have you seen her?"

She nods her agreement, then fumbles with her phone, pressing buttons and scrolling through. She shows me a photo. It is of the girl in the photograph, give or take. At least, the face is. The hair is different, and she looks older. And, if I am honest, not so much like the girl by the pier.

"This is your niece?" the woman asks in an odd voice. "She's in that TV series on the telly. *Game of Thrones*. That's your niece who's gone missing? From *Game of Thrones*?"

I feel my face flush red. I am hot and embarrassed.

A stupid, stupid mistake. I've made myself look a fool. I now understand why the couple reacted as they did.

I snatch the photo back. "They look s-similar!" I snap. Then I turn and walk off, hearing her mocking laughter.

I'VE BEEN on my computer in the corner of the kitchen all afternoon.

Talking with my friends altogether in various social media groups and individually via email.

Seeking their help and advice about what I should do. With the girl by the pier.

It has not been easy. To concentrate on their comments. To pick my words and phrases. To make my carefully chosen replies. I have had the window open a crack for some much-needed fresh air. And there has been noise, endless noise, all afternoon from number five. Where what I call "the perfect family" lives. A young couple and their two small children. It is not a nice noise of children's chatter and laughter. No, not at all. It sounds as though the parents are breaking up. He is marching back and forth to his car on the driveway. And they are arguing endlessly.

"Steer clear," one of my friends writes online. "She'll be on drugs."

"AVOID!!!" another writes, simply but full of emphasis.

"She'll be on the game. Have whatever you want for a fiver. Everything for a tenner." Snide and nasty, that.

Mrs Gedge, an old Suffolk woman, lived at number five for years. On her own since her husband, Arthur, died in the 1990s. She had no children to care for her in her old age, but a young cousin visited once or twice a week, fetching and carrying. Then, as time passed, someone came in from a local charity; eventually, every day. Finally, Mrs Gedge died, and the ramshackle place stood empty for eighteen months.

The so-called perfect family bought No. 5. Had local builders and tradespeople in tearing everything out, doing it up, adding an extension, changing the look, making it modern, getting it ready to live in. The family moved up from London. Her, a little blonde slip of a thing with her two iden-tikit children, two girls of preschool age. He, a bull-necked man who always wears a suit, worked in the city – retired at thirty-five or so. Now working from home as an FX currencies trader. You don't get many high-flyers in Felixstowe. Crane drivers, that's about it.

I learned much of this when the young woman, Emma, came round soon after they had moved in. I'd kept myself to myself, as I have always done. She knocked on the front door a couple of times on successive days, but I had seen her from the dining room window and chose not to answer. I do not want to be in other people's lives, nor them in mine. On her third visit, she caught me as I was out the front, chipping a big lump of bird muck off a downstairs front window, and I could do nothing but have a chat, of sorts, in a polite manner. She was nice enough. Gone within minutes, though. I don't hang about talking drivel.

That was early this last summer. I have not spoken to her since. I've smiled and waved to her and her children when we passed in the lane on odd occasions. *Smile, wave, keep moving,* that's my motto. She acknowledges me and is friendly enough. I've only spoken to the husband once. The Man in the Suit, I call him. After a misunderstanding in late summer. When I say *spoken,* he shouted at me in a threatening manner. I thought he was going to kill me.

It goes quiet for a moment.

Outside.

From number five. A lull, that's all.

I write a reply to one of my online friends. I use an anonymous, but friendly, kind of name online and make it clear I am a man, but I do not reveal my age or any other personal details. We live in a time where men like me are assumed to be a scourge on society – a danger to women and children alike.

I also know that if I say I am a middle-aged man and she is a young girl in her early twenties, some people will jump to the most horrible conclusions. That I am some sort of deviant, wanting her for one thing and one thing only. I am not like that. I am a man who has only ever wanted to love and to be loved. That is all.

The noise starts up again. Him and her.

Him, really. Shouting.

And it brings it all back.

I had been in the garden on a sunny Sunday afternoon in early August, adding some soil and stones under a part of the patio that was uneven and had a smell of the drains. The two little girls, perhaps two and four years old respectively, were playing in a paddling pool on the other side of the fence and, judging by the squeals and giggles, were having a nice time.

I found myself listening to their fun and being drawn into it. I kept myself to myself, as ever, but stopped what I was doing to enjoy these happy sounds. From what I could make out, the girls were on their own in the garden, and the mother was inside with the father. I could only hear the sweet little things. Suddenly, I noticed there was silence, and I had a terrible fear that one of the girls might be face down in the water. I moved quickly to the fence where I could see through a broken part.

All was well. The two girls were sitting side by side in the pool, sucking ice lollies. The mother was stretched out on a sunlounger, sunbathing on her back. She had her top off, and unobserved, I sat there crouched, watching her for some minutes.

I was aroused, and I am ashamed of what I did. No harm would have come from it, though, if it weren't for an extraordinary piece of bad luck. As I adjusted my position, shifting my weight from one knee to the other, I caught a broken piece of the fence with the rolled-up sleeve of my shirt, and it moved slightly, making a noise.

This in itself might not have been an issue – she had her eyes shut, and the children were preoccupied. But by chance, the husband came out at that moment and must have seen or heard me there. I stumbled away, making more noise in my haste, and went back into the cottage, shutting the door behind me.

There was a minute or two's silence, and I thought perhaps I had imagined him spotting me. But then there was banging on my front door. And when I did not answer, obscenities were shouted at me. Very nasty words indeed.

Now, another comment pops up on my screen.

"You're a really nice man. But don't get involved! BIG TROUBLE!"

Then a more restrained one. "What you are doing is laudable, SimpleSimon, but could be dangerous for you. Be careful."

And finally, one that sums up the consensus view. "Donate to charities that help the homeless rather than getting involved personally."

I sigh to myself. All these blinkered, narrow-minded opinions. The assumption, almost from every single one of them, is that anyone who has ended up on the streets must be bad in some way – on drugs or a prostitute or an alcoholic or a thief, or 101 other awful things. No possibility that they may have had an abusive parent or step-parent, that the family may have broken up, or they might be down on their luck, or have lost their job and their home through no fault of their own. These people make me feel physically sick.

I turn off my computer and think about what I should do. There is one last round of shouting from next door, and I hear the woman's high-pitched scream. A long silence as I wonder if this horror is taking place in front of the children. I feel my mouth go dry and my body tense as I debate whether I have the courage to act. To physically go and help her and the children in some way. I do not think I do. But I know I must do something. I could call the police, anonymously, but doubt they'd turn up for days. But then I hear her shouting back, defiant, and doors are being opened and slammed shut. I hear his car firing up and roaring away.

I hope he stays gone. He is a man who scares me. After banging on my door and then storming off in the summer, I have barely seen him since. He has stuck his middle finger up at me twice as I walked by with Fluffy in the lane and he was in the front garden. He also called me a "cunt" on one of those occasions. His children were within earshot. And a few weeks ago, as I was walking up Bluebell Lane with Fluffy, I turned suddenly at the sound of a car accelerating fast on the road behind me. I had to move quickly onto the verge, almost into the hedge, as he raced by in his Audi. I am not sure what he mouthed at me, but judging by his contorted face, it wasn't very nice.

I get up from the computer, deciding I will have one last go at finding the girl.

God help me if I don't.

Left alone with the Lump, Widow Woman and the Man in the Suit, I am going stark, staring mad.

IT IS WELL into the early hours. I am lying face down on my bed, still dressed, with my boots on and Fluffy tucked beside me. I am beyond torment.

I am at the end of my days. I know it. In truth, I have been for some time. The endless descent. This was my last chance of salvation. And it has gone.

And now, I am at rock bottom. I have nowhere else to go. I turn and look at Fluffy, asleep and making his little snuffling noises. I do not know what to do.

I went to the seafront at dusk, one final search for the girl. Back and forth between the pier and the theatre on the promenade. In my haste, I bumped into an elderly woman bumbling along, her husband shouting angrily after me as I ran off, calling back, "Sorry, sorry," as politely as I could.

Working myself into something close to a frenzy as I searched the shelters and the beach huts, and below the pier, and in all the tucked-away places where I thought she could be hiding. Everywhere. Anywhere.

Then further on, down towards the docks and by the

funfair and the amusements all along the front. Faster and faster. I must have looked a sight by this time, so obviously distressed and hot and drenched in sweat, even in this wintery weather.

But there came a point, as dusk turned to night, and I made my way back and headed by the theatre and down towards old Felixstowe and the Ferry, where I simply did not care any more about how I appeared or what people thought.

I could not find her. No matter where I looked.

On the seafront. Towards the docks. Down towards the Ferry. Even up the town.

My hopes raised and dashed. Time and again.

And now, hours later, wet and exhausted and close to collapse, I have to accept that she has gone. This girl who looked a little like my daughter. Whom I would have brought back to my cottage. To look after. To care for. To love; maybe even to be loved back.

I searched in all the places she could possibly be. Hide-aways that nobody would think of. Behind the bins at the back of supermarkets. Underneath the arch of the railway line. The alleyway by the Wimpy in the high street and all the little backyards there.

She has left town. To Ipswich, perhaps. Where there might be more money to be had up by the railway station. Or to Woodbridge. Where they have more money than sense. Richer pickings than Felixstowe, where dockers cut their coupons and shop in Poundland and haggle over every fifty pence at the market.

I have looked everywhere she could possibly be.

She is nowhere.

It is over. And I am finished.

I AM LOCKED UP ALONE.

In a tiny cell.
So small I cannot even stretch out.
I try to sleep.
To shut out the sing-song voice that calls to me.
Behind the bangs.
Beyond the shouts.
And everything all around me.
And I lie here.
In the dark.
Wondering where the sing-song voice is.
Whether it is close or far away.
And what it wants from me.

5

THURSDAY, 21 NOVEMBER, 11.57 AM

I lie here in my bed, dozing fitfully, after another troubled night. Nightmares in my mind. Fluffy restless at my feet.

Other than getting up to go to the toilet at dawn and letting Fluffy outside, I have lain here since I came back from the seafront. I am still in my dirty and crumpled clothes.

Apart from Fluffy, I have nothing to get up for. Nothing to do. I can't even be bothered to finish the half-played solitaire and chess games on the coffee table. Nor use my binoculars to look for the robin. And I have nowhere to go. I just lie here with everything going round and round in my mind.

The girl has gone for good. I know it. I have to leave it now. It was madness, anyway. I realise this. The idea that, somehow, she would change my life. Take me out of my misery. Make me a different person to who I am today. All nonsense. I understand that. And my insanity is rising inside me again. For that is what it is. Just beneath the surface. Only the chance of finding someone to love and be loved by was enough to keep it down. And now that chance has gone.

The medication I used to take dulled my thoughts and

feelings. I would not say the tablets made me happy, nor that they took away the pain. They made everything fuzzy, so that things did not matter quite as much as they might do. Should do. What I have done should matter. It should destroy me. I deserve to die.

I think, without medication, everything is sharper and more intense. There were greater highs as I chased the girl through what was little more than wishful thinking. And the lows now will be deeper and longer. I could just lie here until I die. And why not? These terrible, bloody memories inside my head are too much for anyone to bear.

My daughter is dead. All I see, all I ever see, in my endless, recurring dreams is her face as I look down upon her corpse.

And my wife. All I remember is the screaming, on and on, and then into silence.

The time I spent locked away. On my own. Until I was released, supposedly rehabilitated – and to what?

I just want to be at peace. Yet there is noise all around me. What sounded like a van pulled up next door, at No. 5, an hour or so ago. Lots of men shouting. Loading things, I think. Then a car reversing quickly, the screech of brakes. I assumed, but could not rouse myself to go and look, that the Man in the Suit was back, or that the woman and the children were packing up and leaving before his violent return. I do not know which. I do not care.

And the Lump will be there. By the fence looking over, watching and waiting for me to come out into the back garden. To have an inane conversation, as he tries, with his slow and feeble brain, to recount his news of the day. How he was offered seventy-five pence for a computer game he owned by a second-hand games store in town. How the bakers had run out of the chocolate brownies he so likes. Such important stuff to him. I would smile and frown and pretend something pressing needed doing indoors. But not today. I will not go out at all. I will just lie here, right through.

And there is the knocking. Always the endless knocking. *Tap. Tap. Tap.* Pause. *Tap. Tap. Tap.* I ignore it. It is Widow Woman, taking her fat and smelly dog out across the fields and wanting me to join her. *Tap. Tap. Tap.* Pause. *Tap. Tap. Tap.* Eventually, she stops and moves on. But she will be back, in an hour or so, after the walk. *Tap. Tap. Tap.* Pause. *Tap. Tap. Tap.* Driving me mad.

What's the point of it all?

This wretched existence.

What's the bloody point?

IT IS NOW THE EVENING. I spent all day in bed. Stewing in my own juices. It is the worst thing to have done. I know that.

I am up at last. But I can barely move. Nor function. Washing. Dressing. Getting ready to go out. All an agony for me.

Fluffy wandered about. Then returned and sat there by the side of the bed. And whimpered. And growled at the back of his throat. And did his funny little circular walk when he needs to go out. Now I am walking him over the fields.

It is dark. There are no lights down this end of Bluebell Lane. A few at the top, near the junction to the high road. And there is little to illuminate the fields. The lights of the docks and the outline of the cranes are in the far distance. But I like the anonymity of night. That I can walk head down with my own thoughts. Not that there are ever many people out and about here at this time of the day. Sometimes I nod at those who are. Most times I don't. It is easier since COVID-19; people expect you to veer off and away at the sight of them. And I do.

It is cold and breezy, and the snow is coming and will be here for some time; so they say on the BBC. A week at least, maybe longer, initially, and more after that. Months, possibly. I cannot remember when we last had heavy snowfall, inches and inches of the stuff that stopped the world and trapped everyone indoors and seemed to go on forever. There are comparisons being made now on the BBC to the winters of 1947 and 1963, where life seemed to be put on hold for months on end. I will drive out in the morning and stock up, filling my larder and the fridge-freezer with enough to see me through for weeks.

If it were not for Fluffy, I would give up, as simple as that. I would lie face down in my bed and not get up again. I would just stay there and let myself fade away. Other than Widow Woman and the postman with his junk mail, no one comes to my door. Nobody would miss me. Widow Woman would simply assume I had gone away. I could maybe leave a little note. And lie down to die. But I could not bear to see Fluffy being taken back to the Blue Cross. He is an old dog. No one would take him on. He would die alone in a tiny cage, surrounded by other dogs yelping and barking and scaring him. I cannot let that happen.

Fluffy pulls at the lead, dragging me faster along the path that runs by the main field.

I have my torch held out in front of me, illuminating the path, and swing it left to right to see what Fluffy has seen.

Something darts away across the field, maybe a rabbit, perhaps even a fox – enough to rouse Fluffy to give chase.

These fields and lanes and ditches are creepy at night. In daytime, I have enjoyed the bleak but beautiful landscape stretching out ahead of me. At night, my troubled mind sees movement in the trees and bushes in the distance and imagines bodies in the ditches by the side of my feet. I am a tormented soul, and I twitch and turn at sounds and movements beside and behind me, my head forever twisting to check my footsteps. But no one is there. There never is. It is just my conscience with its hand resting heavy on my shoulder.

These waifs and strays on the streets. So many teenagers go missing from home and are never seen again. They just vanish as if into thin air. You read about them in the papers all the time. I am an avid reader of the local press, albeit much of it online these days. Those who are loved make it into the papers. Many don't even get a mention. Those who are troubled. Unwanted by a step-parent. Forced out, as often as not. The reality is that most of them end up dead soon enough, either through drink or drugs or by their own hands, tablets or a knife. And they are never found.

Some, especially young teenage girls, are taken by predatory older men without love in their hearts. They are used and disposed of in makeshift graves in cellars and gardens and under patios. And elsewhere. Further afield. There are bodies out here, in ditches, buried deep in winter and by summer, with leaves and debris and foxes and other animals, they have all but disappeared. I hurry on my way.

Fluffy squats in or close to his usual place. To do what he does. Over by a ditch that is deep and long and dark. I have walked by it so many times.

I see a red leather glove, stiff and clenched in the cold, beside it. My daughter had a pair of red gloves.

I pick it up and look at it. Cracking the stiff fingers and slipping it into my pocket as I turn and head for home. Glad to be away from this horror of a hiding place.

I AM at the bottom of the stairs in the hallway. I turn and open the cellar door with a big heavy key, twisting it time and again in the stubborn lock before it finally opens to me.

The cellar is a dark and dank place, lit by a solitary 40-watt lightbulb casting more shadows than light in every corner. The room smells. I know why.

There is a single kitchen chair on its side on the ground, a mix of dug-over soil and stones, lumpy and uneven. A broken, rotted beam hangs down at an angle.

I ignore the detritus on the ground – a taken-apart trampoline and its tarpaulin cover, a full bin bag, a torn coat, a length of rope, an axe and a spade – and move to the chest freezer on the far side. It is full of joints and cuts of meat. Two long butchered lengths with white bones and red meat covered in frost are closest to the surface. Other lumps and lengths, some wrapped, some not, are hidden away beneath them.

I do not know what to do. If I am to stock up for weeks, months even, perhaps all winter, this huge freezer is the only place I can store food, nice, cellophane-wrapped chicken breasts and packets of beef burgers and the like. Yet I cannot empty this freezer of its contents. Out with the rubbish bins. Buried in the garden. Maybe burned on a bonfire. Tipped into ditches over the fields. I cannot do any of that.

And I think how long this freezer has been like this. Full of bones and meat. A while now. Without being frozen, I suspect they may have rotted away. Well, perhaps not the bones. Outdoors, those would have been picked clean by birds and foxes and creatures of the night. But still there. The bones. Always there. I think of my wife and my daughter and the happier days we once had. And what I did. Have been doing ever since. Up to and including today, if the girl by the pier had not disappeared. And I am suddenly overwhelmed by it all.

I sink to my knees, my forehead resting against the side of the freezer.

I do not pray. For I am not a religious man. I do not believe in all of that heaven and hell mumbo jumbo.

But if I did, I would surely now be on my way to hell.

I rest there, crouched and sobbing for a minute or two, maybe longer. My emotions, my feelings, my moods are all over the place. I think it is because I have come off the medication. At least when I was taking the tablets, I was steadier. Since stopping – going cold turkey, to use an old-fashioned phrase – there are more highs and lows. Higher highs and lower lows.

I fear these, in a way. The higher highs and lower lows. The highs push me on to greater extremes and excesses – running down the promenade with a copy and pasted photo of the girl took me to the edge of insanity. I know in my heart there is literally nothing I would not have done to find that girl and to bring her back here to live with me happily ever after in Bluebell Lane. Nothing.

And now the lows are lower than they have ever been. The grief. The shame. The horror of it all. Filling my mind. That hand of conscience on my shoulder. Gripping it. Pushing me towards the end. To take my own life. I literally do not know what I will do next. The madness inside almost overpowers me. I must be strong. To keep going. To get through this. One day at a time. Tomorrow may be a better day.

I get to my feet, wiping my eyes and face with the corner of my sleeve.

I look down at all the different butchered parts in the freezer and pull down the lid.

They can stay there. I'll stock up with food that I'll cram somehow into the kitchen larder.

I turn and look up the narrow wooden staircase towards

the half-open door onto the landing. Fluffy is there, and he is pawing the ground, waiting to be called down in the hope of a piece of meat or a bone to chew on. The thought of either revolts me. I make a "tsch, tcsh" noise and wave him away. He ignores the gesture and stands there expectantly as I climb back up the stairs.

I turn back and look down before I lock the door. I have not been in here for so long. I do not know what drew me down there now. The chest freezer is the only place to store bulk-bought items. But I knew the freezer was full and that I could not empty it. Some part of me, deep down inside, made me do it.

I lock the door and make my way to the kitchen. I hang the big old key on one of a row of mismatched nails in the wall by the back door. I vow to myself I will not go down again. I fear what will happen if I do. I could easily go insane down there. I sit at the kitchen table and start making a list of what I need to get for the larder. I will stock it with tins and packet meals to last me a month.

Baked beans. Spaghetti hoops. Ravioli. Soups.

Packets of rice. Things I can put in the microwave.

I will take the car tomorrow morning and drive out to the supermarket at Warren Heath to stock up with supplies. I am ready for this new lockdown.

I AM IN THE FOREST.
It is night-time.
There is moonlight.
Amongst the trees.
And I am standing.
By a grave.
Newly dug.

And filled by me.
But the soil moves.
And I cannot stop it.
And I cannot turn away.
I want to run.
But I know that I must stay.
I awake, tormented as ever.

6

FRIDAY, 22 NOVEMBER, 5.22 PM

I am walking out of the Tesco Express on the high street, laden with carrier bags full of bits and pieces I forgot to bulk-buy this morning. Cupboard stuff such as soya milk and Mr Kipling's cakes. Snow is coming tonight and is expected to last on and off for days, the first of many heavy snowfalls this winter.

And I see her. Just like that.

The girl by the pier is sat, head down, hood up, on the pavement by the side of the road in front of me.

I stop. Surprised. Bewildered. Overjoyed. I stand for a moment, by the Tesco exit, uncertain what to do. An elderly man behind me tuts and huffs, as I am in his way. I apologise. Move two or three steps forward. Put my carrier bags on the pavement. Look down at her.

She seems to sense my presence. Or maybe it's just that my shoes are in her line of vision. She looks up at me, mumbles a request for change, almost mechanically. I am shocked. Her left eye is bruised, her lip cut. I wonder what has happened to her since we last met.

She is wearing much the same as before. A thin and

threadbare fleece with a hood. Jeans. Clunky old-woman shoes. But no blankets or bedding. I am sure she had some last time. They must have been stolen, ripped away from her. She will struggle tonight. The forecast is for sub-zero temperatures and a 90 per cent or higher chance of heavy snow. She needs shelter and warmth.

"I saw you ... on Monday ... down by the pier," I say. Casually, almost conversationally.

"Have you got any change, please?" she replies. I don't know if she heard what I said. Whether she remembers me.

"You gave my dog a treat." I go on. "He's a Jack Russell. I gave you some loose change."

"Have you got any change, please?" she says again, the mantra of every beggar.

I check my jacket pocket. My wallet. A debit card. A credit card. A ten-pound note. A twenty-pence piece and a fifty-pence piece. The ten-pound note is too much, too soon, I think. She will think I want something from her for that. Seventy pence in change is too little these days. You can't give less than the cost of a cup of tea.

"I've only seventy pence in change ... and cards." I hesitate before going on. "I can get you a hot chocolate from the coffee shop if you like, over the way. A sandwich."

She nods – agreement, I think – and holds her hand up for the change anyway. I notice she is wearing fingerless gloves and that her fingers are dirty, and one of them is bloodstained, I'm sure.

I drop the coins into her open palm. "Wait here. I'll get you something nice to eat and drink."

As I turn, she speaks. "Thank you," she says simply. I nod, walk away, towards the coffee shop, ten, twenty metres down the high street.

I have left my carrier bags by her side. To show I trust her. This is the start of getting her to trust me, too, of course. It will take time, be a long journey, but it will be worth it in the end. If I get it right. I have to.

I turn as I enter the coffee shop, to see if she is still there, waiting. She is, her head down again. She has not touched my carrier bags.

I check the sandwiches that are left in the coffee shop. Egg and cress, that's all. The perennial leftovers. As I queue to buy an egg and cress sandwich and a hot chocolate, I wonder what I will do when I return. Hand her the food and drink and walk away, or stop and make conversation as she eats, and tell her I'll buy her the same again tomorrow. If she likes. Maybe also give her a blanket or a coat. If she wants.

Whatever I do, I know I have to do this slowly and carefully. Step by step. I have to show I trust her. Get her to trust me. Then, and only then, do I invite her to stay, to "get herself back on her feet", in the nookery of my cottage at 3 Bluebell Lane.

At the very least, she needs to come back with me and have a warm bath. A wallow. To dry herself on soft, clean towels. Sit by the fire, drying her hair. Put on clean fresh clothes. I have some nice things in wardrobes and drawers she can have.

"Here," I say, my arms outstretched towards her on my return. "Hot chocolate. Sandwich." I pause and add, warmly enough, "Thank you for looking after my shopping."

She takes the food and drink, stuffing the sandwich into a pocket of her jacket. Shifts her position, the hot chocolate between her open legs. No word of thanks. No response to my thank you for looking after my shopping.

I stand there, not sure what to say.

"My name's Philip." I reach out my hand for a handshake. A long pause. I feel I have overstepped the mark. That she will see me as just another middle-aged man wanting rough-and-ready sex with a young girl.

"Rosie," she replies, finally, reluctantly. She reaches out her hand and shakes mine. It is a limp handshake. It needs to be firmer, more assertive. I will teach her, show her, in time, how to do a proper handshake. It's a useful thing to be able to do.

Another long pause as she sips her drink, head down.

I am not sure if that's it, that she is now dismissing me,or whether she is willing to have a conversation. I have to try. To say the right words. Not scare her away. I have to take this chance. If not, that might be it. I may never see her again.

There are so many things I want to ask her. Why she is on the streets. Whether there was trouble at home. A cruel father. A stepfather who wanted to treat her as more than a daughter, maybe.

I wonder how she survives. If she is on benefits, a waiting list for housing. Or whether she has somehow slipped through the cracks in the system. If she is looking for work. What she wants to do, is qualified to do. If anything.

And I wonder about so many practicalities. What she does with the loose change that's handed to her. Is it enough to get something to eat? Can she use it to get a bed for the night? Where does she sleep when she has nowhere to go? I want to know everything about her.

"I've a blanket you can have," I say suddenly. "Blankets. You could come back to my place and get them if you like. It's not far ... my house ... my cottage."

She ignores me, sitting there finishing her drink.

Too much too soon.

I should know better by now. A crass suggestion.

"Or I could meet you somewhere later. Give them to you. The blankets. By the pier. It's going to snow overnight. Heavily. Four to six inches." I am gabbling. I know it. I sound desperate. And creepy. And I need to show her I am just a regular guy.

She gets up suddenly. Holding the empty cup. And she kind of shrugs. And I do not know what the gesture means. I don't think it is dismissive. As she turns to go, I call after her.

"I'll see you by the pier at eight. I'll have the blankets for you."

She does not reply. I watch her walking away, a strange, ambling kind of walk. Almost nonchalant. Defiant.

A police patrol car rolls on by. I turn and go back into Tesco.

I AM CLEANING and tidying the nookery to the side of the cottage.

The thought that the girl – Rosie – might be here tonight in this room almost overwhelms me.

I remain calm and in control by stopping at intervals to do my breathing exercises.

I have a system for making sure everything is clean and tidy and in place, and that it's working properly. I start with the living-bedroom area, dusting and hoovering and using the nozzle to suck up any cobwebs in the corners of the ceiling. I then wipe down the light switches and the plug sockets with a cloth and polish. There always seem to be smeared fingerprints there, and one of the plug sockets had a dark blob of something on it, which I must have missed when I did my last clean. I admonish myself. I must be more thorough next time.

I will need to be careful when Rosie is here. Vigilant.

I do not want her to be seen by the Lump or Widow Woman or the Man in the Suit.

I don't think they need to know my business. And I don't want trouble. The Lump might make a nuisance of himself.

I move to the window and look out through the nets and

into the lane and across to a row of tall conifers that stand strong in the wind. The lane is quiet this evening. I think everyone is indoors, battening down the hatches. Even the dog walkers, usually in procession to the fields and back at this time of night, are nowhere to be seen.

The net curtains are dusty and dirty. I go and dampen one of the cloths under the tap in the kitchenette and come back to wipe at the more stubborn marks. I then pull them this way and that, hoping no one from the lane could see through. I don't want anyone out there to see Rosie in a state of undress.

The rest of the room is easy to do. I pull the bed down and look at the mattress. It has marks and stains on it. But I put a fresh bottom sheet on it and a top sheet and a blanket from the cupboard in my bedroom; it looks clean enough. I take down the curtains that hang from the shelf around the bed and put them in one of the big bins out the back. They are so dirty.

I check down the sides of the chair to make sure there is nothing there. I nudge the coffee table back into place, into the imprints of its feet in the carpet. I move the dried flower arrangement on it slightly to one side so that the pretty rose in the centre of it faces the bed. There is a little radio, an old-fashioned transistor, my late mother's, next to it. I check it is still working. It is. There, that is done.

I wonder if it will be warm enough in here when Rosie undresses for bed.

It's usually nicer here than in the cottage itself.

But I'm not sure how it will be with the cold and the snow that's expected.

I give the kitchen area a brisk clean. Then the shower and toilet. I hurry through, mindful of the time and that I want to be back at the prom by eight. And I need to walk Fluffy before that – although, the weather as it is, he will probably cock his leg against the gate and turn to come back inside. His bowl of Chappie and biscuits waiting for him.

I am bubbling up with excitement. I cannot wait to see Rosie, the girl by the pier.

And I hope that I can persuade her, one way or the other, to come back here to my cottage.

To stay in the nookery. As others have done. This time though, I must get it right. And live happily forever.

I AM BACK at the pier. With a rucksack across my shoulders.

Two blankets. One warm coat. A flask of hot tea.

It is just before eight o'clock. She is nowhere to be seen.

I am sitting on a bench close to where I first saw her. I have not been into the pier amusements. Nor searched around the beach huts or along the prom. I just sit and watch and wait. I said I would meet her by the pier with blankets at eight o'clock. I could not have been clearer.

It's her choice. If she does not turn up, then I have to accept that. I must let her go. I do not want to. But I cannot hunt her down. She might go to the police. Report me. Say I said things to her. Did things. Showed myself to her. And what would happen? Where would that end? I know where it would take me. Back to where I've been before. No. I must walk away.

It's a cold night. A stiff breeze. But still dry. She will need to find somewhere to shelter from the coming snow. And be safe. Out of danger. I have been thinking about her bruised eye and cut lip, and I wonder how that happened. I think she must have been robbed of her belongings by a man. Fought back. Got a hiding for it. Young women on the street are vulnerable to middle-aged men.

I see her suddenly. Strolling along the prom towards me.

Her funny, ambling walk. I was not sure if, deep down, I expected her to turn up. I hoped she would.

Now she is here in front of me. I am sitting. She is standing. She says nothing. Just waits there. For the handout.

I glance around. Up and down the prom. Behind me, the leisure centre, a small car park and the road along to the theatre.

I cannot be seen with her. With any girl, young woman really, on my own. I need to keep my distance, ideally. There are people moving about, cars parking and reversing out and away. Some activity down near the prom. No one is taking any notice of me though. That is good.

I turn slightly to the side. As if she is not with me. Just in case.

Take the rucksack. Put it next to me on the bench.

Gesture with a movement of my head that she should sit on the other side.

She sits down. I wait for her to ask for change or a cigarette or something more. But she does not. She waits patiently. Or so it seems to me.

"I got you some blankets, like I said." I nudge the rucksack towards her. "And a coat. A warm coat. It's waterproof. A flask of tea."

She puts her hand on the rucksack. Goes to unzip it to take a look.

"You can have the rucksack ... and everything in it," I add. I could not bear to sit here whilst she takes out my daughter's coat and looks it up and down. I can imagine her saying, *I don't like the colour* or *It's too big* or *It's got funny buttons* and handing it back to me. This beggar who should be grateful for whatever I choose to give her.

She nods. Pulls the rucksack towards her. "Thank you," she says, quietly and simply.

I expect her to get up, walk off, never to be seen again.

But she stays there, unmoving. As if she is ready to have a conversation. Maybe she's grateful.

I do not know what to say. I am, all of a sudden, tongue-tied. But I have to start a conversation. If I sit in silence, she will think I have nothing to say. And she will leave. And I will not see her again. If she heads out of town.

"It must be really tough," I say, slowly and carefully, in a measured voice. "Being homeless."

She makes no indication she has heard me. Nor does she make a move to go.

"Do you ... get enough money ... in your paper cup ... to get a bed for the night?"

She kind of half-shrugs. I pause. Say nothing. The silence extends. Until she speaks.

"No." I think that's all she's going to say, but then she goes on. "There's nowhere here. A hostel or nothing." I wonder why she stays, then, but do not follow up on it.

"What about Ipswich?" I reply, making my voice sound kind, like a loving uncle. Favourite uncle Philip.

She shakes her head. "Ipswich is ... bad."

I know personally, for a fact, that this is true. I remember once being at the railway station there late one night. A teenage girl had missed the last train home. She had no money for somewhere to stay. I offered her a bed for the night. She walked with me some of the way to my car, parked up a hill and away into the dark back streets. Then she seemed to panic, changing her mind. She ran off. I called after her without success.

If Rosie were my daughter, I would put my arm around her now, pull her close, whisper gentle words to her. But I cannot do that. Not yet, anyway. It is something I will be able to do, one day, if I get this right.

So I simply nod. I do not press the point. About Ipswich being a bad place. It is full of wild-eyed, angry immigrants these days, brutish and thuggish enough in daylight. At night, with a young and pretty girl sheltering in a doorway ... it does not bear thinking about.

I know enough to realise I should not ask her why she is homeless. Or where she sleeps at night. What she does to make ends meet. I am not an innocent. She may steal. She may sell drugs. She may have sex with strangers. None of this matters to me. She has to survive somehow.

And she moves, turning and twisting to put the rucksack on her back. She half glances, as if she is grateful but embarrassed, towards me. Or maybe that's just wishful thinking. She gets up and turns towards the pier.

I had hoped for more. A real conversation. A chance to get to know her. To offer to buy her a meal on the pier. Sausages, beans and chips. Good, old-fashioned, English comfort food.

"Rosie," I say, my voice cracking unexpectedly.

She stops. Turns back. Sort of looks sidelong at me. Her head at an angle. As if she is curious, inquisitive.

"I live at 3 Bluebell Lane. At the Grove. Through the car park. Past the football pitches. Across the fields. Number three. Bluebell Lane. Three. If you ever need any ..."

I think she kind of nods and smiles, almost imperceptibly, as if to say *I hear you*. Maybe a *thank you,* too.

And she is gone.

I watch her.

My heart breaks.

IT IS GONE MIDNIGHT, and I cannot sleep. I am standing in the dark by the window in the nookery, looking out and along the lane.

It is now snowing steadily and settling on the ground.

Rosie will not come tonight, not in this. If, indeed, she ever would have done.

Rosie would not be the first girl on the streets to come here to stay in the nookery. There have been others. At first, I would go to Ipswich railway station, wrapped up warm with a hat, scarf and gloves on cold, wintery nights, arriving five minutes or so after the last train to London, Cambridge, wherever. Every so often there would be girls who missed that train and, with little or no money, would have to sleep on the station platform or close by.

To begin with, none of them took up my offer. One young pudding-faced girl, shivering in the cold, *ummed* and *aahed* for a moment or two, and I could not quite speak with excitement. As I stood expectantly, her quite angry-looking friend, a black girl, suddenly came out of the toilet. "He's offering us a bed for the night," the pudding-faced girl said neutrally. "Ha!" spat the friend, looking me up and down with contempt. Suddenly feeling shamed, I left hurriedly before things turned nasty or the police were called.

I remember the first girl who came back with me. After half a dozen or so visits, I had learned what to say and what not to say. British girls would never consider the offer, most laughing and swearing at me and calling me a creep. But a Dutch girl, backpacking across the UK and ending up in Ipswich, of all places, readily agreed and seemed grateful. I think she had been smoking dope; as she peered at the official-looking Samaritans card I'd put together from the internet, she suddenly seemed to be having second thoughts. I took her firmly by the arm and led her away to my car. To save her from herself.

Another girl, two or three months later, came back with me from the railway station, although I think she might have been sleeping on the streets anyway. She was clearly on drugs; I suspect that, if I had not taken her away, she would have come under attack by any one of the groups of men who were around and close by. After that, though, I had little success, with most of the girls being sex workers. And what with that and the CCTV and police patrols all the time and busybody do-gooders turning up, I felt it prudent to stop my visits.

There are headlights to my left, towards the top of the lane.

An Audi is coming down, edging slowly forwards through the falling snow.

I watch as it turns onto the next-door drive. The Man in the Suit is back. I fear him and what he might do.

After Ipswich railway station, I turned my attentions to Felixstowe and those who lived on the streets here. I took no notice of immigrants, who should not be here. And I rarely saw older women. I doubt they could survive for long. But I found girls who would come back with me to 3 Bluebell Lane.

It took a while, but I learned how to persuade without having to take them forcefully by the arm or rely on their drugged-up state to succumb. Wet, windy and cold weather is the starting point. They need shelter and warmth. In summer, with warmer nights, they are not as desperate. They need to be young, too. Fresh on the streets. Innocent. Ready to be helped. Trusting. I never went near the raddled, skinny things with pockmarked arms in their thirties.

I always felt that a middle-aged woman, a "mum", would have had more success. These young girls wanted an arm round them, a shoulder to cry on. As a middle-aged man, damned as a pervert in this Me Too age, I had to work harder. I am, fortunately, a dab hand with technology, so it is fairly easy to produce a range of official-looking cards for the Samaritans and other charities. Some of the girls would look at my "official" ID, with its photo, stamps and laminated cover and matching lanyard, and believe every word I said.

There is no sign of my admirer tonight. Widow Woman. At the gate. Up the path. Peering through windows as I sleep. Perhaps the grandchildren are there, running her ragged.

It is too cold. And the snow is falling ever heavier. Something close to a blizzard now.

I have been thinking about Widow Woman. She should not be stalking me like this. She angers me. I will have to do something about it. Before she makes me explode. Hopefully, with her grandchildren there, she may leave me alone for a while.

When they came into my little extension, my nookery, the girls would be overjoyed. A gasp. A smile of delight. A clean bed with fresh sheets and puffed-up pillows. A sofa, a desk. Their own kitchenette, shower and toilet. More than they could have ever hoped for. A bit different from living behind the bins at the Co-op supermarket!

And those who came back over the years were all very grateful to me. To start with. They were so pleased. They showed their appreciation. They were so happy. And I was happy, too. And I thought, with each of them, that it might be the beginning of the road to happy ever after.

It was not to be. For one reason and another. They have all gone now. Some sooner than others. They were all a mistake. And I carried on living my life on my own. I had almost given up. Until I saw Rosie, the close image of my daughter. And here I am again, hoping, dreaming, that I might get one last chance to get it right.

I don't want to end up like that oversized freak at 1 Bluebell Lane. Sad and lonely and with nothing to live for.

The Lump. Andrew Lumb. Frankenstein's monster.

I'd like to see him gone. Instead of watching me all the time. He gives me the creeps.

Of course, if you end up on the streets, you disappear from society. You fall through the cracks. Into the gutter.

Down to the drains. And washed away. You are outside of society. There is no network of family and friends. You have gone. Vanished. Never to be seen again. No one knows. Nobody cares.

There are exceptions. I am an avid reader of the local press and watch the regional TV too, to keep up to date with all the news in Suffolk. There was a girl called Abbi from Ipswich, last year, who fell out with her family. Slept on friends' sofas. Dropped out of sight. There were appeals in the papers and on television. It was said she loved Felixstowe and might have come here. But she has never been seen again.

Most just disappear like a puff of smoke, without any mention on the news at all. The Hannahs and Jordans and Beckys and Charlottes and Georgy Porgys. Gone. Just like that. An endless stream of silly, stupid girls leaving home after an argument with Mum or Dad, making their way to the row of open graves waiting for them somewhere out there in the night.

I look up and along the lane. I am surely imagining things. There is a blur of a figure there, walking towards me through the snow. It looks like an angel.

I bring my hand to my mouth. Too late to stifle my sob of joy. I am not imagining things at all. It is real.

It is her. The girl by the pier. I can scarcely believe it. But she is here. Making her way oh so slowly up Bluebell Lane.

Here you are.

Darling girl.

You have come to me.

PART II

THE NOOKERY

7

SATURDAY, 23 NOVEMBER, 12.32 AM

Yes, it is definitely her. This bent and cowed figure. The girl by the pier is walking painfully up the lane through the falling snow. On she comes. On she comes to me.

She slows at number five and moves towards the drive-way, so I cannot see her. She is checking the number of the house. She remembers my words. "Number three." I stressed the three. More than once. Several times, I'm sure.

I wait for her to reappear, to move towards my cottage. And I am suddenly overwhelmed by feelings. The initial excitement. The anticipation. And, as ever, the dread. Knowing where this might lead. How it could finish. Again.

I step back from the window, doubts swirling in my mind. That this is another appalling mistake. Inviting her in. Letting her be here. I know what might happen this time. Police at my door. Coming in.

But I cannot let this madness go. I have no choice. It is a primeval thing. A desire. A need in me. I can deny it. But not for long. I am driven by what's deep down inside.

She is now at my gate. She knows this is No. 3. She has come for help and protection. To me. And me alone.

This waif and stray whom no one wants. Who survives as best she can on the streets. Little more than an alley cat.

I watch as she pushes the gate open and makes her way up the path. She does not see me. But I follow her. Alone and vulnerable.

She taps at the door. Barely even a knock. If I were asleep, I would not hear it. But I have to pretend to be asleep. I cannot go straight to the door, much as I want to. She will know I have been standing there, waiting, hoping. Becoming excited. She will think the worst of me. And that may frighten her. She may even turn and, head down, disappear back into the blizzard. She will only stay here if she believes I am benign.

I wait patiently for the louder knock I am sure will come. I have seen, as she came up the path, that my daughter's coat, the blankets and the rucksack are all gone. Taken from her, I assume. She has nothing but the clothes she stands up in, wet from the snow and soaked through to her skin. She is desperate, completely and utterly desperate, no food, no money, no shelter. It must be minus two or three degrees out there; the snow is coming down hard and fast. She'd die in a ditch by morning.

She knows that. She has no choice. I realise that is why she is here. I am not stupid. I am a white middle-aged man. These days, old white men are no longer a kindly uncle, a friendly neighbour, someone to turn to for a helping hand. We are assumed to be child molesters and rapists simply because of our sex, age and skin colour. She is only here because she has no one else, nowhere else to go. This is the end of the road for her. Live or die. The starkest choice.

Knock, knock. A polite but still quiet knocking.

A pause. A long pause.

And another *knock, knock.* A knock to be heard.

I wait a moment or two, and a while longer, and go and open the door, a feeling of sickness rising in my throat. Half-horror, half-pleasure. She stands there, glancing up at me and away, but says nothing. Not even a smile. She is still wearing the same clothes; they are soaking wet and stuck to the outline of her body. Her left cheek is puffy, as though she has been hit repeatedly. And her left arm hangs by her side as though she cannot lift it. She has taken another beating.

I wonder if she has been attacked, that someone out there has stolen everything I gave her, and whether that was the end of it. Or if that were just the beginning. Someone, a man, an immigrant from Eastern Europe roaming unchecked and unchallenged, dragging her into some bushes. Maybe more than one. A gang. Attacking her repeatedly. Leaving her for dead. She has limped her way here on the brink of death. This cat on its ninth life.

We look at each other, neither of us saying a word. I know that if I speak, my voice will betray me. She has a blank, almost sullen expression on her face, somehow an expectation, an acceptance, that I will help. She shifts her body, slightly and almost painfully, as if to say, *Well, are you letting me in?*

I smile and step back, inviting her inside. Warm and friendly. *Welcome to my haven. Your safe place now.*

She steps slowly into the hallway. Then stops, a sudden wariness about her. And somehow seems to stumble and fall into me. I catch her before her head hits the cold stone floor. Then lower her carefully.

She lies there. Conscious or unconscious, I cannot say. I think it's utter exhaustion, poor little thing.

I SIT IN THE NOOKERY, drinking a cup of milky coffee. The armchair is turned towards the bed.

I am tired, but adrenaline keeps me awake.

I want to see the girl's face as she comes to. What a picture it will be. Happiness. Gratitude.

When she collapsed in the hallway, I checked her body over carefully. Her mouth. That she was breathing. I pinched her arm. To be sure she was unconscious. Her wrist. To see that her pulse was strong. It was. My assessment was that she had fainted from exhaustion, perhaps mixed with relief that she was safe with me, and even the sudden change in temperature from outside to inside – although, in truth, it is chilly indoors. I have a blanket round my shoulders.

I scooped her up in my arms, her head and Bambi-like arms and legs hanging down. I was surprised how light she was. Holding her like this, feeling her body, I could tell how undernourished she had become. Her rib cage was clearly visible. And she smelled. A woman's body should smell sweet and fresh. Of freesias and rose petals. Hers stank of dirt and blood and grime. She repelled me.

I hurried through the living room, into the nookery, and laid her on the carpet, a pillow pushed quickly beneath her head. I stood above her, looking down at this lifeless, stinking thing. Even so. I swallowed hard, and I knew what I was going to do.

All I can see now is her head above the duvet. Hair left scraped back and tied up with what looks like an elastic band.

Her face, even free of make-up and puffed up on one side, is pretty. She is a natural beauty. Eyebrows. Cheekbones. Jawline. And the eyes, when they are open, are most striking. The eyes took my breath away.

One bare foot sticks out of the end of the duvet, nearest to me. It is a dainty, nicely shaped foot with chipped red varnish on the toes. Her ankle above is bruised rather badly, purple and black, as if she has been kicked or stamped on. Maybe during a struggle. As she fought for her honour, perhaps even her life.

I took off her fleece and checked her pockets. I had to. I could not risk her having a knife in there that she might use on me. In one pocket, there were some one-pound coins, six of them, all shiny. A rolled-up five-pound note. In the other, a lip salve, a crushed packet of small tampons, a postcard-sized, folded-in-half sketch of a child's face and, in particular, a passport-sized photograph .

The photograph was old and battered, its edges rubbed away into smoothness. I studied it closely. Two pretty girls, maybe mid-teens, in an embrace, pulling silly faces. One, with a short haircut and a beret, was the girl by the pier. The other, with a similar look but without a hat, was maybe a year or two younger. Or perhaps simply smaller. A sister, maybe. Perhaps just a friend. Or something more. I thought that over for a minute or two, then put her belongings back and hung the jacket over the back of the armchair to dry.

I did what I had to do before I put her to bed. I was gentlemanly, of course, with this dirty, bruised girl. The wet had soaked through her clothes to her skin. The clothes were stained and torn in places. Her body was grubby with etched-in dirt. I attended to her as best I could and laid her out beneath an old but freshly cleaned duvet.

She does not stir. Just lies there, unmoving. A strange and troubled expression on her face.

I get up and move to her, ducking my head towards her face. She is breathing steadily enough. I can feel her breath upon my cheek.

I think for a minute. Lift the duvet and look down at her.

The girls who have come here before have, in their different ways, all been at the end of their rope. A day or two away from swinging from it. I present a kind and gentle face to them. Show an official-looking card. Say some thoughtful, caring words. They are at a live-or-die moment in their lives. Sub-zero temperatures. Drugs. A thuggish man. Their pimp. Whatever. They believe they are streetwise, smart, more than a match for a soft-touch, middle-aged man. They think I am benevolent. A Simple Simon. That is why they come. That they can outwit me, trick me, somehow get the better of me.

That is why she is here. And for warmth and shelter. Some food. Money. Maybe for a night or two. Perhaps longer. When she fell at my feet, I thought at first it was for sympathy or a way of somehow tricking me. To see what I did. That I might run my hands over her body, her breasts, her buttocks and between her legs. She would then fight back and stab me with a knife tucked inside a sock. Kill Fluffy. Stay here until the snow has gone. Maybe longer. Much longer.

But her collapse was genuine. And she has, for the past forty-five minutes or so, been unconscious. And I wonder whether her subconscious, in that strange and troubled sleep, thinks that she is at my mercy and that I am stroking her and probing her wherever I want. The fact is, the girls who have come here have been at my mercy. No one knows where they are. Nobody cares. They have vanished from family, friends, society. They have already gone missing, lost forever, as like as not. They cannot go missing again. They are already dead and gone when they get here. They cannot die twice.

She is asleep for the night. This little urchin.

I lay the duvet back over her as gently as I can. Turn and leave.

I lock the door to the nookery behind me. Slip the key into my pocket.

IT IS two minutes to six a.m., and I awaken, unexpectedly refreshed. I have slept right through for once. No nightmares. Fluffy lies at the bottom of the bed by my feet.

There is that strange stillness that only ever comes with a heavy downfall of snow. It is cold in my room. And there is a lightness to the air.

I don't hear any movement in the cottage. I wonder suddenly if the girl is here, fast asleep. Or if she has somehow woken up and broken out, even though I locked the doors, at the back and into the cottage itself.

I get up. Wrap my dressing gown around me. Push my feet into slippers. Go to the front window overlooking the lane. It is white as far as I can see. The conifers that line the other side of the lane seem to be tipping forward, bowed by the weight of the snow upon them. It is Narnia. I look down to the snow on the pathway. There are no footsteps in or out. The gate remains shut, and the snow, piled up on top of it, makes it look strange and magical, a gateway to another world.

Fluffy stirs and jumps carefully off the bed and stretches, his front paws digging into the rug that covers the battered wooden floorboards. He walks a little stiffly to the bedroom door; I follow him out and down the stairs and through to the back door of the kitchen. "Wee, Fluffy, wee," I say as he stops at the sight of the snow. I push him firmly with the side of my foot, and he walks out a few steps, an odd and hesitant tiptoe-ing, before cocking his leg against a flowerpot, large and misshapen by the fallen snow. Then turns and comes back indoors.

Instead of preparing for our morning walk, I reach into a jar on the side in the kitchen and take out a handful of dog biscuits, dropping them into the bowl by my feet. Fluffy moves forward hungrily. The bowl next to it, half-full of water, has a frosted skim. I take it to the sink and fill it full of sputtering hot water before rinsing and refilling it with cold and putting it back on the floor. This back-of-the-cottage extension is old and primitive; it is as cold as a morgue. You could leave a dead body on the floor here, and it would not rot until spring, maybe even summer.

I watch as Fluffy turns and makes his way by the cellar door to the living room and his basket by the fireplace.

I follow, stop to light the fire, and as Fluffy settles into place, I walk to the door of the nookery.

I lean my head against it, listening. I hear noises, movements, singing in the distance.

She is up already and in the shower. I stop for a moment or two, maybe more, thinking things over. It is a soft and joyful singing; I do not recognise what the song is, and I wonder that she can be so relaxed here. Maybe she just lives in the moment, and the hot water on her body, the shampoo in her hair and the soft soaping of her skin are all momentary delights for her.

I wonder what the girl will do, coming out of the shower, drying and wrapping herself in a towel, most likely. Walking across the bedroom to the door to the living room. I locked it when I left her. I do not want her to know that. She will guess she is my prisoner. I do not want her to think that. I listen. There is silence. She may already be out of the shower and walking through the room to the door.

I slip the key into the lock as quietly as I can. There is a slight jangle as my hand shakes. It is coming off my medication that causes that. I will persevere. I want to be happy and normal, like other people are. I know I can be. I turn the key slowly to the left, as gently as I can, unlocking the door. Then slip the key out, another jangle, and into my pocket. I stand there, still listening, imagining her inside the room. I hear her.

I rest my head against the door, tortured. A minute passes as I listen to her doing what she's doing in the bedroom.

Then I turn and walk away, whistling through my dry mouth for Fluffy.

I will take Fluffy for a walk. She will be here when I get back. After all, she has nowhere else to turn. And she believes she is safe here. With this kindly old man.

8

SATURDAY, 23 NOVEMBER, 6.42 AM

T he snow lies deep on the ground, and the sky is white, and the temperature is cold enough for me to know that more snow is coming. Sooner rather than later.

I have taken Fluffy along the lane and by the side of the fields, up and all around. The usual route. Even with his coat on, he is a reluctant walker, hip-hopping through the snow. But he needs to get out and do what he needs to do.

Now we are coming back, and I am both excited and fearful about the day ahead. Spending it with Rosie. Getting to know her.

As I pass by No. 1, I glance across and see the Lump standing indoors by the front window, watching the lane. As he seems to do most days, whenever I am walking. Sometimes, he stares out trance-like, and I am never sure if he is looking at me or not. He is today. He raises a mug towards me in some kind of celebratory manner, triumphant and mocking. I do not know why. Perhaps it is because he is in the warm and dry and I am not. The boy is an idiot. But he does not know it. He thinks he is normal. He does not see himself as everyone else does. There's a bit missing somewhere inside his head. The "on" switch.

I stop and look back, a blank expression on my face as if I am waiting for him to gesture, indicate something more, to explain the celebration. I cannot think what there is to celebrate in his squalid little home. His father dead and his mother too, after succumbing to COVID-19. Maybe he's had some sort of payout for that, her being an NHS hero and all, standing six feet behind a Perspex screen, handing out prescriptions.

I wonder how he will manage in this snow. We must already be cut off from getting a car in or out of the lane. He does not drive anyway. And no van can get down to deliver groceries. Walking into town is possible, I think, but it would be slow going and dangerous with the snow soon packing into ice underfoot. And the BBC reports that more snow is on its way later today; I suspect we will be isolated here for days, maybe a week or more, until the weather eases. Perhaps temporarily. There is talk this snow will go on and on, through Christmas and beyond.

I do not know what he will do about essential supplies. Milk, bread, toilet paper and all. I hope he does not come knocking on my door to help him out. I do not want to get dragged into his misery of an existence. Become some sort of father figure. He must manage somehow. On his own. Until eventually he leaves the gas stove on and blows the place up, and then is taken into care, where he belongs.

I smile at him. The stupid great dollop.

Turn to go and follow Fluffy up the path.

To home. My happy home. With Rosie.

I step into the hallway, stamping down hard, partly to shake snow and ice off my boots. Partly to feel my feet are still there. I take the boots off, followed by my hat, gloves and coat, which I put on the hooks by the cellar door. They hang there, dripping slowly. I have a sudden, vivid image of blood oozing out onto and down the steps into the cellar.

I ignore it, bending to pull off Fluffy's coat. He stands stiff and unyielding, so I have to tug at the coat to get it over his legs. He is no help at all, lifting the wrong leg each time, as if he is being deliberately slow-witted to annoy me. Finally, he shakes himself free and potters towards the kitchen to see what's left in his bowls.

The cold gets into the bones of you in this place. The windowpanes are lined with twisting and distorting shapes; pretty if it weren't for the chill. In the hallway, I can see my breath. I move towards the living room for some heat.

And then I stop.

Expecting to hear noises from the nookery.

But it is all quiet.

I put my ear to the door. A minute, maybe more. There is no sound at all. Not from the bedroom. The kitchenette. The shower room. I wonder suddenly whether she may have collapsed again. Some underlying health problem. I put my hand on the door handle and hesitate. She may be in bed. She may be on the toilet. She may be undressed. Then again, she may be fighting for her life. I open the door and go in.

The bed is folded up against the wall. The coffee table has been moved slightly from its position, and the flower arrangement is facing in the wrong direction away from the bed. The transistor radio is next to it, resting on its side. Other than that, it is as if she has never been here. I move to the bed, which is stood up against the wall. Tug out the bed legs. Bring the bed down. The pillow, duvet and sheet are still in place. I pull at the duvet. There is a smear of dirt on the sheet. The only sign that she has been here.

I move quickly to the kitchenette, opening cupboards, drawers, to see what she has taken. There is only cheap cutlery, no sharp knives. All seems to be in place. I move on.

The shower is clean and tidy. So is the basin. And the toilet. She has vanished. Rosie. The girl by the pier has left.

I move out of the nookery, hurrying through the living room to the stairs and up them two at a time.

To my bedroom. Money. Jewellery. Personal possessions. Private things I don't want anyone to see. They are all there. Maybe now gone.

As I get to the top of the landing, I stop.

There are noises – movements, really – from the other bedroom. What was my daughter's room.

I take one, two, three steps across the landing. I am back from my walk sooner than expected; I think I have caught Rosie unawares. I move to the doorway. The door is slightly ajar. I look in to see what she is doing.

Rosie is standing with her back to me. In front of a wardrobe.

Naked.

Other than her dirty pants and pink socks. My daughter's socks.

I stand there for a moment. And I see myself with utter clarity. I know, in that instant, I am middle-aged and she is young. And that it is wrong of me. To look at her the way I am doing. But I cannot help myself. It has been a long time. And I am a normal, healthy man. I cannot stop my body reacting. I cannot control it. But I can control myself. My natural urges. Of course I can.

She's not aware I am here. She is absorbed, singing quietly to herself and looking at the clothes hanging up in the wardrobe. Pretty clothes that I cannot bear to throw away. She is standing, her right hand touching, almost playfully, each dress in turn. A little black dress. A red one. Another cut low at the front. A shiny one. This thieving magpie is choosing one to suit her mood. I do not mind. I am at ease with it. I think she is in a happy frame of mind as well.

I know if I make a noise, a cough to announce my presence, that she will jump, be startled, and will turn towards me. Her face. Her breasts. Her body. Her long legs in those pretty pink socks taken from the chest of drawers in the far corner of the room. And I do not know what I should do. What I would say. How I would handle it all.

Nor do I know what she would do. To her, I am an old man. Twenty-five years or more older than her. My attentiveness is her creepiness. She will not react as she might with a young man. A smile, a bashful, downward gaze, reaching half-heartedly for a dress to cover her nakedness. Inviting him in. Wanting him.

She may be angry, spitting fury. At me. A voyeur. A deviant.

Pushing and shoving me out of the door. Shutting it in my face. The movement of her body. The smell of her freshness. Overwhelming me.

Then getting dressed and leaving. Storming off. Making her way through snow up the lane. To God knows where. And to what end.

And I cannot have that. Not now. She needs to stay. I think she can be happy here. With me. And I can be too, at long last. She is what I have been waiting for. If I can get it right this time. But it cannot be rushed, nor forced.

So I step oh so carefully back, across the landing, waiting for the creak that will give me away. But it does not come, and I edge my way back down the staircase, slowly but surely, one step at a time. The second-to-last step creaks loudly with my full weight suddenly upon it, so I shout, "Hello, I'm back!" as cheerfully as I can as I reach the hallway and move towards the kitchen.

And the new day begins.

The two of us together.

At the start of a long and winding road to happiness.

IT'S ALMOST HALF past seven, and we are having breakfast together. Me and Rosie with her little puffed-up face and our warm, matching blankets wrapped round our shoulders.

We are in the dining room with the heater turned up to the maximum and water running down the windows and onto the sill.

Working our way through the food and drink in something close to an awkward silence.

I bustled about the kitchen once I had crept downstairs, making plenty of noise as if I'd just got back to the cottage. I normally eat in the kitchen with Fluffy at my feet. But it is too cold there now, so I put the gas canister on in the dining room to warm things up and busied about making everything look nice. Naturally, Fluffy sits as close as he can to the canister, hogging much of its heat. He can be rather selfish at times.

I then prepared breakfast. I decided not to cook my traditional first breakfast together – my "Full English". The white-ridged bacon and plump sausages bursting out of their skins that I get from the local farm may repulse her. There are moments, with the meat and big, juicy tomatoes, when it looks a little like an autopsy on a plate. Not that this sort of thing bothers me. But Rosie might prefer something less gory.

I put out a pot of tea and cups and glasses and small jugs of water and orange juice. Various cereals, too. Bran flakes and a banana for me, as I like to stay regular. Half-full boxes of Coco Pops and other chocolatey cereals from the back of the cupboard. I also made two bowls of my usual porridge with big flakey oats and lashing of piping hot milk. Bananas on the side. Toast as well, brown and white, with jam and marmalade and honey and a pot of chocolate spread that young people like. What a feast. I called Rosie downstairs as I put the radio on quietly, Radio 2, so we don't have to force small talk.

She is dressed in my daughter's favourite sweatshirt and short denim skirt. She has long, bare legs and those little pink socks. Neither of us comment on her taking the clothes.

She has her head down and is spooning porridge into her mouth like it's her last meal before her execution. On and on, as if she is embarrassed to look up.

I say nothing about the clothes. My heart just bursts with happiness sitting opposite her. Even though she seems in a hurry to finish and be gone.

I have to be quick to start forming a relationship between us. So that she stays of her own accord when the snow goes. I need her to see me as a kindly uncle figure, sincere and genuine, ready to listen to her thoughts and worries, and to help her to resolve them.

But I have to draw her out of herself gently, without pushing or prodding her for information about her life, her background and how she has ended up here.

I have done this before. And I know what to do by now. To talk generally, neutrally, of things that do not seem to matter much, but are close enough to lead into conversations about more important things. About her.

"I love porridge," I say eventually and as cheerfully as I can, taking a spoonful and rolling the warm slop around my mouth. "I've had it for breakfast every winter's morning, when it's cold, since I was a small child."

She says nothing, no response, no inclination of her head to acknowledge my words. No suggestion of what she ate for breakfast when she was a child. No opening into a conversation about her family. She takes my words as a statement, not as a question, and carries on eating. She's like a thin stray cat gobbling up her food while she can, never knowing if this will be her last meal.

"And toast," I add a moment or two later. "For breakfast. After my porridge. Toast and marmalade. Thick cut." And, following another longish pause, "I've put some of that chocolate spread out for you. Do you like it?" I gesture towards the pot of Nutella and suddenly hope that, if she opens it, there isn't a smear of congealed butter or any mould across the top. It has not been opened for nearly three months, and I forgot to check it.

She looks at it and nods briefly as if to say *yes I do, thank you*. Then scrapes her bowl with her spoon, not wanting to leave even the slightest smear of porridge. I ask if she'd like another bowlful – I can make it easily enough – but she shakes her head and reaches for a piece of white toast. She picks up the pot of Nutella and unscrews the lid. She looks inside it for a moment or two, and I wonder if it is full of sprawling mould.

"I love Nutella," she says simply, dipping her knife in and spreading the chocolate on her toast. "I've had it before."

I nod, not sure how to reply. This seemingly inane but crucial conversation could go either way. It's the start of everything – or, if I get it wrong, possibly a sudden, brutal end. She could get up to go. What would I do? I can't have her walking away right now. So I don't ask her if she had Nutella as a child. A lead into a more personal talk about her mum and dad and family. Instead, I sit back. We eat in a more companionable silence.

Now and again she glances up at me when she thinks I am not looking. She is reluctant to make eye contact. And she is still shovelling in food as if there were no tomorrow.

I keep my face bland and neutral. I will not comment on her manners, which are appalling. This starving creature. I have a naturally kind face; that helps in moments like this. Like a young and sympathetic George Clooney (but with twinklier eyes).

She is going to say something. I know; I can tell. I just have to wait whilst she builds her confidence. And ploughs through all the food left on the table.

At last we have finished eating our toast, and I am sipping my cup of almost cold tea, and she is swallowing her last mouthful of orange juice. She fills her glass again, a nervous glance towards me as if I might slam my fist on the table and shout *"that's enough!"* at the top of my voice. I nod: *go on, please do.* And then we are at the end of eating and drinking and kind of look at each other once more, both of us seeming awkward again.

She glances out of the window towards the lane and the snow and the fairyland beyond, and looks back at me. She swallows.

"Do I ... have to leave now?" she says almost forlornly. Her voice hesitating.

I choke on my words of reply. "No. You can stay here ..." I pause and think, but do not add *until the day you die.* Instead, I simply say, "U... until the snow has gone."

She looks at me and smiles.

A grin. Her pretty face. Her childlike glee.

Here we go. Again. I pray I get it right this time.

———

WE SPENT THE MORNING APART, Rosie and I. She was in the nookery, and checking regularly at the door, I could hear Radio 1 playing on the little transistor radio. I enjoyed imagining what she was doing in there. I finished off a game of chess I'd been playing with myself and followed my usual routine of tidying and cleaning around. I worked through my list quite quickly. My timetable is very important to me. I don't like to sit around and think. To dwell on things. And, whilst tidying, I came across something to give to her as a little present. A welcome gift. It's too soon for jewellery, of course, but this box of goodies is just perfect.

Now it is one o'clock, and we are at lunch. A Tesco vegetable quiche and one of their mixed salad bags. Salad cream and mayonnaise, in small bowls, are to the side of the plates. Orange squash and lemon barley water in jugs in-between. We are in the dining room again. The sun is shining, and it makes this dim and dreary room slightly more bearable. The little box is on my lap, and I am waiting for the right moment to give it to her. A surprise.

There is some sudden movement outside by the gate and path, and Rosie looks out of the window and moves her head sharply to see who it is. I don't think she does see. She leans back just as quickly. There is knocking at the front door. Rosie looks at me with her troubled little face bruised on one side. Her expression says everything: *That knocking must mean it's important – urgent – in this freezing weather; why don't you answer the door?*

"Ignore it," I say. "She'll go away. It's just a widow woman from up the lane. She's got a thing about me."

She replies, "Okay?" She speaks with a questioning tone, as if she doesn't quite believe it. That there's a woman at the door. Or that someone might be interested in me that way. I'm not sure which.

A silence.

Between Rosie and me.

As we wait for another knock.

And it goes again, the door. *Knock. Knock. Knock.* Polite but insistent. The wretched Widow Woman who won't leave me alone. Even in this weather, with snow laid thick on the ground, she is at my door on some pretext or other: to walk the dog with her, to look at her dripping tap, fix her window that won't shut properly and lets in a draught. Whatever.

"What does she want?" Rosie asks.

"She's lonely. She wants company, that's all." I push my fork into the quiche, breaking off a corner. As if we should get stuck in. That it's something and nothing.

"What's wrong with that?" Rosie says.

I shrug. I want to say I don't find the woman attractive. Just the look of her. The whole bloody package. Her little busybody face and her short arms swinging enthusiastically at the sides. And everything about her, really. But I cannot say anything like that at all. It might seem rude.

Nor can I comment on the size of her backside, and the thought of that bare white mass pushed up against the middle of my back at night in bed. That's where it will all end if I let her into my life. My back warming her cold white slab of an arse.

"I'm happy on my own," I answer simply, and before she can ask me questions – difficult ones about my wife and daughter, and where they are – I add, "She'll be gone in a minute."

She knocks again. More insistent this time.

And I feel Rosie tense. She sees me glancing at her and lifts her glass of orange squash, swallowing a mouthful. A pretence of normality. I can almost hear it sticking in her dry throat tight with tension.

"How do you know it's her?" she asks. "It might be urgent. It might be the police ... someone you know may be ill."

"She knocks the same way most days. The same pattern. The same number of times. It's her, alright. She walks her dog this way, wants me and Fluffy to go out with them across the fields."

Rosie nods and looks towards the window. Even though she can't see who it is on the doorstep. And she cannot be seen either.

"She might look in," she says. "If it's her."

I nod and shrug, not sure how to answer that. Widow Woman might.

We sit there in an uneasy silence. Rosie reaches down to pat Fluffy on the head. He is there on the off-chance that she might give him some of her food. The little beggar.

He used to do the same with me, but he has transferred his affections to Rosie. I am not bothered by this at all.

We are both equally tense, waiting for the knocking to go again – or to stop, and we can then relax into silence.

And it stops.

A minute or two passes, and Rosie turns slightly towards the window as if she sees movement, then leans back, not wishing to be seen. I instinctively do the same. A moment or two and Widow Woman has gone; we start eating again.

I am looking over at Rosie. With my troubled thoughts.

Wondering why she does not want to be seen in my company.

I think that maybe she is embarrassed or ashamed to be here with me.

We continue eating. She seems to start relaxing again, and when she thinks I am not looking, she slips Fluffy a piece of quiche, which he takes and eats noisily. I pretend not to notice. She does it again a few minutes later, but Fluffy drops it on the floor. She glances down when she thinks I am not looking and uses her foot to move it further in, under the table. I can only think it must have tomato in it. Fluffy has a thing about tomatoes. I am the same with boiled eggs. I cannot bear the smell of them. They remind me of sick.

I take out the box I've been hiding below the tablecloth on my lap all this time. "Here," I say. "For you. Your face." I gesture towards her cheek, but do not ask anything about it nor comment further. Her arm seems to be better though; or, at least, is not troubling her. I will not mention it.

I push the box across the table towards her. She takes it

and opens it and looks inside. It's my wife's old make-up box. I found it at the bottom of the chest of drawers in the corner of my bedroom. Lipsticks. Face powder. Mascara. Old-woman stuff, mostly. But beggars can't be choosers.

Rosie rummages through, a look of suppressed pleasure on her face, and picks out a lipstick and a mascara. I gesture towards the face powder, and as she looks at it and me, I touch my cheek on the same side where her face is puffed. I smile gently at her as if to say *go on, take it, cover it up.* And she sort of grimaces a little, as if to reply, *yes, okay, I will.*

And a minute or two later, we finish eating, and we smile happily at each other.

And she is up and away to the nookery, clutching the make-up box tight.

Her room. Her own happy little place.

JUST GONE SIX P.M., and we are back sitting in the dining room, Rosie and I, about to eat our tea. Rosie is now wearing mascara and lipstick, applied too liberally on her little child-like face, and a thick layer of make-up over her damaged cheek. Coco the Clown. Fluffy sits by Rosie's feet. Having spent the afternoon with her in the nookery whilst I tidied my room and put things away in the loft, he now seems devoted to her. That's fine by me.

The door is shut, and the heater is turned up, and it feels almost warm in here. The moisture runs down the windows again and, beyond that, the snow still lies heavy and has a kind of shimmering effect in the darkness. There may be a further fall later this evening or overnight. I pull the curtains together for warmth and for privacy, in case Widow Woman pays another visit.

Tea is a simple affair. A vegetable lasagne from the Tesco

Premium Range with some peas and carrots that I boiled myself. Two bottles of water, one sparkling, one still. An apple crumble and custard for pudding. Packet and tinned respectively, but very nice brands. I don't skimp on these things.

I am a competent cook if I stick to basics. I like plain fare. I am a meat eater – chicken or beef or pork, mince, too. I don't eat hearts, livers, kidneys or offal. None of that. I am not Hannibal Lecter.

She sits there in front of her full plate, knife and fork in hand, like a small child, waiting to be told to eat – shovel, in her case. It is rather endearing.

"Still or sparkling?" I ask, gesturing towards the bottles.

She looks blankly at me.

"Ordinary water or fizzy water?" I put my hand on the top of one of the bottles and turn it round so she can read the label.

She moves her glass towards the bottle closest to her, and I lift it up to see which one it is. "Fizzy," I say. "You like fizzy water?"

She does not answer, so I pour the water into her glass. She takes a mouthful, a big one, without thinking. Pulls a face. Wrinkles her nose like a little Disney rabbit. Kind of gasps.

I laugh. "I can put some orange squash in it if you prefer ... have it as fizzy orange?"

She sort of gulps and nods as she splutters. All from a mouthful of sparkling water! Maybe some of it went up her nose.

I go to the kitchen and fetch the half-full bottle of orange squash. As I return and push the dining room door closed behind me and splash a little squash into her glass, I note she is composed again. She takes two or three big sips of the fizzy orange and chokes the words, "That's better," almost under her voice, as if to herself.

We sit and eat in silence, on and on, working our way through the main course. She has her head down, eating quickly with a fork in her left hand, her right hand curved around her plate as if she is protecting it. I want her to slow down, relax, to sit back and chat between mouthfuls, so we can get to know each other better. Talk about things. I reach out to put my hand lightly on her left arm and to say sweetly, "Whoa, slow down."

She rears back instinctively, her fork falling and clattering across the table. She looks at me suddenly, an instant mix of fear and anger, then somehow seems to blank her face as she sees my own benign expression.

"Sorry," I say, reaching for her fork and giving it back to her.

She takes it and hesitates and, after a moment or two, speaks. "I jumped."

I nod. "I didn't think. I'm sorry." I'm not sure what else to say other than repeat my apology.

Realising what I was trying to do, she then sits up straight and starts eating slowly, carefully, with her knife and fork.

We move on to the pudding, me scooping big spoonfuls of crumble and still-warm custard into her bowl before taking the rest for myself. We continue eating. Slightly mannered at first, and then relaxing again, until I feel ready to speak.

"I was wondering ..." I clear my throat. "If you are staying for a while, until the snow clears, maybe." I hesitate, but she does not respond, so I go on. "If you needed anything ...?"

She looks at me, and I cannot read the expression on her face. I am worried that she may be thinking I am talking about what my mother would call "women's things". I would not want to make a reference to tampons or sanitary matters to Rosie. It is too intimate. I need to clarify what I mean.

"A book to read?" I say, gesturing at the bookcases in the room with my spoon. I am not sure, what with my crime novels and my boys' own adventure stories, whether my tastes will appeal to her. Packed away in the garage, I have books and magazines belonging to my wife and daughter, but I do not want to draw attention to them nor talk about my family yet, even though I am well rehearsed about what to say.

She looks at the shelves and seems embarrassed in some way. I can see she is unsure what to say about my Dan Browns and old Alistair MacLeans and all. There is a moment of awkwardness between us. I go on, and I feel that I am gushing my words as she finishes her pudding, scraping the bowl as clean as she can. She is listening, though.

"It must be boring ... will be ... being in ... your room all day, just listening to music and ... and just doing your make-up ... you can come out with me in the mornings if you like ... to walk Fluffy ... and there's the TV. I only have the free channels, but, you know ... and board games and cards in the chest of drawers over there ... please make yourself at home."

I can see, from her face, a sudden flush of pleasure. I think it is my use of the phrases "your room" and "make yourself at home". I eat my last mouthful of crumble as I wait for her to speak. I know she is going to. And as she puts her spoon into her empty bowl and thinks twice and removes it and puts it to the side, she does.

"Would you ... do you have some paper and pencils?" she asks, then adds simply, "I like to draw." She says nothing else, but there is a plaintive, little-girl-lost look about her that tears at my heart.

I nod and smile. After putting my cutlery onto my plate, I rise and go to the chest of drawers, rummage in it and return with a pad, a Basildon Bond notepad, and a couple of pencils. I hand them to her.

She looks overwhelmed, so much so that it is impossible not to smile. Such a wonderful gift! I resist the laughter that's bubbling inside me as she gets to her feet, all dizzy and excited. By a pad and pencils!

As she is about to turn to leave, she stops, and I think for one glorious moment she is going to step forward and kiss me. I think that is what she intended to do, but I may have slightly swayed backwards in my surprise, and she seemed to check herself and think twice.

And she is gone.

But I am happy.

Our relationship has taken another step forward. A big one.

IT'S GONE EIGHT P.M., and we're already getting ourselves into a nice little routine.

Rosie and I.

We are playing cards, and I think we're going to get along ever so well.

After tea at six, Rosie retired to her room for a while. To wash or shower, have a lie down, to do whatever women do when they are alone, and to draw in my Basildon Bond notepad. I imagine her drawing Disney characters. Princesses. Unicorns, maybe. Pretty things.

After I had washed up and put everything away in its place, I finished off a game of solitaire that had been sitting there on the coffee table for ever so long. That got me thinking, and I knocked gently on the connecting door at six thirty and suggested we might meet back in the dining room at eight o'clock to play cards. A moment's silence, and I heard a clear and simple "yes". A further pause followed by a "please." I took the time after that to potter about, check my CCTV and what have you to see what I had recorded, and to lie down in my bedroom and relax.

Washed and with another change of clothes, and a fresh dab of make-up to her other cheek, Rosie looks and smells much nicer than when she arrived. She wears her hair scraped back. I think it would look much better if she wore it down and fluffed out. As it is, it gives her head a slightly skull-like appearance, which is not so attractive. Her eyes are most striking, though. Deep and brown and soulful. They are, in their colour at least, identical to Fluffy's – although, of course, I would not say that to Rosie. She may misconstrue the compliment.

Her face is nicer than her body, which, understandably, is thin and scrawny. She needs fattening up a bit, and I will make that my job over the coming days and weeks. I think, filled out a little, she will be a very attractive young lady. I have noticed, as all men would do, that she does not wear a bra; that would be something of a distraction for most men, although I will not show that I have noticed it. I am not like that. Not at all.

I suggested we played cribbage or gin rummy with my trusty pack of cards. Or solitaire, which I have always enjoyed playing on my own.

She did not know how to play any of those. The only card game she knew how to play was called "shithead".

I had not heard of that one, so we compromised and are playing snap. Everyone knows how to play snap. Even a five-year-old.

"Snap," she goes.

Then "snap" again, a moment or two later.

"Snap." One more time.

She wins more than me and seems enthusiastic about it.

At least, she is concentrating and saying "snap" as fast as she can. And loudly, too.

Truth is, she is quicker than me. But I hold back a little anyway and let her win. I'm like that. I am a good sport.

It will make her happy, and she will have good feelings about me. Fluffy sits by her feet. We are like a happy family.

"Snap."

"Snap."

"Snap!"

There comes a point, of course, when the inane and endless game becomes irritating. I do not show my feelings, though.

Instead, I see the happiness on her face – that childlike pleasure – as she leans forward.

And she beats me – *snap, snap, snap,* again and again. Until she sits back, as if to say, *that's enough; we're done. I'm through.*

Ten games to six.

First to ten.

Rosie won (with a little help from yours truly).

As she gathers up the cards to put them back into the box, I sit and wonder what we could do next. It's still quite early, and I would normally read my Ludovic Kennedy book for an hour before watching the latest news on the television and going to bed. I sometimes have a hot milky drink and a custard cream (occasionally two) with the news. I'd like her to stay until then. Really, I would.

I am thinking what we could do between now and then, and it occurs to me that it might be rather fun if I read to her. It is something I used to do with my daughter when she was little. But I read *Winnie The Pooh* to her. I am currently finishing *10 Rillington Place*, and there is nothing in there that makes nice bedtime reading. I make a mental note to see if I can find a *Winnie The Pooh* book in a box in the garage for the next evening.

Before I can speak my thoughts out loud, she is up and on her feet, gathering up the pad and pencils by her side, and saying goodnight. And she looks me straight in the eyes and smiles at me. A really warm and affectionate smile. She is going. Off to her warm little room. And I do not want her to. But I cannot think of any reason for her to stay. Fluffy gets up to go as well.

"The morning," I say, and I think I sound almost desperate as she stops and turns back and looks agreeably at me. "How about making some cakes?"

She pauses and has a funny expression on her face. "Um," she goes. "Er," she says. It is almost as if she is teasing me, playing with me.

"Yes," she answers finally. "Okay." And I look at her and swallow and agree. And she is gone and on her way to bed. There will be sweet dreams tonight. For both of us, hopefully.

I AM IN THE CANAL.

Cold and wet and struggling.
I have to find something to hold on to to survive.
I keep trying to reach for the sides.
And falling back.
Again.
And falling back.
I have my arms around something.
I have been searching for it in the dark.
And I turn it about in the water towards me.
The face is close to mine.
This bloated mush of rotting flesh.
I wake and scream.

9

SUNDAY, 24 NOVEMBER, 7.35 AM

The moment comes, as I knew it would soon enough, as we finish what has been a quiet and reflective breakfast. Eating and drinking steadily, quite happily, as we listened to Radio 1. Rosie's choice, this morning.

Rosie smiled to herself once or twice at the presenter's comments and jigged ever so slightly in time to a couple of the livelier songs. I sat there, mostly baffled by it all.

And she speaks, right at the end of the meal, as if she has been preparing for this all the way through. "What's your daughter called?" she asks, politely enough.

"Lucy," I answer without hesitation, for I have had this conversation before. Many times. I would not state that everything I will now say is rehearsed. But I have said it all so often that I know what to say. More importantly, I know what not to say.

Rosie nods. Sips her orange juice. Asks the next, inevitable question.

"Where is she?" Still an innocent and trusting question with an upward inflection at the end of the sentence. The unspoken assumption that she is alive and happy and out there somewhere living a fulfilling life. That she would not mind Rosie borrowing her clothes whilst she is away.

I know not to say, *She is dead.* That is too blunt. Too dismissive. Too uncaring. People give you a strange look when you say something like that about anyone. Let alone a daughter.

But I do not like phrases such as *she's passed away* or *passed over.* I do not believe in an afterlife. It is errant nonsense. And I dislike the word *passed*, as if it were a simple and effortless thing. It was not.

"She's not here ... any more," I reply, a little crack in my voice halfway through. A touch of emotion.

She stops and glances across at me, then away, when she sees my anguished face.

I drop my head down. My body tenses with emotion.

"Do you mean ... she's ..."

I nod my head. Bring my head up as I gasp out a single word. "Yes."

Dip my head down again. This is a difficult moment.

She moves her glass and bowl a fraction to one side and back again. A touch of nerves. Some uncertainty. What to say. But I know what the next question will be and what I will say. I just have to wait. It comes, finally.

"What happened?" Of course. What else could she ask? It had to be that or a variant of it.

"Lucy went to university up north. She wanted to be an engineer. But ... when she got there ... she ... struggled with her mental health ... anxiety and depression. We never knew. We just assumed she was happy and well and getting on with things."

I stop and draw my breath in loudly. I think maybe Rosie will reach out and rest her hand on my arm. But she does not.

And after a moment or two, I continue talking, now more composed. But still vulnerable.

"That, the depression, eventually rolled into anorexia. And from there ... looking back now, I think ... the end was inevitable ..." I stop. I do not need to say any more. Rosie can join up the dots and draw her own conclusions. She will feel sorry for me.

There is more I can say. So much more. A different story. But this is what I present to the world. To anyone who asks. And who did ask, when I was locked away. I keep to it precisely.

Rosie makes a strange, whooshing noise with her mouth. I do not look up. I do not want her to see my face. A moment or two passes. And I feel her hand resting lightly on my arm. Just as I had hoped.

"I am sorry for your loss," she says simply. As if she has been taught to say this at such moments. She does not add to it. She does not need to.

We sit there, my head down, her hand on my arm, for something close to a minute. I then get up, sobbing quietly, and start gathering together the plates and bowls and everything else. Rosie takes her hand away; I am aware that she is watching me sympathetically. She then gets up too and helps me take everything over to the sink.

I start washing up the breakfast things, rinsing each one under the running tap before handing them to Rosie to dry with a tea towel and put away in the cupboard. We do this in comfortable silence. I sniff noisily once or twice, and on both occasions, she reaches out and pats me gently on the back.

As we finish, I say quietly that I'm going to spend a little time on my own. That she should maybe do some drawing in her room. And we will meet up again mid-morning to make cakes? She agrees.

As she turns to go, I think for a moment, as she is closest

to me, that she may reach out and kiss me on my cheek. I would then embrace her. But she hesitates and pats my arm in a reassuring manner instead. I hold back, my face ever so slightly contorting in pain as she glances at me. I struggle to say, "Th ... Thank you."

And we smile at each other. And look into each other's eyes.

She is encouraging. I am being as brave as I can.

And then we turn and go. I think our relationship has taken a leap forward. A really huge one.

MID-MORNING, after Rosie has been in her room drawing and listening to music, and I have been resting quietly and doing the household chores, I knock on the connecting door.

"Ready?" I ask, smiling, as she opens the door, encouraging her out.

"Something for us to do. It will be fun," I add.

Rosie follows me into the kitchen. *Ta-dah!* (I think this, but do not say it out loud.)

I used to make cakes with my daughter once a week on a Saturday afternoon. When she was a little girl. To have with tea in front of the telly. Any leftover ones to be eaten on Sunday.

Little packet mixes for children; you'd put a blob of icing on the top of each cake and a sticker on that. Disney, mostly. Mickey Mouse and the like.

And here I am now. With Rosie. Ready to make cakes with her. She stands by the kitchen table, seeming awkward and embarrassed.

I get the mixing bowl out from a cabinet. Butter, sugar, eggs, flour. A sharp knife from a drawer. A wooden spoon. All put on the table. She looks at them.

I have a tray for twelve little cakes underneath the sink. I take that out and rinse and wipe it over with a tea towel and put it on the table too.

Reach for a half-empty packet of cake cases in another cupboard. I've no idea how long they've been there gathering dust. Years. I switch the oven on and turn the dial to 180.

"There," I say, looking at what's on the table. "Now, what have I forgotten?" I'm half-teasing, half-checking to see if she knows.

She seems to redden slightly as she looks at the table. "Um." That's all she says. Then, "Um," again.

"I don't use scales," I say before she can answer. "I know the amounts to put in."

She says nothing, but watches as I cut off some of the butter and put it into the bowl, followed by rough-and-ready amounts of flour and sugar. I pick up the wooden spoon and offer it to her, then pull it back, teasing, as she slowly, reluctantly reaches for it.

"We've both forgotten something," I say cheerfully as I put the spoon on the table in front of her. She watches as I open and reach into a drawer for my folded-up Michelangelo's *David* apron. She looks down at it and up at me as it falls open. I see her smile to herself as she dips her head back down again.

I am tempted to lean over and flip the apron over her head before going the back of her and tying the cords around her waist. But I hesitate, feeling that this gesture might be seen as too intimate, creepy, even. So I simply hand it to her.

We stand there as she puts it over her head and ties it around herself. I am waiting for her to start mixing. She has her head down, looking at the bowl.

She puts the spoon in the bowl and stirs the flour and sugar slowly around the lump of butter. It is soft enough to mix, but even so, she won't mix it like that.

I reach my hand across towards hers, and she drops the wooden spoon in the bowl. I take it and start mixing the ingredients together properly, squashing and spreading the butter vigorously. She watches me.

"Have you made ... cupcakes before?" I ask, hesitating halfway through the sentence as I realise how foolish the question is. Surely every child has made cupcakes at some time in their life. But she's oddly ill at ease.

"Not for ages," she replies, not meeting my gaze. I think she hasn't. Not ever.

"Did you make them with your mum when you were small?" I press on as I continue stirring the cake mixture.

A long pause. I do not think she is going to answer. But as I look down into the bowl, she speaks. "She died when I was little."

I nod. Unsure what to say next. I think and go on: "Were you brought up by your dad ... or a granny and grandad?"

She shakes her head and stands still, and for one awful moment, I think she is going to turn and run. There is a sense of panic. I push the bowl towards her quickly with a gesture as if to say, *Go on, you do it*. Something to distract her.

She takes the bowl and copies what I was doing, spreading and stirring and folding the mixture up and over and into itself.

I stand there not sure what to do, whether to wait for her to go on or to busy myself, pottering about, maybe getting icing sugar and sprinkles from the cupboard and water in a teacup to start mixing the toppings. Just to act normal.

Slowly, without looking up, she speaks. "It was just me and my mum ... and uncles ... and she ... I was taken away when I was eleven ... I saw her twice after ... and then she died ..." A pause and one more final, meaningless sentence. "I didn't see her again after that."

I watch her as she keeps stirring the mixture.

My heart aches.

And swells big enough to give her all the love that I can.

I nod and sigh, but do not ask her anything more nor add any comments of my own. It would, I think, be natural to push on now that we have bonded over my daughter and her mother. But it would be wrong to do so. I do not want to force our relationship. I would prefer it to grow naturally. So that it will go on. And endure. Last a lifetime.

Instead, I busy around. Then, when she has mixed all the ingredients together well, I grease and put the tray in front of her. I hand her a large spoon, inviting her to drop a spoonful of mix into each of the twelve spaces. She does so, making some spoonfuls larger than others and dropping some of the mix on the tablecloth. "Oops," we both say at the same time and laugh together. It is a nice moment.

When the tray is ready to put in the oven, she reaches out to the teacup I have by my side, full of the icing to put on top of each little cake. Without thinking, I put my hand out and rest it on hers, as if to say *stop, not yet ... we do that after the cakes have been baked!* She does not pull her hand back this time, nor seem to mind that I have my hand on hers. She laughs and says, "Oops," again. And I tell her we will do the toppings later, once the cakes are out and have cooled. We can have them after our lunch instead of pudding.

She smiles at me. I smile back, taking my hand away as naturally as I can.

Pals.

Becoming good pals now.

As we finish our lunch – more Tesco Luxury Range Lasagne and salad – I bring the cupcakes across to the table.

Push the teacup full of icing towards Rosie. Hand her a spoon.

"Go on," I say. "You do it ... then we can eat some of them." She takes the spoon and dips it inside the teacup, scooping out a blob of icing.

I watch her and decide this is the time to tell her about my wife. A version of it, anyway. To fill in a gap, so to speak. Rosie must be wondering about my wife since I gave her the make-up box. And as I have talked about my daughter and she has talked about her mother, this is the natural time to do it. If I am honest, I am surprised she has not asked.

"Blob it," I say. "Just a bit on each ... that's got to go between twelve."

She looks at me and smiles. The look of concentration on her little face – the determination to get it right – makes me want to laugh. But I do not. We are not yet at the stage where we can tease and have fun with each other. It will come soon enough.

"If you put a teaspoonful in the middle, you can then turn the spoon over and spread the icing across to the edges."

She slows and turns the spoon over on the cake and gets in a muddle, the icing oozing over the spoon onto the table-cloth. She laughs to herself, happy in the moment. Wipes it off the cloth with her fingers.

She looks at me. Her sweet face.

I smile back.

These happy times. And so many more to come.

She licks the icing off her fingers with her tongue. It distracts me, this. Her tongue, long and pink, slightly repelling me, but fascinating me too, the way it runs over her fingers one at a time.

"I'm a widower," I say, my voice wavering slightly. An expression of sadness.

She glances up at me, her tongue wrapped halfway round her index finger.

She nods as if to say, *yes, I know, I guessed that.* As though it does not really matter all that much. To her, anyway. If anything at all.

I am shocked a little. Maybe *disappointed* is a better word. That a death is just *yeah, whatever* to her. Perhaps I should be angry.

She was interested in my daughter. I suppose, being much the same age, what happened to my daughter – at least what I said happened to my daughter – is of more relevance. An older woman dying is, I suspect, of little concern. Old people die. It's the way of things. Someone of forty-seven is ancient to Rosie.

"She ... passed away ... after my daughter." I have talked previously about my wife, many times, and to different people, and use certain phrases that put it over well. *Never recovered. Took her own life. I have been grieving ever since.* And other descriptions that gloss over the truth of the matter. The heart of things. The reality of it.

But Rosie has already moved on, dipping the teaspoon back into the cup.

Taking out more icing.

Dropping it on the cake, turning the spoon, spreading it about.

And the matter of my wife and her death and what happened is dismissed. Just like that. I had expected questions and had my prepared answers. I know what to say. I do not doubt that Rosie, had she listened, would have been moved and would have felt protective of me.

Never mind. She has accepted the deaths of my wife and daughter as perfectly natural and nothing out of the ordinary. And she is happy here and all is well. And I am happy. All is well with me, too.

Neither my daughter nor my wife cast a shadow.

Over us.

Nor anything else for that matter.

WE ARE SITTING at the kitchen table. Rosie and I.

The lunchtime things have long since been put away. Fluffy is asleep in his bed.

And we are ready to have some fun.

I keep scrapbooks. Of cuttings from newspapers and magazines over the years. Anything relating, one way or the other, to yours truly. And other things. Mementoes. Souvenirs. Stuff you can stick to a page. My little collections would probably seem odd to someone who sat there and flicked through the books at random. They might think I was a strange man.

It's something I started doing as a young boy. I was an only child and lonely, especially in the school holidays. I was not allowed to bring friends home. My father's work. Not that I really had any friends. I don't know why. I guess nobody liked me enough to want to come round. I have always been a solitary person, even when I had my own family.

I have continued scrapbooking all my life. It's a habit. A hobby. Perhaps more. Most of them are stacked up in the loft. The childhood ones are gone, of course. My father burned them when I left home. I went to university and never returned. More recent ones are stored in roll-out drawers beneath my bed. I take them out from time to time and look at them, thinking things over.

Rosie sits opposite me at the kitchen table. She holds scissors in one hand. A glue brush in the other. A pot of white sloppy glue is by her side.

She has a clean, fresh scrapbook I have given to her. And

a stack of magazines that I have bought and read and kept over the years. There are articles in them that I like to revisit from time to time.

I have a half-filled scrapbook in my bedroom, but I do not want Rosie to see what is in it, so I have a new one in front of me. I have a pile of old local *East Anglian Daily Times* and *Evening Stars*, too, and will see what's in them. Some bits have been cut out, but there are plenty of pages left.

"You've never had a scrapbook?" I say in a light and friendly manner. Conversational. Not interrogative.

She shrugs as if to say *no* or *I don't remember*; a negative either way.

"You can do all sorts with a scrapbook," I add cheerfully. "You can keep clippings of any stories you're in yourself. Or cut out pictures of scenes. Or follow a story through press cuttings. Or do what I do, and mix pictures together." I don't actually do that, but it's an idea I have for getting friendlier. I've used it before. Twice. With some success.

I pull one or two magazines towards me, flicking through the pages. One's a farming magazine. There was an article in there that caught my eye when I saw it in WHSmith. About composting. The other a lifestyle one, which I bought back from the dentist's, as there was an advert in it that interested me. Some liquid for rotting tree stumps. Rosie watches me, slightly puzzled. She is young, naïve even, in some ways.

I take my scissors and cut around a photo in the farming magazine and glue it in the middle of the first page of my opened scrapbook. Rosie leans forward, looks at it, and laughs. I think maybe she knows where I am going with this.

I then flick through the lifestyle magazine, an upmarket one full of photos of weddings and other events in grand houses and barns and stately homes across the county. And smug, self-satisfied people full of their own importance. The Wills and Cordelias who think they are much better than the likes of me. I find a photo similar to the one I had in mind, give or take, and cut a twenty-pence-piece-sized part out of the middle of it as carefully as I can. I stick the part on the front page of the scrapbook.

Rosie laughs, derisive laughter, and suddenly snorts and brings her hand to her mouth. She continues to laugh. An almost jeering sound.

At the sight of a fat bride's face inside a veil stuck onto the body of a Holstein Friesian cow.

And I know, at this moment, with that one silly act, that I have got through to her. And that things will move quickly from here.

WE ARE GOING to do our scrapbooks for most of the afternoon, up to teatime and Fluffy's walk. Maybe into the evening, too.

I cut out photos of cities and faraway beaches. The Eiffel Tower. A beach in Antigua. The Empire State Building. Rosie goes for photos of babies and small children.

We do this all quite happily, mostly in silence. I am a quiet and solitary person. I think Rosie is, too. We fit together well.

I notice that she has cut out a photo of a small baby and stuck it in the middle of the first page, and drawn sketches of a baby from different angles all around it. Then, on the next page, a photo of a slightly older child, a toddler, in the middle with her own sketches to the top, sides and bottom.

I stop what I am doing and watch her. She does not seem to mind the attention. She hums to herself as she flicks through magazines until she finds a photo of another child, a slightly older one now, a boy. She cuts that out and sticks it in the middle of the next page and starts sketching again.

I speak with my head down as if focusing on my own scrapbook.

"Do you have a brother?" I say quietly. I think she said she was an only child, but I am not sure. Sometimes my memory plays tricks with me. I have had tests to prove this. It is not my fault.

"No, just me," she replies, quite matter-of-factly, whilst carrying on with what she is doing. I expect her to add, *I told you*, but she does not.

"Me too," I answer, pleased to confirm the connection.

A moment's silence.

"Were you lonely?" I ask. "I was. I spent hours on my own during the school holidays. I used to cycle to different libraries."

"Not really." She sighs as if she does not want to talk about it. Would rather carry on sketching. She does not add to it.

I do not say anything else. I do not want to push her into a corner. She will open up to me, as and when she is ready.

"I like drawing," she says suddenly, unexpectedly, a minute or two later.

"You're good at it," I reply and add, "Do you always draw babies and children?" I am about to laugh, but see her serious face and decide not to. I wonder if she has been pregnant and maybe lost the baby. She seems so young to me, but it's possible.

"Not always. I like drawing things that change but stay the same."

I am not sure what she means by that. But I am reluctant to ask her, to question her too much. She senses my confusion.

"So I would draw a kitten." She sketches the outline of a kitten's face on the pad by her side on the table. She then draws the eyes. "And I would draw it as a cat ... see, the eyes are bigger, but still look the same."

I look at her. *Uh, okay?* is what I think, but I do not say it.

"So, this ... and this ... and this." She points to the sketches of the baby and of the toddler and of the small child. "Are the same boy. My drawings, not the photos. You can see how his face changes ... but stays the same. His eyes. His nose. His ears. Well, they get bigger." She laughs.

I have no idea what she is talking about. I am not sure she does, either. But she is happy and enthusiastic; I like her chatting away. Even if it is nonsense. It will lead to other conversations.

"What I'd really like is a notepad with about eighty pages. I can draw a face on each page, starting from a baby. You can then flick the pages and see them getting older ..."

"But staying the same," I tease.

She does not pick up on it. "When I was little, my dad showed me two photos of his mother ... my grandma ... as a young woman and an old woman before she died. I did not think they were the same person. But he pointed out how the eyes were the same in both photos."

"I see," I say although I don't. Not really.

She flicks through another magazine, presumably looking for a photo of an older boy to cut out. One who is similar to the photos of the boys she has already stuck in the scrapbook, although none of these are the same boy. Except her sketches are. Or whatever. None of it makes sense to me. But then I am not artistic.

I am watching her when I hear the sound of the helicopter again. It is further away than last time. And the noise is not as loud. But I can still hear it clearly. And I wonder what it wants. Why it is there. And whether it is going to come closer.

Be seen this time. Circling overhead. Whoever is in it is

looking down across the landscape through binoculars. Searching for something or someone. There is a prison over at Hollesley Bay, for men and young offenders. They are always escaping, and the public are warned not to approach them. But I do not think any of them would get out this far.

I look at Rosie to see if she has heard the helicopter. I expect to see her head cocked at an angle, listening, a puzzled look on her face. But her head is down, and she is sketching again. I wait, listening. The helicopter comes closer. Lower, maybe. A louder noise either way.

"Do you hear it?" I ask.

"Hear what?"

"The helicopter."

She stops. Angles her head. As I expected. Listens carefully. "No." Then she adds, "You must have better hearing than me."

She then points at my scrapbook, still open at the centre pages. It is full of little photos spread across the two pages. All sorts of well-known places around the world. I have always wanted to travel. Somehow I never have. Early on, there was never enough money. Later on, I had nobody to go with. I did not want to be the solo traveller whom happily married people shun: *Look out, darling; it's that boring little man again.*

"Have you been to all these places?" she asks, a note of interest in her voice. She stops sketching to look at each of the photos in turn.

"No ... I'd like to ... some day." It strikes me, quite suddenly, that I must seem like a sad man who has never done anything or been anywhere or achieved anything in his life. And that would be true. The thought suddenly flattens my mood.

"They are on my bucket list," I say.

"Bucket list?" She laughs.

I suddenly feel old and hopeless and out of touch.

Knowing that expressions I use, once so commonplace, are not used by younger people any more. And our happy time teeters on the edge of turning sour.

I turn the scrapbook around, trying to stop my mood plummeting even further.

"How many do you know?" I ask.

"Um ..." She hesitates.

"Point to the ones you recognise," I say cheerfully enough. And she stays quiet.

And I wonder how she can possibly not know some of them – the Taj Mahal and the Eiffel Tower, at the very least.

There is a long pause. To avoid further embarrassment, I start naming each of them, telling her a little about each.

She listens closely enough and expresses interest, and we are soon at ease with each other again.

And I can no longer hear that helicopter. I wonder whether it was ever there in the first place.

ALL IN ALL, we had a nice afternoon with our scrapbooks, a pleasant and jolly tea, and exhausted by our fun, we spent the evening apart, Rosie drawing and listening to music in her room, me reading my book in the living room.

Coming up to bedtime at 11 p.m., I am sitting on the sofa, finishing *10 Rillington Place*. I am undressed other than my fleecy dressing gown and a pair of striped socks. Although it is still cold, I do not have a blanket around my shoulders tonight.

The fire is blazing, so Fluffy has chosen to sit with me. He hogs the heat, as usual, but there is enough left over for me. I am happy. I am content. I am at peace.

Rosie suddenly barges in, pushing the living room door open with her right foot.

She is wearing a pair of my daughter's pyjamas. Disney PJs.

Rosie has wet hair. A hand towel in her left hand. A hairdryer and a hairbrush gripped tight in the right.

She sits down cross-legged in front of the chair nearest the fire. Wraps the towel round her shoulders. Brushes her hair. Glances at me once or twice. I pretend not to notice. I am not sure why she is looking at me. She leans forward and plugs the hairdryer into the nearest socket. Moves a switch on the hairdryer up and down. Then the other. It does not work.

She looks at the hairdryer. Shakes it. Switches it on and off at the plug socket. Fiddles with the switches again. As if that will make a difference. She has a look of disbelief on her face. I go to say it may just be the fuse, but realise I don't have any spare ones. Would need to find a small screwdriver. Take a fuse from something else. All a nuisance to do. And leaving the kettle or the microwave or the vacuum cleaner without a fuse. And, anyway, it gives me another idea, a better one, now that we are getting along so well.

"Do you have another one?" she asks, holding the hairdryer up towards me. "My hair's dripping."

She puts the hairdryer down, pulls the towel across her shoulders up around her neck.

"No," I reply. "It's the only one I have." Then I pause, hesitating, before going on: "If you want to come over and sit here, I'll do you a scrunch dry." My most light-hearted voice. And a phrase my wife used with my daughter. I don't know if it's in common usage.

Rosie looks at me. Hand on heart, I expect her to shrug and say *no thanks* at best – maybe even to recoil at worst. Repulsed by this old man sitting in front of her with his dressing gown and veiny legs.

But she doesn't. She stops for a moment until, turning her back to me, she moves on her bottom towards me, stopping an inch or two from my knees. I open my legs wider so that she can sit between them.

She hands me the brush over her shoulder.

I take it. I am nervous and, to be frank, aroused too. By her closeness. Her arms almost brushing my thighs. But I am a gentleman, and I know how to behave. I slowly run the brush through her hair, above her left ear, the centre of her head, and by her right ear. I try to be as no-nonsense as possible, as if this is a chore. I do it gently.

Rosie adjusts herself slightly, sitting up straight and hugging her knees. She is a little further away from me, but moves her head back at an angle so that her hair is still as close to me. She is not repulsed.

The fact is, I think she is starved of affection, a human touch. As am I.

I edge forward a little, pulling my dressing gown back up over my thigh as it slides down. I cannot close my legs, as her shoulders are in the way. I hope she does not turn round.

I put the hairbrush on the armrest and reach for the towel around her neck, taking it off and holding it in my hands.

"To scrunch dry, you have to scrunch the hair ever so gently." I scrunch the hair at the back of her neck as carefully as I can.

"This is just to remove any excess water." I dab the towel over her head two, three, four times.

"Never rub. Rubbing can break hair ... fine hair like yours." I keep dabbing. Waiting for her to pull away at my touch. Or to lean back into me.

"Rubbing can make your hair go all frizzy." She leans back, ever so slightly, just a touch, but it is enough. She is relaxed with me.

I dab a little more. My hand is shaking slightly. Lifting and patting her hair. Once, twice. Three times. That is enough. I need to be careful.

And so I stop.

I know that I am treading a fine line. Between kind and thoughtful and being too close.

We both sit there for a minute, or maybe longer, and she then edges forward, away from me. Embarrassed, possibly. I am not sure. I close my legs, pull the dressing gown over my thighs, covering myself. She stands up, and there is a moment of silence, possibly awkwardness, between us.

She then turns and takes the towel from me and moves towards the fire. She sits back down, looking into the flames, one hand resting on the sleeping Fluffy. She hums to herself as she pats her hair with the towel.

I sit back and open my Ludovic Kennedy book.

Rosie turns and looks at me.

I smile at her. She smiles back.

I SEE THE BLAZING TANKER.

I feel the heat of its flames shooting skywards.

I cannot move.

Neither closer nor away.

Can only watch.

Car after car smashes into the inferno.

Because I do not move.

I see shapes in the cars.

Melting in front of me.

I hear the screams as they burn into silence.

And there is nothing I can do.

But stand here.

Dying inside.

10

MONDAY, 25 NOVEMBER, 7.46 AM

Our third morning and breakfast together. I am happy and content as we settle into our new life. Knowing where it might lead. Given time and patience. Forever together. Never to part.

I still want to ask her why she was on the streets. Where she comes from. What happened to her. I think, after last night, that the time is coming when she will open up to me. I just have to be patient a little longer. I know not to press. What might happen if I do.

As I finish my toast and marmalade, she pushes her cup and plate to one side and reaches for her pad and pencils. I continue to eat, taking a sip of my by-now cold tea in-between mouthfuls of toast, as she starts sketching.

I am thinking of what to say to her, something trivial, to have a conversation, to fill the silence. We have become at ease together over meals, sometimes with the radio on, sometimes with it off. We have not had the radio on this morning, and I rather wish we had. It eases us along through mundane comments and lengthy silences.

"I like that jumper," I say inconsequentially, nodding towards her top.

She looks down at it, puts down her pencil and pulls at the jumper, tugging the material away from her body.

"It's warm," she replies.

I nod. "It's always cold here ... rackety old place, really ... I need to get heating put all through properly. Maybe I'll get it done once the snow has gone." I doubt I have the money for it, but still, we'll see. I may be able to get a loan.

She thinks for a minute and adds, "I'm about the same size as your daughter. Her clothes fit me." A pause as she seeks the right words. "Do I look like her?"

"Yes, you do ... a bit." I smile. "I have some photos of her somewhere. I'll dig them out later and show them to you."

She nods and says without hesitation or any trace of embarrassment, "I've seen her driving licence and passport photos."

But she does not add to that, perhaps realising she has said too much. That taking my daughter's clothes without a *by your leave* may be acceptable, but rummaging through drawers, looking at private things, as she must have done, may not.

I wonder where she has been looking whilst I have been out walking Fluffy. Everything I would not want her to see is packed away in the loft.

I do not say anything.

Things are going well between us. I do not want to damage our growing relationship.

I carry on eating. She sketches some more.

"Do you miss her? Your daughter?" Rosie says.

I nod. Not sure how to answer.

"Yes," I say finally. I am not sure where this is going nor what more to say. I think of ways to lead her towards telling me about herself. The words *Do you miss anyone?* are in my mind. But I hesitate. A crass question.

"You don't have any photos up," she says. A statement. But one that sounds more like a question: *Why?*

The answer – the *why?* – is because there are no photos of us as a happy family. Nor any of us individually smiling happily at the camera. And those that I do have of my daughter, I do not want to see.

"No." I laugh, although the sound is not a happy one. "I always seemed to … have my eyes shut." The words come out all wrong. I am slightly tongue-tied.

Rosie tears carefully at the edge of her paper. Turns to show me what she has been drawing. A young girl with big sensual eyes, a coquettish smile, bare shoulders and cleavage.

"You can put it somewhere so you can see it every day," she says, handing it to me as she gets up to clear the breakfast things away. "It's your Lucy."

I smile and take it. I thank her and tell her I will put it on the mantelpiece above the fireplace in the living room. I cannot help but think the sketch looks more like her than my daughter. And that bothers me. I am not sure why.

———

WE SPEND THE MORNING APART. Rosie in the nookery with Fluffy, listening to music and drawing.

I took some time fiddling with the back door of the kitchen, which keeps blowing open whenever there is a strong wind. It really needs a new fixing. I will get one when I am next in town.

After a brief lunch of soup and warm, buttered toast, we agree to play games in the afternoon, through to teatime.

We are in the dining room, Rosie and I. Wrapped up warm

in blankets, as usual. Ice has formed in strips on the windows. They look like jagged bars. Locking us in. Fluffy has sneaked off somewhere, my bed upstairs, most likely, although he sometimes struggles to jump up on it unassisted these days.

I have picked out an old Trivial Pursuit box from a cupboard. I suspect some of the questions will be outdated now. But I have a little quiz pamphlet of up-to-date questions and answers from a recent Sunday newspaper we can use instead.

Either way, we will muddle through for a little bit of fun. To pass the time. To become closer.

I have opened the box. Unfolded the board. Laid it on the table between us. Taken out the cards, which are all muddled up. I start sorting them into their proper piles. Rosie takes the coloured pie-shaped pieces out of the box and the dice, and she sits there playing with them in an offhand kind of way. She seems distant. I reach for the instructions and pass them to her. "Go on," I say. "Have a read. Have you played before?"

She shakes her head. "No." I think she is not someone who has played many board games, but it is enjoyable, and I will let her win if I need to. I will *um* and *ah* over a decisive question towards the end, get it wrong, and watch her as she punches the air with joy. That's how I imagine it will be.

She holds the instructions leaflet in her hand without looking at it. I can tell straightaway something is wrong. She glances at me and then rests the instructions on the table. I think she is ever so slightly red-faced, but cannot tell for sure. She is putting on a brave face, that's for certain.

"You're dyslexic," I say gently before going on, "No matter; I can remember what to do, pretty much." I am dismissive, in a nice way, rather than making an issue of it and embarrassing her. It is nothing to be ashamed of. Once we have settled in together, I can help her with her reading.

Before she can reply, something catches Rosie's eye. I

follow her gaze out of the window. She leans back so she cannot be seen as I lean forward to see who it is. I am expecting to see Widow Woman at the gate again, making a nuisance of herself. If she has seen us, I will have to go out and send her on her way. Say Rosie is my niece, staying for the weekend. Until the snow clears. *Now, if you'll excuse me ...*

But it is not, this time. The Man in the Suit's car, a black four-by-four, expensive and full of swagger, has pulled up alongside my front gate. I can see him inside on his own. He is looking at the cottage, up and down, checking each of the four big windows in turn. Like he owns the place. The lane. The whole wide world. I hate this arrogant, thick-necked brute, hiding behind his smart suits and handmade shoes.

"Who's that?" Rosie asks, more curious than concerned.

"Neighbour. That side." I nod towards 5 Bluebell Lane. I'm tensing up, at the sight of him, but do not want her to sense the tension in me.

"What's he doing?" She looks puzzled. She finds it odd, not alarming or frightening.

"I don't know. He had a massive argument with his wife. In the back garden, before the snow fell. He left. I think she then went off with the children the next day. I heard a van loading stuff. He's now come back. I guess he's looking for her. He's ... nasty."

I don't add anything to that. I hope that final comment is enough for her to keep well away from him. She does not seem to want to be seen anyway, slipping back out of view when Widow Woman turned up the other day. I had assumed she did not want to be spotted with me. Now, as she sits there leaning back and looking awkward, I wonder if there might be more to it than that.

Rosie says, "If she loaded a van and left with her kids, she'd not be here, next door." A simple statement, but an obvious one. She then adds, "He might think you know where she is. She might have talked to you before she left."

I watch him sitting in the car. Brooding. Studying one window followed by the next. Upstairs first, then across and down to the nookery.

He knows I am here. My car, snow-covered but clearly visible, is still parked on the other side of the nookery.

His gaze turns to the dining room window, and he seems to be looking straight at me. I sit there looking back. He scares me to death, but I will not show it.

"What's he doing now?" Rosie asks.

"Sitting. Watching."

"Weirdo," she says.

I do not know if he has really seen me and is staring me down, spooking me. If he has, he has succeeded. This man is so full of fury, his response to the misunderstanding last summer wholly out of proportion. Most men would have laughed it off. A jovial *clear off!* and no more. Secretly pleased that his wife could still draw admiring looks.

His attempts to drive me off the lane when I am walking down it reveal his violent nature. Accelerating towards me until my nerve breaks and I jump out of the way. One day, when this snow has gone, I will not move, I will just walk normally as I am perfectly entitled to do. I will hold my nerve to the last minute, and he will have to brake hard. An emergency stop. If his brakes and tyres are less than perfect, his car will end up rolled over in a ditch. Serve him right if he breaks his fat neck.

"Ignore him," I say. "Let's play."

She looks at me uncertainly.

"Put the round thing, like a pie plate, in the middle and roll the dice. It's like snakes and ladders. You move round the board and have to collect six little wedges. Whoever gets six wedges into their pie thing and completes the pie is the winner."

She still looks unsure.

"Go on; choose a colour and roll the dice."

She takes the yellow pie and puts it in the middle where I pointed. I take the green one and put it next to hers. I glance out of the window and see the car is still there. I assume he continues to watch me. It takes all of my nerve not to stare back. I fear what he will do next. Come up the path and bang on my door, most likely.

I do not know what I will do if he does that. I cannot ignore it. I do not want Rosie to think I am scared of him. I am, though, and I am not ashamed to admit it. He is full of suppressed violence. If he comes to the door, it's because he has seen me here staring back. My own fault.

"Open the door, you fucking coward," he would shout. I would be diminished in Rosie's eyes and more terrified than ever to answer it. I can imagine him pushing me to one side, bowling me over, and coming in to search. I wonder what he would say when he saw Rosie. What he would do. That frightens me most.

"Six," Rosie says suddenly, "I got a six ... where do I go?"

I count six places out on the board and point to where she should move her piece. She does so and looks at me expectantly. As if I know what to do. I am not sure. I have not played it for years and never really liked it that much. And I have half my mind on the game, half on what's happening outside.

"I ask you a question from this booklet ... from last Sunday's paper ... the game cards are years old," I say. "If you get it right, you put that piece of pie in the pie itself." I am not sure that is correct, but try to sound convincing.

I look at where she's landed and say I have to ask her a general knowledge question. I look down the questions in the booklet – 101 of them in all – to find one that is suitable. And maybe just a little bit easy.

"Who was prime minister before Boris Johnson?" That's about as easy as you can get.

"Um," she says. "Um ..." A pause. She brushes an imaginary strand of hair back from her forehead. And blows air out of the side of her mouth. Another long pause into an embarrassing silence. Then she speaks. "Um. Can't think ... sorry."

I shouldn't, I know, but I give her another go. Sport this time. She'll know this. Everyone does. "What's the name of Andy Murray's tennis-playing brother?"

"Andy Murray ... Oh, I should know that," she says. "Um, tip of my tongue ... no, it's gone again. Brain freeze." She laughs a little, but it is an embarrassed noise.

One more. Another easy one for someone of her age (although it is meaningless to me).

"In Harry Potter, what animal represents Hufflepuff house?"

She sits there in silence. Something close to sullen now. A slight shrug indicates she does not know. I am not sure how to respond. I don't know the answer. I'm sure she should.

Outside, the four-by-four revs up, and we both turn anxiously to see what's happening. For a long, horrible moment, I think he is going to somehow do a three-point turn and ram the front of the car into my gate, up the path and against the front door. The utter ferocity of the man. There is a screeching, snarling noise from the car as he tries to push it into the correct gear. The man is jerking back and forth in his seat in frustrated fury.

He finally jabs the car into gear, and it reverses rapidly, the speed far too fast for the gears as he zigzags his way back towards his house. Rosie swears to herself under her breath: "Fucking hell." I suddenly find myself gulping in air, as if it is the first proper breath I have taken since I first saw the car outside. I do not speak – my wavering voice would betray my emotions.

As I turn back towards Rosie, to try to appear calm and in control and ready to resume the game, she catches the edge of the board with her elbow and sends everything flying onto the carpet. I think this was deliberate, although I say nothing to her as I bend to start gathering it all up. She is dyslexic, so reading questions out to me, and checking the answers, was always going to be something of an issue for her.

I am happy to pack the game away.

I sit in the living room by the fire, reading my book, whilst she draws in her pad. Or sulks in her room, most likely.

Until teatime. When we can be happy chappies again.

JUST BEFORE TEA, I rummaged around and found some more make-up items of my wife's in a chest of drawers.

Lipsticks, mostly. Not as bright as the red one that Rosie keeps wearing.

I pull a handful of lipsticks out of my pocket and roll them like marbles across the table to Rosie. She is eating her way through a plate of white bread and butter. That's all she wanted. She stops and looks at the lipsticks scattered in front of her.

"My wife's," I explain. "All sorts of –" I search for the right word "– shades."

Rosie reaches across and jiggles the six lipsticks into a row in front of her. She then takes a mouthful of bread and butter and, as she chews, unscrews each one in turn to see how much is left.

"My wife did not ... has not used some of them. Some of them were new from the Christmas just before ... she died.

The others are about half used, but you can wipe the ends over with a tissue," I say, prattling slightly. I am suddenly nervous, but am not sure why.

Rosie looks at each lipstick and reorders them from left to right, the complete lipsticks to the left, the others, in their different sizes, to the right. "I've never had ..." she says through a mouthful of bread and butter. "Your wife had so many things."

I nod, taking this at face value, as an observation rather than, as many people would, some sort of envious criticism. "You're welcome," I reply, although she has not said "thank you" as such. I take it for what it is. She is a funny little thing at times. I cannot get the measure of her.

She finishes her bread and butter and takes a mouthful of water from a glass by her side.

Then reaches into her pocket and takes out a hand-sized mirror. I have not seen it before. I wonder where she got it. It must have been my daughter's or my wife's. If it is my wife's, it means she has been in my bedroom when I was out walking Fluffy.

She purses her lips. Brings the first lipstick up to her mouth. Rubs it round her lips. She checks her appearance in the mirror. Purses her lips again. I cannot do anything but watch.

I bite into my cheese and pickle sandwich. Then take a mouthful of milk from the glass by my side. I try not to watch her as she wipes her lips with the back of her hand and applies more lipstick. Pursing her lips time and again. Looking into the mirror. Her head this way and that. Pouting. I have thoughts in my head. Swirling round. I do not want them there.

She works her way through all of the lipsticks. Wipes her lips a final time. My eyes are drawn to the lipstick smears all over her hand. My mind full of imaginings. She applies lipstick, from the second in the row, one final time, checks her appearance and turns to me and smiles. She has lipstick on a tooth, and I cannot look away. There is something about it.

"You have so much," she says suddenly, blurting out the words.

"It's all yours," I answer instinctively.

"Thank you," she replies. I look at her. I am not sure if she is joking. And whether or not I am.

"I don't have that much," I add.

"You have this big house."

"It's not that big. But I do own it. The mortgage got paid off when my wife died." I am not sure what to add to that. She looks blankly at me. Talk of mortgages and life assurance policies. She has no knowledge of nor interest in these sorts of things.

"And I have some savings." I go to say *but not much* but stop myself. I don't want her to know that I am running out of money, that I will need to go on benefits soon, and the thought depresses me. I do not want her to know I am a little man. A failure. A loser.

I want her to think of me as a smart man. Who has made a success of his life. Has taken early retirement. Can afford to do whatever he wants. Travel to exotic places. Tick off all those things on his bucket list. I want her to feel proud of me.

"And I have no family or friends. It's just me and Fluffy with my cottage and my money."

She looks at me warmly.

"And you can stay here just as long as you want."

She laughs.

"And everything I have is yours."

She smiles widely at me.

IT IS the coldest night so far. And the snow is coming down
hard and fast again. BBC weather suggests this will be the last
big fall for now. Another three to four inches or so. We must
wait to see what happens next. It may go on and on, this
weather, for some time.

Rosie, Fluffy and I are all huddled round the fire, staring
into the flames. Fluffy's bed takes centre stage at the front, so
close that embers spit and fly towards him. Rosie and I take it
in turns to pat them out on Fluffy's fur before they burn into
his skin.

There is a sense that we are under siege. Widow Woman.
The Man in the Suit. And the Lump is never far away. That
this moment of quiet is a lull before some sort of storm.
There is a feeling of closeness between us. We both feel it.
Rosie pulls her blanket tightly around her shoulders, sips her
hot chocolate, and then rests the beaker on the arm of her
chair.

As we sit there quietly with our own thoughts, she kind of
jiggles about. I sense she is ready to speak about herself. I have
been waiting for this moment since she talked of her mother. I
have wanted to know more of her childhood and who raised
her after her mother died. If I had pushed her with questions,
I might have driven her away. But I have judged it perfectly.
She is about to take me into her confidence.

"You remind me of my dad," she says unexpectedly,
glancing shyly at me.

I think about this. I did not believe she had a father, as
such. That she had never known him. She spoke only of her
mother and "uncles", and in such a way that I assumed they
had treated her badly. And maybe more than that.

"What is your dad like?" I say as neutrally as I can, not
conveying my assumption.

"He was nice. Kind. He was always smiling." She pauses,

and I think she is going to add *like you*, but she stops as if she is remembering him. *Was* suggests to me she knows he is dead.

"Where is he now?" I ask, realising she is opening up to me, perhaps fully.

"He left when I was five. At Christmas ... Boxing Day night," she answers. "He had a drug habit. I haven't seen him since."

I nod, waiting for her to go on. The assumption that he is out there somewhere, just waiting to be found. An improbable happy ending.

"We came here on holiday once. A caravan park by the railway, near some amusements. The trains kept me awake at night." She half-smiles at the memory.

I smile too, imagining her as a small child, playing on the beach in the sunshine with her bucket and spade. The innocence and pure joy of it.

"He said he'd like to live here. As a deckchair attendant. His name is Martin Beech." She looks up at me as if asking me if I might know him. Or have somehow heard of him. She is watching my face, my reactions.

I shake my head slightly as if to say sadly, *no, I don't* and *no, I haven't*. I stop myself from adding that I don't think they have deckchair attendants here any more.

She reaches for her beaker and sips the hot chocolate from it. Her whole body is suddenly stiff and formal. I think she is screaming in pain inside.

"What happened after your dad left?" I ask as gently as I can. I want to see if she will elaborate on what she said before.

She sighs as she puts the beaker back on the armrest. I wonder what she is going to say. She looks down, her face troubled by her thoughts. Then up, her face full of I'm not sure what; unease, I think. Here it comes. Her truth. Out it gushes, unexpected in its emotion.

"My mum was into drugs. Because of my dad. She ... the police were always round ... and she was in and out of court ... she never had any money. I always had to answer the door. She'd hide behind the sofa."

She moves in the chair, curling up into herself. I cannot tell if she is distressed or angry.

"She worked as ..." She stops, as if not sure what to say nor how to say it. "I had a lot of uncles ... she made me call them 'uncle' ... sometimes I had to ... do things."

She stops again. The horror revealed in her simple, stilted words. And more to come. It pours out of her in ragged breaths now, close to tears.

"There was a little boy ... next door ... Louis ... I didn't mean to ... he died, and they took me away. Said it was my fault. They couldn't find my dad. My mum died of an over-dose. I didn't have any family."

She won't look at me. My mind reels at what she is saying. She has taken a life. That's what she is confessing. She has killed. I cannot help but respond.

"You ... this boy ... you ... took his life?"

She looks at me. A sudden clear and steady gaze. "That's what I was accused of. They put me away. No one helped me. I had nobody when I came out. I came here to find my dad."

"You didn't mean to ... or you didn't?"

She shrugs slightly as if she does not understand, to say, to ask, *what's the difference?* Then she answers, almost gushing her words.

"People were in and out all the time. From all over. Next door. And down the street. I was ... he was strangled ... and they said it was me. I don't remember ... I wanted to be ... good. I just wanted to draw. I had to have sex with men. I don't know what happened to him ... how it happened."

I am breathing heavily, taking this all in. Part of me recoils at what she is saying. And another part is heartbroken. For her as much as the little boy. This young girl who was passed from man to man by her mother when she was no more than a child herself.

She pauses. A deep breath. "Please help me."

I am not sure how to answer, my mind is reeling from what she has just said. But, deep down, regardless of my feelings now, I already know that I will. I am, one way or another, in love with her. In some sort of way, anyway.

I nod my reply, once hesitating, twice more firmly, confirming that I will. Rosie sinks back into her chair as if exhausted by her confession.

We sit there staring into the fire for what seems like ages, taking it in turns again to pat the sparks on Fluffy's back before they catch fire. Later, as the fire dwindles and ebbs away, Rosie picks Fluffy up, and with shy smiles of understanding, she heads off to bed.

I can't help thinking that, in some way, our relationship has changed.

Somehow turned on its head.

For better or worse, I do not yet know.

I LIE IN MY BED, wrapped up tight in the duvet. Rosie and Fluffy are downstairs in the nookery.

I cannot sleep, my mind going over what Rosie said. So little. So much. I am weighing the words. Balancing the sentences. Running over it time and again.

Making sense of what she said. I work through it point by point. Stopping. Starting again. Understanding things.

Rosie is a vulnerable and damaged woman. I know that.

She is little more than a girl, really. Only a few years out of childhood.

She was brought up by a drug-addict father and mother. The drug-raddled father left when she was small. Even though she hopes he might be here, he is almost certainly long-since dead.

She clearly loved the father and has come here to try to find him. I think she sees me as some kind of substitute.

Her mother was a sex worker. And Rosie was forced to have sex with different men from a young age. I do not know what age. I suspect a pre-teen age. My heart breaks for her.

Rosie needs my help. And she has asked for it.

I feel responsible for her.

I cannot just abandon her. I have to absolve her.

The little boy who died troubles me. Rosie said she was accused of killing him. That no one was there to help her. No father. Mother on drugs. Men at the house demanding sex. From all over, Rosie said. I wonder if she were the scapegoat – another victim – for what was happening there. That someone else did this terrible thing and blamed her.

I didn't mean to is what she said. The suggestion in her inarticulate words that she *did* do it. But that it was an accident. Unintentional. That she wished she hadn't. "I don't remember." She said that too. Maybe she had been given drugs. Somehow sedated before being forced to have sex with a man. Or several men at the same time.

I see her in my head as a young child of ten or eleven, stumbling from her bedroom, from the debris of second-hand toys and old comics, and away from two or three men there. In the dark, lashing out in fear at someone, the next in line to have sex with her. But not a man: a young boy. He falls backwards, bangs his head on the wall. Lies there. She runs. A man steps forward. Strangling the boy to silence him. As Rosie ran away.

I think it is possible that she did not do it. I believe in her. I don't know why, but I do. In my heart.

If she did it, she was without doubt a victim of circumstance, and she surely cannot be beyond saving. She can become a good and decent person. I am sure of it.

I can help her.

We can save each other.

Rosie and I.

I AM BACK in the cell.

I cannot hear the sing-song voice that calls for me.

But I know it is there and will come for me soon.

I roll off my mattress.

Crouch down.

Empty my bowels.

The indignity of it.

There are whoops and hollers all around me.

Madness and insanity.

But I cannot hear the sing-song voice, and I want to.

I wipe myself.

Hang my head down.

In shame that I have come to this.

PART III

THE LUMP

11

TUESDAY, 26 NOVEMBER, 7.32 AM

I t is the morning at last. It has been a torrid night. Nightmares when I am asleep.

Thinking of Rosie when I am awake. Turning it all over in my mind.

I am determined to save her. And myself. To live a happy life together.

Rosie stands by the front door, on the doormat, looking back at me as I put on my coat, hat and gloves. She has Fluffy on his lead, waiting patiently.

She is wrapped up well. In my daughter's red coat, which is almost the same shade as mine but thick and woolly, plus a striped bobble hat and matching scarf and gloves. We both have wellington boots on. Hers are a little too large, I think. She does not say.

She has the look of my daughter at times, and it almost overwhelms me. I glance at her and can see how excited she is. A walk in the snow! I wonder when it last snowed like this. I think it must be a decade or more.

"Can you remember such heavy snow?" I say to her as we push open the gate and turn right down the lane.

She shakes her head, then pulls the bobble hat down to try to cover her ears. Pushes her hands deep into her pockets. Head down into the wind.

I walk on her right side, between her and 1 Bluebell Lane. With the distance and my body in-between, I don't think the Lump would see her even if he is watching. It is none of his business anyway. I would say she is my niece if it came up in conversation. Just in case.

We walk on, Rosie and I, stomping and striding through the snow.

She starts to move ahead and pulls away.

I am not sure whether to take longer strides to catch her up or simply follow in her footsteps.

I walk behind her by the trees as we approach the open field, just a long stretched-out blanket of white.

I cannot see the trodden-in paths to either side that I usually walk up and across and down and back home. She ploughs straight on, towards the centre of the field. Her head is down, and I cannot tell if she is concentrating on her foot-steps or is troubled or perhaps even angry in some way. I feel I have done something wrong.

I am not sure what that might be. Perhaps I should have addressed what she said more fully. Expressed sympathy and concern. I am now ready to do that. But I do not know what to say, nor how to say it. I do not want to push or probe. I must show that I care. If she wants to say more, I will listen to her. I am here for her.

We carry on in a straight line across the field. On and on we go. One foot down. The other pulled out of the snow and forward. Next foot pulled out and another step on. And so on. Each time, the snow threatens to hold tight to my boot, drag-ging it off.

She is pulling further away from me almost with every step.

And I am struggling already to keep up with her pace. My legs are heavy and my breathing increasingly ragged. I hear myself breathing heavily. Puffing in and out, louder and louder. I sometimes forget my age and my health; I need to remember I should be on medication for this and that and the other. I've stopped taking the cocktail of tablets, but it takes time to come off them completely.

I wonder what would happen if I fell to the ground now, face first in the snow. What she would do. Whether she would make her way back to the cottage. To find my old-fashioned telephone on the sideboard in the living room. Call 999. An air ambulance helicopter hovering over the fields as I gasped my last breath.

Or whether she might leave me there dying, soon to be covered by another heavy snowfall, and make her way back to the cottage. I have a sudden mental image of her sitting by the fire, a tea cake on the end of my toasting fork. Fluffy would lie there, his head on her lap, gazing up and waiting for her to give him a corner of the tea cake, as I have always done.

She stops suddenly and turns and looks back at me. A serious expression on her face. She's been thinking about something important. Worrying. That she now needs to share with me.

I am here for her. I will be supportive. Whatever it is.

"I can't really read and write. Not properly. Will you teach me?"

And I find myself feeling relieved. Not being sure what I expected her to say at that moment.

And I am nodding and smiling and saying I'd love to. I feel happy. There's a sense of relief. I don't quite know why.

WE SIT, side by side, at the dining room table. The breakfast things have been cleared away. We are ready to begin.

Paper, pencils, rubbers and pencil sharpeners in front of us. Dug out from the backs of drawers.

And a *Winnie The Pooh* book, too. A favourite of Lucy's.

I must admit I was surprised Rosie could not really read or write, but delighted that she asked me to help her. That she would share such an admission with me. That she sees me as a father figure. It took all of my willpower not to hug her on the spot.

Instead, I led the way home through the snow. She followed eagerly. Bumping into me once or twice from behind. I had no idea how to start teaching an adult to read or write, nor which came first. Reading or writing? Chicken or egg? I really did not know.

Once we got back to the cottage and had taken off our hats and gloves and coats and boots, I headed straight for my old computer on the desk in the corner of the kitchen. Rosie stood by my shoulder as I started it up and entered my password. As she leaned forward, I thought she might rest her chin on my shoulder in her excitement to find out more. But she did not.

Lots of conflicting advice, as you'd expect from Professor Google!

But most seemed to suggest starting by learning the letters of the alphabet.

Writing them out and matching them to simple words. Apple. Bird. And so on.

A rushed-through breakfast, and here we are. Rosie watches me as I write *A a, B b, C c* and so on, carefully across the paper. She sits up and then back as I continue through the alphabet and down the sheet of paper. She's huffing in frustration as I get to *K k, L l, M m*. I slow a little just to tease her. I think she realises and sits still. I am not sure whether she is playing along or being a sulky madam. I speed up, and she sits forward and seems pleased when I get to *X x, Y y and Z z.*

I finish bottom right on the paper with *Z* and a long zzzzzzzzzz whilst making a buzzing noise like a bee. "Zzzzz, zzzzz, zzzzz," I say, imitating a bee. "'Zed', we call it here," I add. "In America, they pronounce it 'zee'. Rhyming with bumblebee." I glance at her; she does not seem to know what to say. She licks her top lip with her tongue as if she is focusing on the alphabet.

I draw, on a separate piece of paper, an *A* followed by a little *a,* and draw an apple although it looks more like a peach to me. "A is for ... a peach." I laugh, turning my head from side to side at what I have drawn. She looks at me blankly. "A is for apple," I add. "You draw an apple and do a capital *A* and a –" I search for the correct word "– small *a.*"

She draws an apple that looks like an apple.

A slightly stilted *A.* And a rather scrawly *a.*

She looks satisfied. A glance and a half smile towards me.

I'm not really sure what to say or do next, other than to think of words that begin with a. "Words starting with *A,*" I say. "Have an 'ah' sound ... apple –" I look round the room "– armchair ... ah ... armchair ..." My mind wanders, trying to find something else. I glance out of the window.

Widow Woman is walking by. The fat Labrador on a lead. The two grandchildren, too. Older boy. Younger girl. I cannot remember their names. They are on their way to the fields. They do not look this way.

Widow Woman has her head down and is concentrating, not wanting to fall over. Forwards or backwards.

"Arse," Rosie says and laughs. I laugh, too.

"You know some words, then," I say cheerfully.

She smiles and nods and drops her head down shyly. Then back up with a look of mischief on her face.

"Only rude ones." And she laughs again, easy with
me now.

"Spell it, then. Arse," I say. Why not? Have to start
somewhere.

She puts her head down, the tip of her tongue poking out
of her mouth as she concentrates. She writes slowly and carefully. A stop-start scrawl. A back-to-front *r*, I think. A pause
for thought. Letters rubbed out. Another go. A sense of frustration. She scribbles over what she has written. Then, in
block capitals, writes F U C K. Looks at me to see what I say.

"Well, some words are easier to spell than others," I say
neutrally, then add, "Why not write down the words you
know how to spell. Rude ones, if you like."

Rosie looks at me and, head down, writes OFF next to
FUCK. Glances up. Sees my bland face. Writes SHIT. Then
CUM. Then TITS. I smile benignly, which seems to
encourage her. One after the other, she writes down all sorts
of swear words, in block capitals. I watch her until she stops,
and I then check them.

"I think that's O-C-K-S, not O-X," I say, pointing to one
word. "But other than that –" I count up the words "– it's nine
out of ten." I write "9/10" and put "A" next to it.

She leans forward and writes "STAR" next to the "A" and
draws a little star, too.

I laugh. She has some reading and writing ability already.
Whatever she has said.

Has had some teaching. Somewhere. Sometime.

I wonder if she can do joined-up writing. Read a simple
book.

"You're smart," I say. "Can you do joined-up writing?"

She looks at me.

Writes oh-so-carefully on her sheet of paper.

Turns it towards me. Has that serious expression on her
face again.

She has written what I assume is her real name. Alice Beech.

"Hello, A ... A ... Alice. B ... B ... Beech." I smile widely.

I offer her my hand. She hesitates and reaches out to shake it. Then laughs.

"I prefer Rosie," she replies. "Call me Rosie."

And we carry on. *A* is for apple. *B* is for bird. *C* is for ... I ignore Rosie's suggestion and write *car* and do a little scribble. Rosie repeats what I have done. Her car looks better than mine.

On we go, working our way through the alphabet. I think we will try to get through a third of it today before stopping to prepare for lunch.

And we look at each other on and off and smile. We laugh at my drawings. And admire hers. She has a talent. No doubt about it. There is more to this young lady than meets the eye.

HAVING FINISHED our first reading and writing session, Rosie goes back to her room with Fluffy.

I hear Radio 1 playing loudly. She will be gone until lunchtime.

I sit quietly at my computer. Searching for "Alice Beech".

There are so many. Just a cursory glance down the first page shows dozens of them on Facebook and LinkedIn and Instagram and Twitter. More than thirty on some sort of people's directory. I click and click and click, looking at faces and places. All a waste of time, of course. I know this Alice Beech is not going to be on any of these sites. This outcast from society. Who probably has little or no knowledge of social media.

I try again; amending my search to "Alice Beech", I hesitate and add the word "murderer". So, "Alice Beech Murderer". There are pages and pages and pages of entries to look through. Most linking "Alice" and "Beech" and "Murder", but none together in the same case. I go through all of them. Searching. Always hunting for the correct entry.

One more go. This time searching for "alice + beech + murder". Heart in mouth. There are cases. But as I trawl down them one by one, most have a line at the end, "Missing: beech+ | Must include: beech+" I try variations. *Alice Beech Child Killer. Alice Beech Louis. Alice Beech Case. Alice Beech Trial.* I go round again, including her father's name, Martin, this time. On and on without success.

I click to "images". Enter the same mix of names and words. Over and again.

Page after page after page. One after the other.

I see no faces that resemble Rosie now or as I imagine her as a child.

I sit back. Thinking. Then start over. Searching for child murders over the past decade or so. Sickening. But I have to do it. And Louis Child Murder and Alice Louis Child Murder. And so many variations of the names and words. Martin Beech included again. Alice Rosemary Beech. In case Rosie, Rosemary, might be her middle name. On and on through Wikipedia, until I have seen so many stories and so many innocent little faces and so much unrelenting horror and misery that I stop, my head hanging, unable to read on.

No Alice Beech.

No Louis. No Rosie.

And I wonder why that is.

WE SIT TOGETHER side by side. After lunch.

On the sofa in the living room. Rosie and I and Fluffy.

Perhaps that should be side by side by side.

Reading Winnie The Pooh. *When We Were Very Young,* which I think may be the first Pooh book. I turn the pages over slowly, going back and forth, pointing to various poems and sketches and words. Saying the simple words. Rosie repeats them and draws in her little notepad.

We stop at "The Four Friends" poem, and I read it aloud and point in turn at the elephant and the lion and the goat and James, a very small snail. Rosie repeats the words *elephant* and *lion* and *goat* and tells me conversationally that she used to like stepping on snails and hearing the cracking sounds that made. I move straight on.

I look at the "Daffodowndilly" poem and point to the daffodil and say, "Da ... Da," and Rosie interjects and says, "Daddy-long-legs." She laughs. I think she is in a silly mood, and I am not sure whether to persevere with my teaching (such as it is) or to join in the jolliness.

Rosie draws a daffodil in her pad.

Shows it to me.

It's a perfect match for the one in the book.

There is a poem called "Hoppity", with a little girlish figure in three sketches: one with a blue hat, another with a green hat and a third one in a red hat. I think these must all be Christopher Robin.

"Christopher Robin," I say, pointing. Rosie does not respond. "A. A. Milne's son ... the author ... his little boy ... Pooh's friend." There is something about the spindly figures that remind me of Lucy as a small child.

Standing next to me in a river somewhere on holiday. Devon, I think. Her bare feet and tiddly toes, trying to catch fish with a small net. Me next to her, watching, encouraging. Happy days.

And I turn the page. To another poem, "Happiness".

John and his waterproof boots, hat and mackintosh.

A smear of a jammy fingerprint on the page. Lucy's.

I stop, struggling now with my emotions. This was Lucy's favourite poem; I remember reading it to her over and over on that holiday in Devon. A caravan on a clifftop in the corner of a caravan park. Brixham, I think. Looking out across the bay.

Her on my lap at the table, toast and jam in front of us, me reading the poem to her. She pulls at the book with her jammy fingers to see the sketches. Here is the proof of that memory in front of me now. Taking me back in time to those precious moments. I can barely breathe.

Rosie does not seem to notice my anguish and presses on cheerily. She touches a sketch of John in his hat and coat and boots on the page and says, "Wellington boots," with an air of triumph. The poem states "waterproof boots", but I do not correct her. She draws a picture of the figure of John as I pretend to cough and splutter and wipe my eyes with a handkerchief from my pocket.

And then the moment has passed.

We move on to another poem. One that is not familiar to me.

And the lesson continues on its way.

AFTER TEA, we sit, Rosie and I, in the living room with blankets around our shoulders.

I am in the armchair, finishing the last few pages of *10 Rillington Place*. Rosie is on the sofa, drawing in her pad with her pencils, Fluffy stretched out alongside her. He has transferred his affections very quickly.

We are at peace, the two of us.

Rosie glances up, looks towards the window into the dark of night and sits back, startled. She then turns her head away and pulls the blanket around her.

The Lump is at the window, his stupid face pressed against it. "Hello?" he calls out, as if he cannot see us in there. "Hello?" Louder now. It's something important, maybe even urgent. Life-threatening.

I move quickly out of the living room to the hall and front door, pulling it open in my controlled fury. How dare he sneak up on us like that, spying, peering through, expecting to see God knows what.

"What do you want?" I say sharply as he steps back from the window and onto the path, his face dull and uncomprehending. I do not turn the outside light on. I do not want to make him feel welcome. He can stay in darkness.

"Tea bags," he says in his raised, slightly high-pitched voice. The campness in contrast to his huge bulk. "I've run out of tea bags. Do you have any ... and milk?"

No *please*. No *thank you*. No manners at all. I can barely suppress my anger. I am able to control it these days. Even though I am now off my medication. So I can live a happy, balanced life.

I stand there looking back at him shivering in the snow in his ridiculous bobble hat and coat. If I tell him to go away, to clear off, politely or not so politely, I wonder what he will do. I have heard him lose his temper before, over the fence, when both his parents were alive. The shouted oaths, the sudden rise to fury, the sound of glasses and crockery being broken. The storming off. And then the silence of the Lumps.

If I agree and go and get him a handful of tea bags and a jug of milk, this will be the start of a series of visits, for bread, for washing powder, for goodness knows what, as he starts to rely on me rather than making the long walk into town and back. He will forever be at my door. Disturbing Rosie and me.

"Have you got any?" he says quite abruptly, interrupting my thoughts. There is no politeness there. He is not asking a favour. He is demanding his right. This ignorant simpleton of a man.

"Wait there," I answer as firmly as I can without sounding angry. "I'll see what I have." I just want him gone as quickly as possible.

I walk to the kitchen. There is a two-thirds full box of 240 tea bags on the side. I tip all but a handful out onto the worktop surface. Go to the fridge where I have four bottles of fresh milk, two opened, one green top, one blue top for my cereal, both half full. I empty half of what's left of the green one into the blue one, leaving a quarter-full green bottle of milk for him.

"Here," I say, thrusting the teabag box, with its half-dozen bags, and the two-to-three-inch full bottle of green-topped milk at him. "It's all I have; take it." I suppress the urge to add, *And don't come back. Ever, you cretin.*

He stands there for a moment or two, holding the box and the bottle, as if processing what I have just said.

"What do you want?" he says.

I shake my head, not understanding.

"I have money," he says. "In my pocket." He nods to his left side, but makes no move to reach for it with the box in one hand and the bottle in the other.

"I don't want anything for them," I answer. Even if I did, I would not put my hand in his pocket. "*Gratis* ... free ... they're yours." I wave my arms about. *That's it. Sorted. Please go.* He just stands there.

"Well," he says finally, and I expect him to add something conciliatory about having half each, that we should share it, and I am ready to reach in and take a few of the tea bags back. Just to be rid of him. But still he stands there. On and on. And does not add anything to it.

He then takes a sudden, unexpected step towards me. I resist the urge to step back. He smells of cheese. His breath of onions. It is hard not to recoil from him. But I stay steady and look calmly at his face.

He gazes at me with his dim, staring eyes, but his face is flushed, and his mouth is twisted. It is as if he is aroused. I glance down at his half-open coat. I think he is. The utter horror of it.

"Who is she?" he says conspiratorially, his head inclining towards the living room window. He winks.

I imagine him, whilst I was inside, stepping forward to take another look, touching himself, squeezing, and then standing back as I came back out. Before I could see him.

I really want to tell him to fuck off; he makes me that angry. I want to put my hand on his chest, shoving him so hard that he falls onto the path. I want to take the tea bags and push them into his mouth and down into his throat until he chokes. In that moment, I want to kill him, standing there, spoiling everything.

But I know I cannot do anything like that. I have to be normal, relaxed, indifferent. That this is something and nothing. That his comment is little more than polite conversation. Even though he stands there now with his excitement clearly visible to me through his half-open coat.

"She's my niece, staying for a few days, until the snow clears," I answer, turning away and going back indoors.

"Oh ..." He is about to say something else, something conversational, as I shut the door on him, hoping this will be the end of it.

Knowing, as he stands there in silence before trudging off, that this is just the beginning.

I must not let it spoil things. But I know it will worry me all evening, as we spend time reading and drawing, and until we go to bed. He will come back.

I HOLD the body close to me.
The bloated face next to mine.
Cold and clammy against my cheek.
If I can tread water long enough.
Until someone comes.
I think I can save us both.
But no one comes to help us from the water.
And I cannot hold on much longer.
I have to let the body go, or we will both go under.
But I cannot let go.
And I know why.
I wake up.
And I am sobbing.

I AM in and out of sleep. As I so often am at night.

Living my nightmares.

Reliving my life. The absolute truth of it.

I loved my daughter. Lucy. But I never told her. Not even once. I wish I had. People said she would have known. I don't believe she did. If she had, I do not think she would have taken her own life. How could someone so loved do something so terrible? So final. Ruining so many lives.

I love you. Such a simple thing to say.

Three words that will always haunt me.

And the thought of how things might have been if I had said them.

I have some happy memories of Lucy. From when she was born. The midwife holding her up in front of my wife. Our baby's squashed and bloodied face. My arm around my wife as she held Lucy close to her. I leaned forward to kiss Lucy on her forehead. I should have whispered *I love you* then. But I did not. I don't know why. I was an only child and always found it impossible to show emotions. Everything bottled up.

An early birthday party at home. A pink pony theme with bunting, balloons and cake. Lucy's solemn face as she waited to blow out the candles. Little friends in a circle around her. Her look of delight when the candles magically relit themselves.

Her first day at school. Running ahead to the playground without looking back. Her straw hat blowing away in the breeze. Stopping to get it as we ran to catch up. Her shyness when meeting the teacher. Hiding her pretty face in my wife's skirt.

Lucy took her own life. The open verdict was no more than a kindness.

She walked into the river late one night. She had stones in her pockets. She could not swim.

Neither my wife nor I were swimmers. We did not teach her. She did not have lessons.

At the age Lucy should have had lessons, the drink already had me. I had discovered alcohol as a pre-teenager, only child of distant parents, sipping from bottles in their drinks cabinet during the long summer holidays when I was left alone whilst they went to work. I did not like the taste then and was sick more than once, but I believe that's where it started. My alcoholism.

I drank regularly in my late teens, going to pubs with fellows I worked with on a Saturday job in a furniture store. Pints, mostly. Never spirits. I continued to drink heavily – weekend benders, mostly – when I was at university. I got a 2.2, the aptly known drinker's degree. I never thought my drinking was out of the ordinary. Just what young men did.

I stopped drinking for a while, when I fell in love, got married, went to work, had baby Lucy. But then the stresses and pressures of life – the wrong spouse, the responsibilities of parenthood, a dull and poorly paid job – led me back to alcohol. Birthday, Christmas and New Year drinks became more regular. Weekly. Then daily. And more frequent. Nightly. Early hours drinking, eventually. Trying to unscrew the bottle top without making a noise.

The drink made my life easier to live for a while.

I managed my drinking around my life, my job, my family.

Things turned, inevitably, and I managed everything else around my drinking. For a while.

I don't remember as much as I should about Lucy's childhood as she moved towards her teenage years. I have a memory of sitting with my wife in her car in a field as a sports afternoon was about to begin at school. Arguing. I had been drinking. My wife wanted me to stay in the car. I would not. There was some embarrassment. I remember having to return to the car and being sick beside it. And being seen by some of the schoolchildren.

As a teenager in her school holidays, I would sometimes ask Lucy to phone in sick for me at work, leaving a message on an answering machine, sometimes getting a call back, speaking to someone. My wife refused to do it. Lucy did it. I do not think she wanted to. I remember sitting close to her so I could hear what was being asked and telling her what to say in reply. I was already too far gone to realise the woman on the other end of the line could hear everything I said. Shouted, more like.

And I remember how, as days turned into nights and back into days again, I would lie curled up beneath the dining room table for hours on end. I do not know why. I think it made me feel safe, in some way. And I felt hidden from view. One afternoon, Lucy brought two friends back – the last time, I think, so it must have been in her mid-teens. And they came into the dining room for a board game, or some such, and found me there. Later, I was told I had wet my trousers.

By now, my marriage had long since splintered. Little more than a polite pretence in public. Shattered in private.

And Lucy had turned away from me. At least, given up.

But I did not realise any of this, so lost was I in drink with bottles in the cistern and the loft and at the bottom of the old bin at the back of the garage. So many hiding places.

My last clear memory of Lucy was at her school after what must have been her A Levels. I had tried several times to stop drinking over the years. The threat of my wife leaving. Taking Lucy with her. Losing my home. My job, too. I do not think I really wanted to stop. It has to come from inside, not from outside pressures. But I did stop for a while. Short periods of sobriety. Lucy won an award, the person who had done the most for the school, or something like that. As she was announced, I stood and clapped loudly, too soon and too much. I may have whistled. I can still see the look on Lucy's face in my mind even now. Mortified.

I have no idea how or why Lucy chose to go to the university she did in the north-east. I have no recollection of visiting it. Nor talking about it before she made her choice. These years were a blur, if even that. For much of it, I have no memories at all. Something went wrong in her first year there. She had her first serious boyfriend, and that wasn't really for her, I don't think. Boys. Men. She was confused about herself. She didn't come home during the holidays, as she had a job there in a bar. Somehow, moving into her second year, she began to suffer from depression – and eventually anorexia – and then things started to fall apart.

She had to travel by train for a term's work placement, and one night, she missed the last one home. She was sexually assaulted and left for dead by the station car park. The man was never caught. She did not tell us any of this at all, nor reach out for help. Not that I would have been any use. I learned all this later, of course. Much later. Far too late.

There was the knock at the door. The police. We learned that Lucy had gone missing. We drove up there in utter silence. By the time we arrived, they had found her body and dragged it from the river. I remember sobering up and walking back and forth, collecting her things, being surprised that she got into such a good university. I did not know how bright and smart and clever and funny she was. This is what friends said to my wife and me at her funeral. I think they were being kind. But truthful, too.

I remember the funeral. Shocked into sobriety, I listened to the vicar, and then one friend after another sobbing through their carefully rehearsed words about Lucy. Halfway, I decided to get up and say something. My wife watched me rise to my feet. By this time, she was far beyond anger. And sorrow and pity, too. She looked at me with the strangest expression. I stood there and said the words I should have said so many years ago. *I. Loved. Lucy.* But I stammered and choked on her name and struggled for breath until the vicar, assuming I was drunk, took me gently by the arm and guided me back to my seat.

And all I have left now are memories. More gaps than memories in truth. For a while after, as our marriage disintegrated completely, people would occasionally share a story about Lucy. All new to me.

Her left-behind clothes stayed untouched in her bedroom. Her clothes and possessions from university packed away in boxes in the garage.

And I have scrapbooks filled with her cards and drawings from when she was small. There is one there, from a Father's Day when she was at nursery, with the spindly words "I love you" in her own hand, guided by a nursery assistant. I can hardly breathe when I read it. Yet I have to look at it now and then.

I lie here in my bed. Waiting for the morning.

The cold getting to my fingers and toes.

Yearning for sleep. And a better day tomorrow.

12

WEDNESDAY, 27 NOVEMBER 1.17 AM

I am awake, suddenly, unexpectedly, and turn to my bedside clock to check the time. The illuminated screen shows it is 1.17 a.m.

Something has woken me. I don't know what. I look down the bed. Fluffy is not there. I cannot remember if he came upstairs with me or not. My fragile, collapsing mind.

I think Rosie may have come through into the cottage. Called Fluffy to her. He has left me for her nice warm bed.

I lie here in the dark, my duvet up round my chin. Just listening. But there is silence in the cottage. Rosie must have shut the connecting door. She now lies back in her bed. Fluffy is by her feet. Maybe under the duvet with her. Snuggled up close.

I turn on my side, curling under my duvet, my arms around me, my legs drawn up into a foetal position. Waiting for warmth and for sleep to embrace me again.

As I descend back into the depths, there is another noise. Hardly anything, a metallic click, not even a clang, but I hear it in the cold night air. It disturbs me. Then there is silence again.

There is someone or something in the front garden. I get up out of bed, slip on my slippers, move to the window. Pull a curtain back slowly with my right hand. As carefully as I can. Just enough to see out through the nets.

In the moonlight, I see the hulking, slightly stooped silhouette of the Lump. He stands inside the front gate and then steps forward into the moonlight. Bobble hat. Overcoat. Boots. The first noise, the one that woke me, must have been the sound of him forcing the gate open against the snow. The second, just now, the click of the metal latch falling back into place behind him.

He stands there, unmoving, as if waiting to see if he has been heard. I am holding my breath, hoping he does not look up at my window and see me there.

He looks up. I stand stock-still. A statue.

His head moves ever so slightly, checking each window in turn. Two or three seconds at each. The same at mine.

And he turns his head towards the nookery. And I count in my head as he stands there. Ten. Twenty. Thirty seconds.

He moves now, one step at a time, slowly and surely, towards the nookery. At his sixth step, he moves out of my sight, too far down and too far to the right for me to see.

I do not know what to do.

Go and confront him, this Frankenstein's monster of a man.

Or wait and listen, going down if I hear him breaking in.

I put my fingers on the handle at the side of the window, easing it up. Then reach down, lifting the latch that sits on the windowsill. I get ready to push the window open a crack so I can hear more clearly.

I am holding my breath again. Hoping the window does not creak. If it does, the Lump will hear it. I do not know what he will do if he does.

I feel sorry for him in a way. This strange and freakish

boy-man. I fear him, too. His strength. His anger in a rage. The violence.

There is no creak. I breathe again, listening. My breath sounds loud inside my head.

I hear his heavy footsteps in the snow, the crunching of his steps into ice as he approaches the nookery.

I imagine him, by the window, peering in. I know why he is there. This grotesque creature who has never had a woman. Rosie. My so-called niece staying in the nookery. He wants her.

He is there now, looking through a crack in the curtains. Watching as she sleeps.

I imagine what is going on inside his head.

I lean my forehead against the window, struggling with my thoughts. Then gather myself and step back so that he cannot see me. I count the seconds into one minute and towards two. I wonder if her duvet is flung back and she lies there naked. He is by the window, looking through, touching himself as he looks her up and down.

I imagine her rolling over in her sleep onto her back, and he watches her. She moves a little, and he steps forward, his face pressed against the window. His breath on the pane. She then moves again. And he stands, moving towards ecstasy. I shut my eyes and think my terrible thoughts.

Open them again as I hear the click of the gate.

The Lump glances back as he shuts the gate behind him. Then looks up at my window. Stands and stares. I am not sure if he knows I am there. I do not move; I just wait.

Suddenly, he is gone. I return to my bed.

Restless and more troubled than before.

I HAD my usual early morning walk with Fluffy, studiously ignoring any signs of activity at 1 Bluebell Lane. I enjoy our walks, despite the snow.

We listened to Radio 1 over breakfast (although it might as well be in Swedish for all I understand of the gibberish).

And we cleared the breakfast things together as usual. I washed. Rosie dried and put away. I like our companionable silences.

When we had finished, she stood there unmoving for a moment or two. I could tell by the way she cleared her throat, the way she hesitated, that she was going to ask something of me. I thought it might have been to do with the reading and writing lessons that we'd agreed to do one hour each morning and one hour each afternoon whilst we are shut away in the snow. But it was not.

"Would you teach me to cook?" she asked ever so politely.

I could not help but feel pleased. My Eliza Doolittle.

"Not cakes," she added. "They're nice but ... meals, like ... proper meals."

I nodded and smiled. "Yes, of course."

And so here we are now in the kitchen, after the usual morning of cleaning and tidying, ready to "give it a go". I had said that spaghetti bolognese was an easy meal to cook, and she said she liked it, so that's what we are starting with.

Rosie asked if we could look up the recipe online so she could see the ingredients. She sat there all excited by the computer, turning it on and waiting for it to warm up and wheeze into life. She kept turning and looking at me, as if to say *Hurry up!* Then she looked blankly at the screen, which needed a password to go any further.

I said she could find the password at the top of my note-book – "my little book of passwords" as I call it – in the top drawer of the desk. She did and carefully entered Q1W2E3R4. She took an age searching the keyboard, pressing each key carefully, like a child. But she got there in the end.

I then clicked on Google on my home screen and did a search for "spaghetti bolognese" and went through each entry until I found one that listed and showed the ingredients. As I did this, I leaned in close to Rosie, my head to her left side and my right arm reaching around her to touch the keyboard. She sat very still, but seemed to be at ease with my close proximity.

"Onion," she says cheerfully, pointing to one picture.

"O-n-i-o-n," I reply. She nods.

"Carrot," she says next. Quite jovially.

"C-a-r-r-o-t," I answer. She nods.

And so we work our way through the ingredients, stopping and stumbling a little over cloves of garlic (where I did a brief impression of Dracula, and she looked back at me without comment) and pancetta cubes (neither of us knew what they were). I said they must be like OXO cubes, but she did not seem to know of them either.

There's knocking at the front door.

Loud, demanding, insistent.

And I am striding through into the hallway and wrenching the door open. Furious at the interruption.

It is him again. The Lump. And I have no time for any of this nonsense. He wants this. He wants that. And he expects me to get it for him. To give it to him. And all of it just an excuse to come indoors. To have a closer look at Rosie. To smile vacantly at her. To say something inane. To stand there looking like the stupid freak that he is.

"I'm busy," I say before he has a chance to speak. "I ..." He goes to reply, but I hush him down. "I'm on the phone to someone right now. It's important. Okay?" I add. I can tell from the look on his face that he is taken aback by my raised voice and abrupt words.

"So, unless your house is on fire ..." I say. He looks blank-faced, but goes to answer. I just carry on over his hesitant "No."

"You'll excuse me, then, as I'm going to finish my conversation." I shut the door in his face. I don't wait to see if he stands there or trudges back down the path and away. I go back to Rosie and the computer in the kitchen.

I am about to comment on the Lump. But she has her head down, looking at the screen, concentrating.

Turns, seems flustered, clicks a button, and the page she was looking at is gone. I could not see what it was.

"I'm looking at other recipes," she says, flushing red. "I've lost the page."

She gets up out of the chair; I slip in and see that Google is no longer there. I go back in again and bring it back. I resist the urge to click further to *history,* and instead re-enter a search for "spaghetti bolognese" and work my way through to where we were.

Rosie has gone over to the fridge and the larder in the corner and comes back with two tomatoes and two carrots and two onions. One each, I guess. She hands them to me.

I laugh and put them on the desk beside me. "We can do better than that," I say. I go to the cupboard and get two tins of Tesco minced beef and onion, a bit dusty but perfectly usable, and a packet of spaghetti from under the sink.

"We boil this," I say, showing her the dried spaghetti, "for twenty minutes. In fifteen minutes, we put these two tins into a pan and heat them through. We can then mix in some tinned vegetables and sweet corn, and there we have it."

She laughs. "That simple?"

"That simple," I reply. "When you've got tins ... always have a stack of tins."

We both laugh.

WITH THE SPAGHETTI bubbling away and Rosie putting on make-up in her room and changing her lipstick for the umpteenth time, I am back at the computer, Fluffy at my feet. I want to know what Rosie was searching for. I am not sure what I expect to see.

Signing in. Clicking on Google. Going to history. There are only a handful of searches on the list. I clear it every time I finish. Habit, I suppose. The last but one is what I am looking for. I glance and see "Martin Beech".

I sit back. Thinking. She still believes he is alive. Wants to find him. I am not sure how I feel about that. Not good. But I don't quite know why. Maybe it is because I am distracted right now. My mind keeps returning to the Lump. He is a problem. And I do not think he will go away.

The Lumps are – were – an odd family. All six foot plus, with identical long arms and legs and large heads. The mother and father were so similar they could have been brother and sister. Maybe they were. "Suffolk born, Suffolk bred, strong in arm, soft in head" was never more apt. And Felixstowe is notorious for its rabid inbreeding. Cousins are fair game hereabouts.

The Lump was the strangest child. I first noticed him as a teenager, walking to school and back again with his long, marching stride, always alone. Other times, I'd see him in the garden, from my bedroom window, staring into space. Occasionally, I would hear him singing in his curious, high-pitched voice. Hymns, mostly. After leaving school, that was it. He seemed to spend all of his time at home. Hard to imagine anyone employing him. This half-witted fool.

As he became a man, in body anyway, I heard him in the garden one day with his parents. He must have been about eighteen. It might even have been his eighteenth birthday. I sat there listening quietly. His childlike, excited talk of getting his own place, of marrying, of living a happy life. The father laughed, not in a nasty way, and said something to suggest that could never happen. A nonsense. There were more words. Raised voices. The Lump flew into a rage. I heard chairs being kicked over, glasses and crockery breaking and the mother screaming.

Rosie comes back in. She smiles at me. Then points at the oven.

I smile back. Pretend I am doing something and nothing on the computer.

She goes across to the tins of mince and onions. I nod for her to go on, to empty the contents and heat them up.

There was a terrible struggle between father and son, with the Lump swearing furiously, using the F- and the C-words over and over again and threatening to kill him. The father was knocked to the ground, and I heard the mother's voice, trembling but defiant, shouting, "Don't you touch me, Andrew, don't you touch me." A moment when I thought he was going to attack her. But then he was out of their gate, slamming it hard, and was storming along the alleyway and was gone.

Still I sat there silently, too scared to move. I heard the mother talking to the father as he came round. His muffled incoherence turned to words of anger as she helped him up and into the house. I expected to hear the sounds of an ambulance and a police car as I went back inside. But I heard neither, and later than night, I watched the Lump striding back home as if he didn't have a care in the world. Whistling, he was. Life resumed. I never heard anything else. But I remember. I'll never forget.

And I fear what he is capable of. Driven by a mix of child-like dreams and man-sized urges.

I must keep him away from Rosie.

As I get up to sort out our home-made spaghetti bolognese lunch, I have to think how to do that. To stop him before it all goes too far. Before it spirals out of control.

AFTER LUNCH, I walked Fluffy across the fields and beyond. An hour, maybe more, the longest walk we've had since the snow fell. I needed to clear my head.

Over near the farm where I buy home-made sausages and beefburgers. To gather my thoughts. To work through my worries. Calm down. Get things in proportion.

I did not see the Lump on the way out. Nor on the way back. I did tell Rosie not to answer the door whilst I was away. To lie low. Just in case. But I did not mention the Lump specifically. I did not wish to alarm her. I want to keep her safe. I wish her to feel secure as well. I am simply going to shield her from him. That is what I will do.

When I came back, she was in the dining room, looking out of the window towards me. Waiting. I think she must have missed me. She was restless and out of sorts. Fiddling about with knick-knacks on the side. Clearly bored. So I suggested on the spot that we make a cheesecake.

Cheesecakes are something of a speciality of mine. It all came about when I bought a so-called luxury one from a local supermarket (which I will not name). I had expected, given the word "luxury", that it would be a light and fluffy, creamy affair. Something like squirty cream foam. With a soft and tasty base. But it was not. It was a stodgy, lumpy thing, and a large piece of the base got stuck in my throat, and I gagged on it. Fortunately, learning the Heimlich manoeuvre is about the only thing I can remember from first aid training during my workdays. And so I performed it on myself before anything untoward happened.

I threw the rest of the cheesecake in the swing bin straightaway and decided there and then that I would make my own. And I would make it to perfection! And I have done so, every fortnight or so, since then. My special mix of digestive biscuits, butter, cream cheese, sugar and double cream. You can put fresh strawberries or raspberries on the top. But in their absence, I have used strawberry jam, marmalade and – a particular favourite – lemon curd.

"Top or bottom?" I ask Rosie, pointing to the biscuits and butter in one bowl and the cream cheese and sugar in another, with a tub of double cream next to it. And an empty tin ready to take the cheesecake.

"Um," she says. "Top?"

"Okay," I answer, pushing one bowl towards her and pulling the other towards me.

We both start our spreadings and stirrings.

I think now may be the time to talk to her a little more about herself. I have waited. And waited. And waited some more. Not wanting to push nor pry. To risk damaging our growing, loving relationship. But she has visibly relaxed so much with me lately. Letting me dry her hair. Revealing what happened to her. Admitting she cannot read nor write properly. Seeking my help. My advice. My love. It is now time for us to progress.

"We moved here twenty-five years ago this year, funnily enough," I say conversationally, out of nowhere, looking about the kitchen. "I was from south London originally. But ... there were jobs here then. We bought this place with an inheritance ... well, that and a mortgage. Bit beyond us otherwise."

She says nothing, just carries on stirring the biscuits and butter.

"Where are you from?" I say gently, almost in an it's no-big-deal, just-something-to-say way, as I stir the ingredients in my bowl. "You have an accent, but I can't quite place it."

"Lutterworth," she says, then adds, as she sees my quizzical face, "Near Leicester ... the other end of the A14."

I nod. That makes sense. The A14 is a long road, 120 or so miles, stretching from the Midlands to Felixstowe. It brings all the lorries thundering into the port and back out again.

"So that's why you used to come here on holiday? Along the A14?" I ask.

"Yes." She does not say anything more. Her head is lowered, and she is stirring the ingredients for the top of the cheesecake round and round and round.

I hesitate and press on carefully.

"Did you hitch-hike here? This time?" I ask.

She nods, but still keeps her head down, looking at the bowl. She stabs at the mixture with the wooden spoon, as if checking its consistency.

"Yes ... but not from Lutterworth. I got moved around places a lot. I got released earlier this year ... on licence ... and was in a bedsit in Rugby. Doing a shit job. Packing stuff."

She glances at me but does not add to her comment. Just pushes the bowl back towards me as if to say, *There, it's done.*

I pass her my bowl and tell her to squash the mixture into the bottom of the tin on the table with the back of a spoon. I hand one to her.

As I do this, I hear a helicopter above. It's back again. Searching.

I look at Rosie. She has not heard it. At least, if she has, she does not show it.

I ignore it. If it is there, above us, it's just out doing whatever it's doing. Nothing to do with me. Or us.

"Anyone know you've come to Felixstowe?" I ask quietly, finishing stirring the mixture and waiting for Rosie to press the rest of the biscuit base into place. "Anyone know you're here?"

She looks at me, and it is an unsettling look.

"Friends you had in Rugby? The lorry drivers who brought you here? Anyone, anywhere, you've been asking about for Martin Beech?"

She pulls a face and shrugs. She says, "No," but her body language hints at a *yes*.

Rosie watches me as I pull the tin back towards me. Press one or two places a little harder with the back of the spoon. Then pour the cheesy mixture onto the biscuit base in the tin and spread it out evenly.

I am not sure what to say to Rosie. Someone, somewhere, knows she is here. A friend from the bedsit, most likely. And someone, somewhere, will come looking for her. The police, I would expect. She must have broken the terms of her licence, for sure. They will want her back.

And I wonder, as I put the cheesecake in the fridge and say we will have some for dessert after our tea, what that means for us.

The helicopter comes in closer.

I smile at Rosie. She smiles back at me.

Our rictus smiles.

───────────

WE SPENT the rest of the afternoon together. We did some reading and writing. Then she drew, and I finished my book. I took Fluffy for another long walk whilst Rosie had a shower.

And we made some cheese on crumpets for our tea. I showed her how to add some onions to the cheese and melt them into the crumpets in the microwave oven.

We had some cheesecake, too. Then spent the rest of the

evening drawing and writing again. We talked a little bit, now and then, but about nothing of consequence.

And then we went to bed.

I have stayed awake tonight, sitting up in my bed, duvet across my lap, blankets round my shoulders.

Waiting for him. The Lump. Whilst Rosie and Fluffy lie sleeping, safe and sound, in the nookery.

I know he will return, and I know what he will do. And I know what I will do. If I have to.

I sit here with a poker from the fireplace across my lap. It is a heavy one, with a ball at one end resting in my palm and a twist of metal at the other end for poking the fire. It could be used in a number of ways. You could, for example, hit an intruder – a menacing burglar – on the back of the head with it. That would bring them to their knees. A second blow, by an innocent homeowner fearing for his life in the dark, could fracture their skull. Self-defence, really.

Or it could be useful as something like a sword, with the twisty end being used to parry, to jab or to stab. If someone broke into your home in the dead of night, you could use it to defend yourself and others too. If you had to, for protection, you could hold it up straight and true as the burglar ran towards you in the dark. No one could blame you for that.

The Lump will come here. For Rosie. At some point soon. This strange man-boy with his big slab head and dull, lifeless eyes, and with the childlike obsession of a fifteen-year-old boy. The wants and desires of a grown man. Standing there aroused and touching himself, almost as if he does not know what he is doing. If he breaks in, to force himself upon her, I will need to act. And I will do whatever I have to do. I do not know what will happen after that. I do not want the police here.

I get up and move to the front window, looking out of the darkness towards the snow-lined trees.

I stand there a while, listening to my measured breathing, in and out, waiting for him to arrive. And he will. Any time now.

He is not at the front. There is no sign of life at all, just a slow and steady sprinkling of dust-like snow falling.

I move to the back window, looking down its full length towards the fields beyond.

And there he is. Already. As I knew he would be. He has pushed the back gate open, into the snow. He is by the glazed window of the shower-toilet room at the back of the nookery. He has his hands up above his head as though he were surrendering to armed police. In reality, he is leaning his hands on the window, his face pressed childlike to the pane. Hoping to see what is already in his mind.

A minute passes as I stand there watching him. He moves, very slowly, to the nookery door that opens into the little kitchenette. And I do not know if the door is locked or not. I locked it last. I think. But Rosie may have opened it to come outside at some point, to let Fluffy out. If the door opens, he will be in the nookery, and I will have to act fast. I wait, my mouth so dry. I suddenly feel frightened at the thought of taking him on. But what else can I do? I won't have the police here.

I imagine, can almost see, his hand on the handle. He pushes it down, and I wait for the door to swing open and for him to disappear inside. He will push his way through into her bedroom and be upon her as she wakes. There will be little she can do to protect herself. As he pins her down and rolls his great heavy body onto her, I will have to force my way in and confront him. Now it is almost upon me, the moment. I do not know if I can do it.

Suddenly, he is stepping back and away. It is over before it even started. The door must be locked. He's turning and leaving, pulling the gate shut behind him.

I can sense his thwarted lust as I see him disappearing into the passageway and through his own back gate.

He will return. I am sure of it. And I fear for what will happen then.

THE TANKER STILL BLAZES, its flames up into the sky.

And the sun is so hot and beating down.

And the cars are crashing and burning.

The shapes are melting, and I can hear the screams fading away.

Before the next car crashes, and it starts over again.

There is a shape coming out of the inferno.

And this melting thing walks towards me.

It is speaking, but I cannot understand what it says.

And it is pointing at me.

And it beckons to me.

It wants me to come into the flames.

To burn and die with it.

And I move towards it, to embrace death.

I AWAKE WITH A START.

Another nightmare. My recurring sorrow. This endless night.

I lie here, thinking.

I loved my wife. Laura. Once upon a time. Unreal, fairy-tale times, when our lives lay ahead of us and everything seemed possible.

I told her so, too. That I loved her. In the early days. More lust than love, really. Young men are driven by their desires.

There was no real chance of a happy and long life together. Too young. Too ill matched. It is as simple as that.

We met at university in the Midlands. I studied for a business degree. She did English literature. Mine was practical. Hers was artistic. Mine led to a job, a series of jobs really, in low-level marketing in local authorities. Never well paid. Not even half decent. She had dreams of creativity. Poetry. Amateur dramatics. Singing. But nothing came of any of it.

She did a teacher training course after university and worked at various dead-end pub and restaurant jobs. She then spent years teaching in one primary school after the other. I think she was frustrated. Teaching the same things to the same children at the same times, year after year. The children always the same. Her forever changing – ageing steadily.

But I get ahead of myself. We met through mutual friends at university. I forget who they were now. Started going out in a crowd. A couple of times, just the two of us turned up at the pub or the cinema, and we kind of fell into seeing each other. I found her attractive. Tall and slender and seeming so comfortable in her own skin. I was always worried about fitting in and being seen as normal. I don't think I ever have been. I have always felt an outsider. She knew I went out drinking some nights, and did not seem to mind, but never came along. Parallel lives, even then.

After university, we stuck together. The alternative would have been to go back home to indifferent parents. She was an only child too, with an equally distant family. About all we had in common. Living together, the dreariness of day-to-day living, nine-to-five jobs, little money, no common interests – lust soon wears off after a year or two, and what's left, in our case, was not much.

Our marriage stop-started along. I think we both thought about separating. But we did not. Instead, we got married. I must have gone out drinking one Friday night with people from work. Got horribly drunk. I don't really remember it that much. I just recall the conversation on the doorstep when I got home.

"I'm pregnant." She sounded more disappointed than excited.

"You're pregnant," I stated, a drunken echo. Trying to take in the enormity of it.

"I'm pregnant," she repeated, a strange tone to her voice.

"Oh," I said, pushing by her to the toilet. She told me later that I had said, "Oh shit," but I do not recall it like that.

The early years of our marriage, raising Lucy, were happy enough times. I was happy enough, anyway. My drinking was, if not quite under control, not yet taking me over. I have memories of us – a small family – enjoying simple pleasures. Paddling in the sea by the pier at Felixstowe. Having fish and chips at Aldeburgh. Walking up and down Southwold Pier and throwing pennies off the end of it. There was drinking. Nights spent on the sofa. One or two in nearby fields, waking up to see cows looking down at me. But not too many. My alcoholism was there, though. Waiting not so patiently. Restlessly.

We did not try for another child. Laura said she did not feel she could. At the time, I took that to mean she could not physically face it; the pregnancy and birth of Lucy had been difficult. I did not mind. I never wanted a son. I did not want to replicate my relationship with my distant father. And we had Lucy and did not need another girl. That was how I felt at the time, as I spiralled downwards. I think now that Laura knew which way things were heading with me. And she did not want to bring another child into the world.

I do not know, looking back, why my wife stayed with me all through those years up to Lucy leaving for university. I think she must have done it for Lucy's sake. She did talk now and again of going, taking Lucy with her, maybe to try to shock me out of my drinking. But nothing she could say or do made any difference to me. By the time Lucy left, and I have no real memories of it, I was gone completely. By then, our lives were separate. She did whatever she was doing. I drank.

"I wish it were you who was dead," she said to me, on the stone steps of the building after we had identified Lucy's body.

And she turned and walked back towards the hotel. I slept on the back seat of the car, an old blanket from the boot covering me, in the hotel car park overnight.

We drove home in silence the next morning. She wept and shook uncontrollably most of the way. I wanted to get home to drink myself unconscious.

Somehow, we kept going. Her in the routine of work, day after day. Me working my way to oblivion on a daily basis. Both of us still living in the cottage. Her sleeping downstairs in the nookery. Me in what was our bedroom. Separate meals. Separate lives. Easier not to say anything to each other after a while. Just moving around the other like ghosts.

Neither of us could face Lucy's room. Neat and tidy, with everything she did not really want, or had outgrown, left in the wardrobe and drawers. It all stayed there untouched, part of a shrine. In a rare moment of sobriety, I stood there once in the doorway. Breathed in stale air. Touched my finger on the chest of drawers, leaving a print in the dust. Picked up the discarded cellophane wrapper of a small tampon from beneath the bed, illuminated in a shaft of light. Rolled it round my fingers, dropped it back.

We went on like that for a while. My wife disappeared at times. More than I noticed, most likely. Sometimes, she was gone for days. During school holidays, I think, looking back. To friends, maybe. To parents, elderly and living in an apartment high upon a hill in Edinburgh. I don't know. The idea of a lover crossed my mind. But I did not think it was likely then, and less so now. She was following the same path as me in her own way, ever downwards.

I kept my job at the local council all this time.

In truth, it was not a difficult job to do. I turned up as often as not. Pushed papers around. Sat in group meetings. Filed things. Waiting for five o'clock to come round so I could go home and start my proper drinking.

But there were asides and conversations and one-on-one meetings, and more formal interviews, and I knew the end was coming. Sooner rather than later.

Then, one evening, just after I had opened a bottle of whiskey and downed glasses one after the other, there was a knocking at the front door. An echo from before. With Lucy. I opened it, to get whoever was there gone as quickly as possible, and saw two police officers standing on the path. A middle-aged man who looked steadily at me. A younger woman who seemed to be holding her breath. I knew straightaway that Laura was dead.

After a few polite words, the policeman as good as confirmed it and took me to identify her. I remember sitting in the back of the police car and watching the young policewoman. She seemed to be sweating, even though it was a cold night. I recall thinking, quite clearly, that she must be a special rather than a regular officer. She seemed more nervous than I was. Some silly banter came over the radio, and the older policeman turned it down before saying, "Sorry," over his shoulder to me. I smiled back. More dazed than drunk.

They only let me see her head, the rest of her body below the sheet looking odd and disjointed. I thought the shape was not quite right, that it was not all her. That, somehow, something had been added to make her body look whole. Her face was bruised and battered, although someone may have applied some sort of make-up to make her look better. All I remember thinking is how old she looked with her grey hair roots and lines cut in around her eyes and mouth. She never used to look like that.

Laura had waited, quite calmly, by the side of the A14. In amongst a copse of trees. For ten to twenty minutes, based on statements taken from car drivers over the following days.

As a petrol tanker gathered speed, she stepped out and strode into the middle of the dual carriageway. Her head down. Body turned away. I don't know what she must have been thinking at that moment. Whether she could somehow calm her mind. I doubt it.

Four people died in all, including her, and the blaze of the tanker and the cars and the bodies could be seen far away over the fields, towards the pretty little village of Kirton.

I look at the illuminated clock.

Coming up to two a.m.

I must try to get some sleep.

13

THURSDAY, 28 NOVEMBER, 7.10 AM

E arly morning, and I am walking Fluffy through the snow towards the fields. The air feels more damp than chilly, and I think a thaw may be coming, at least temporarily.

The Lump is at the window of the front room of his house. Inane smile on his face. Mug of tea in his right hand, raised up. Taunting me.

I think he is waiting for me to disappear into the distance before he sneaks across to the cottage to try his luck.

I hesitate, not sure what to do. I want to march up his path, bang on his door and tell him to keep away from Rosie. That's all. Just stay away. But I am not sure how he would react to that. Whether he would meekly agree. Or if there would be an argument, a brawl, with me ending up flat on my back and humiliated on the path.

I could walk Fluffy further on and turn towards the trees, hiding behind them, watching. But I do not know what to do if he comes out of his gate and turns left. I could chase him off, send him away, as he approaches the cottage. But I wonder if he might lose his temper and lash out at me. Knock me unconscious. That would then leave Rosie at his mercy.

I could call the police. I don't know what I would say. That the man next door is bothering my niece? But they might not come for days. If at all. I do not want the police here, anyway. Looking. Talking. Assessing. And Rosie would run just as soon as she saw a police car. And the police cannot arrest someone on the basis of what they *might* do. Only after they have done it.

I stop at the top of his path. Look towards him, unmoving.

He looks back. His big stupid face.

We stand there, as if locked together, neither of us wanting to move first. He then turns and disappears from sight.

And he is opening the front door, striding down the path towards me in his dressing gown and pyjamas and slippers. He still clasps his half-full mug of tea in his right hand. This idiot of a man. This dim-witted fool I have to engage with.

"Yes," he says in his high, nasally voice. A question, really: *What do you want?*

"You must be cold," I say mildly, conversationally, looking him up and down.

"I'll be alright for a minute," he replies, then stands there looking at me expectantly.

"My niece," I say ever so blandly.

"What about her?"

"She's not for you."

He pulls a face, makes a noise at the back of his throat. This simpleton who thinks he is normal. He shakes his head slightly from side to side, and I wonder if he is rising to anger already.

"She likes me." His eyes are locked on mine, as if staring me down.

"She doesn't know you," I say instinctively, derisively. And go to add, *You've never met.* But then I suddenly realise that they have. That he must have called round when I was walking Fluffy. Maybe twice yesterday. That they have talked. I do not know what to say. I am taken aback by this unexpected development.

"She likes me," he insists, his voice rising higher. "She said so." He will brook no argument. "And I like her." As if that settles it.

His tea sloshes over the edge of the mug onto his fingers. He does not seem to notice.

He seems to be shaking.

I know I should back away. But the anger is rising within me. I must subdue it.

"You're a ... a nice man, but, you know ..." My voice tails off as he stares at me. I am not sure how else to put it. Diplomatically, at least. That he's not all there. He thinks he is normal. Nobody else does.

"She likes me more than you," he says. "She said so."

I sigh loudly, involuntarily, suddenly realising the pointlessness of this conversation.

"She's told me about you," he goes on, a look of satisfaction on his face. As if he is oh so smart. A clever debater.

I pause, thinking. I turn away, my back to him, pulling at Fluffy's lead. "Come on," I snap at Fluffy.

"I know," he says loudly, following me down the path to the lane. He is so close he could reach out and touch me. "All about you." Louder still.

I ignore him.

"Get your dog off," he yells nonsensically. "Dog shit everywhere."

I laugh at this. His incoherency.

I feel the spray of tea across my shoulders.

I turn back angrily. "You come round again, and I'll have

the police on you." It's all I can do not to swear and call him a freak.

His face contorts. He throws his mug on the ground towards me. It breaks. Fluffy backs away.

I turn away too, anxious now to be gone. This can only end in a fight. And I will come off the worse.

"Cunt!" he yells as I walk away. He repeats it six, seven, eight times, louder and louder, like a small, angry child who has lost his temper.

I do not know what will happen next.

If he will turn up at the cottage.

And, if he does, what I will do.

BREAKFAST IS A QUIET AFFAIR. Radio 1 is turned up louder than ever. Rosie seems happy just to listen to it. I am stewing over what the Lump has said. I'm not sure how to raise it with Rosie. If at all.

She looks across at me occasionally. Smiles. As if everything is the same. Nothing has changed. Of course, I know it has. She does not yet realise that I know.

I am going to sit back and look and watch and listen. I do not doubt they have spoken. But I do not know if they have talked in the way the Lump has described it. Whether she has betrayed me. Told him about me. Quite what she has revealed.

She goes upstairs as I start my dusting and cleaning and tidying.

Comes down with something that she slips into her pocket as she passes me in the living room.

Goes through to the nookery, shuts the door behind her. I can hear the shower running.

I busy about as usual, dusting one room at a time. In the

living room, I shake the dog blanket and the cushion over the fire, watching the fur and the dust and the dirt dropping into the flames. Fluffy is stretched out on the sofa, ignoring me.

I move into the dining room, rubbing my cloth at the edges of the ice that has formed on the inside of the window. I cannot chip it off. I peer out through the glass and out to the snowy lane. My face, from the other side, must look twisted and distorted. The Phantom of the Opera. There is no one about. I wonder how long it will be before the Lump appears at the gate.

The kitchen always seems a mess, with too many packets and bottles on the sides dotted between the kettle and the toaster and the other pieces of old and dated equipment. I wipe over the surfaces, which seem to be covered with crumbs of toast and smears of butter today. And flakes of porridge.

I dust and polish. Hoover about. Room by room. Except the nookery, of course.

Pick and rub at odd marks and smears and stains.

Killing time, really. Waiting to see what will happen next.

I tense, expecting the knock at the door. The Lump. I imagine him sitting in his house, thinking about Rosie, obsessing, working himself up into something close to a climax. Then storming round here. Only me standing between him and Rosie.

But there is nobody out there. No Widow Woman. No Lump. No Man in the Suit. It is like Christmas Day, everyone inside and getting on with their own lives. It will not last. This stillness. This quiet. This peace.

Christmas is not so far away. I wonder what Christmas Day will be like this year. I drank my way through so many. The last year or two, I have struggled along with Fluffy by my side. I gave him a whole plate of sausages from the local farm for his dinner last year. He spent the evening breaking wind and looking at me in something close to disgust as he hurried away before returning later to repeat the process (more than once). I cannot imagine Christmas dinner with Rosie and me eating and the Lump's face pressed hard against the window.

The door from the living room to the nookery is suddenly pushed open. Rosie comes through. Her hair has an odd blonde-gingery hue. A touch of orange at a certain angle. She must have found a packet of hair dye somewhere in a drawer.

I am not sure if this is the colour her hair is meant to be. I suspect the hair dye may have been years out of date. Or that it has reacted with whatever she already had in her hair.

She kind of tiptoes by me like a model on high heels – her interpretation of a sensual walk – and makes her way to the kitchen. Puts the kettle on to boil. She does not look at me, but expects me to look at her.

I do not know what to say. My wife, many years ago, in happier times, once had a dramatic haircut, going from long brown hair to a short blonde bob. I did not comment on that at the time, although, later, she claimed that I said, "Fucking hell," without thinking when I first saw it – apparently, in a derogatory manner. I do not recall that.

Instead, I get up and follow Rosie into the kitchen and watch her as she prances and preens. She reminds me suddenly of my daughter when she was little and had her ears pierced. She walked about just like this. I breathe in hard – these sudden flashbacks move me unexpectedly. Tear at my heart.

Rosie puts two mugs on a tray and fusses about with teabags, sweeteners, milk and teaspoons. Adds boiling water. Looks at me and beams, her face all lit up. She gathers up books and pads and pens, ready for our next reading and writing session. Fiddling about, getting everything just so.

And I look at her and see a happy girl. Someone who is at ease. Has shaken off her troubles and worries. Is settling into her new life here with me. And can go on, as I had hoped, to lead a good and kind and fulfilling life. As we make our way to the dining room, she turns and looks at me and smiles. I smile back.

"Your hair looks nice," I say, a lilt in my voice. "Really nice."

She seems to swell close to bursting. "Thank you." She laughs.

Then it hits me. I wonder who she has done it for. Herself? Me? I think it is for the Lump.

WE SPEND an odd morning together reading and writing.

She is jolly, silly, even childlike at times.

I am on edge, constantly watching for the Lump.

I decide to talk to Rosie about the Lump over our lunch. I think I have to. To warn her. As gently as I can.

I turn down the music on the radio next to me. Clear my throat. She looks across at me, her mouth open and full of baked beans.

"There's something I need to tell you," I say. Her face is blank and neutral. I do not know what she is thinking.

"The boy next door. Well, man, really. He's simple, but I think he might be a bit of a nuisance."

Rosie angles the fork she is holding to her right, towards No. 1, as if to ask, *That way?* She swallows her mouthful of beans.

I nod.

"The one who wanted tea bags?"

I nod again.

"He's early twenties, but, like, fifteen in his head. He's ... not quite right. He's lived on his own since his parents died. He should probably be in assisted living or a home or something, but I think he's somehow slipped through the net ... he probably needs reporting." I add that last almost as an afterthought. I pause.

She carries on eating.

I continue. "He got some sort of payout when his parents died, I think, so he can afford to live there on his ... anyway ... I think he must have seen you when we walked Fluffy the other day. He's got a bee in his bonnet about you ... that's why he keeps turning up."

She tips her plate towards her, scoops up the last forkful of baked beans and puts the fork in her mouth. It's as if she is not listening to me.

I look at her. She looks at me blankly.

I don't know what to say. I don't want to scare her.

She chews and swallows the last mouthful and speaks. As if it's something and nothing.

"He's knocked a couple of times when you've been out on your walks." She looks at me with a steady gaze. She then shrugs, as if to say *it's no big deal; don't worry about it.* She reaches for a piece of toast on her side plate.

I reach slowly for a slice of toast, too, butter it carefully and dip it into my bowl of tomato soup. I am thinking what to say. I need Rosie to hide away, to stay safe. But I do not want to say that. To make her feel she is in danger.

I see him for what he is. Very clearly. A simple boy with strong urges and a raging temper. He is alone next door. With nothing to do. I imagine him on his computer, looking at photos of young girls, watching videos of them. Pulling at himself, fuelling his urges, stoking his obsessions.

Then he comes here. To peer at her through windows. To imagine her. To watch her in her bed at night. And, at some point, when he is close to boiling over, he will force his way in to have her. I will need to stop him. But I do not think – given my age and size and his utter brute strength – that I will be able to do so.

"He'll make a nuisance of himself if you let him." My words taper off as I feel myself repeating what I have already said. I then try to add something different. "He'll keep coming back now he knows you are here … if you talk to him."

She pulls a dismissive face as she chews her toast. But she does not speak. She glances away.

"How many times has he come knocking?" I ask as casually as I can. I make my voice nice and calm. A little chat.

She shrugs. "Twice. Once yesterday. Once this morning." She laughs, as if she thinks he is rather sad. "When you walk the dog."

I nod, suddenly angry at the thought that he must have come straight round here after we clashed first thing. He has no respect for me at all. None whatsoever.

"Do you –" I do not know quite how to phrase it "– lie low?"

She is thinking how to answer, what to say. I can see that. She finishes her toast. Reaches for her glass of water. Swallows a mouthful.

"I answered the door. He'd have just kept knocking and ringing otherwise. I –"

"What did you talk about?" I interrupt, knowing I sound worried. I need to make it as casual as I can.

"Nothing really. He wanted some coffee … and, um, something else this morning … I can't remember. I said he'd have to come back."

There is a silence. I am formulating my thoughts and questions.

What else did he ask? What else did you say to him? Did you talk about me? I am not sure how to put these questions to her in a casual manner.

But before I can speak, she is up and out of her seat,

clearing away the lunchtime plates and bowls and glasses, and the moment has gone.

ROSIE WANTS to spend some time alone this afternoon. Listening to music, she says. She is cheerful. Perhaps more cheerful than I have seen her.

She disappears into the nookery with Fluffy walking stiffly behind. He has a touch of arthritis today. He will need lifting carefully onto the bed.

I sit in the dining room, my new book, Agatha Christie's *And Then There Were None*, open at the table. It is an old favourite. I like the judge best. There is snowfall again, a steady sprinkling, enough to cover footprints and give us a fresh clean sheet of white by morning.

I am not really reading.

I am watching the lane.

Waiting for his imminent arrival.

I can hear the shower running in the nookery. I shut my eyes, thinking my thoughts. I open them again. I must not be distracted.

The Lump will be sitting alone in his house.

Thinking of Rosie.

Working himself up to come here.

There is silence in the nookery. The shower has been turned off. The toilet flushed. The door between the shower and the bedroom shut. Then nothing. It is the silence that torments me most. Thoughts of what she might be doing.

He will leave his house any moment.

Dressed in his coat and boots and stupid bobble hat.

And he will walk to my cottage. Stand at my gate.

I hear Rosie come out of the nookery. Footsteps on the stairs. Into my daughter's room. Back and forth across the floorboards. Then down the stairs again. The door to the nookery shut carefully behind her.

The Lump will look at me. His hand on the gate.

I will stare back.

It will be a battle of wills. I will not give in.

Rosie is out of the nookery again. Through the kitchen, into the bathroom this time. I imagine her rummaging around in the bathroom cabinet. And in the cupboard under the washbasin. Searching for powders and ointments.

He will march up the path.

Knock on the door.

I will ignore it, willing him to go away.

Rosie is out again, back upstairs into my daughter's room. I hear the creak of the wardrobe opening and shutting. Hurried footsteps coming back down the stairs. The nookery door shut loudly this time.

Knock. The Lump will hit the door hard.

Knock. Knock.

Knock. Knock. Knock. Knock. Knock.

Rosie comes out of the nookery, and I hear her footsteps as she walks towards the dining room. She stands in the doorway. And looks at me, smiling. She has spent an age getting ready, and now I can see why.

She is wearing my daughter's best special-occasions dress, all black and slinky. A prom type of dress. Her hair is brushed and groomed and tied back. She wears high heels.

I have a sudden memory of when my daughter was small. Collecting her from a playdate with a friend and getting there too early. My daughter and her friend had taken women's clothes from a playbox and strutted up and down, five-year-olds playing at grown-ups. And that is how Rosie appears now.

The make-up of a clown.

The yellow and purple bruised arm and ankle at odds with the dress and heels.

And yet ... it is oddly endearing.

I do not know what to say. Whether I tell her she is beautiful. That her hair is lovely. Her make-up perfect. Her dress an utter joy.

But I hesitate, knowing I will stumble over the words, stuttering out clumsy sentences. But she waits there, expecting something from me. Compliments. Words of praise. Encouragement. And so I simply say she looks *so* nice, and that seems to be enough for her. She smiles and waltzes away. I hear her in the kitchen, clinking glasses and bottles and making orange squash for the two of us.

So I follow her there, my heart full of hope and expectation. But I see her glance at the clock on the wall. Just gone a quarter to five. Then a look at me, with her anxious little face, and she says she will make tea whilst I walk Fluffy.

She says it quite lightly. As if in passing. Like it means nothing.

She hands me the dog lead.

I know what she is doing. She wants me out of the way. By five o'clock.

And that suddenly makes me angry. So very angry.

———

Rosie is not happy. Then again, neither am I. Not at all.

I told her it was too cold for Fluffy to go for a walk. That his arthritis was playing up. I put the lead on the side. Said I would make tea. Soup and bread. Let him out in the back garden later.

She has gone back to the nookery. Leaving Fluffy with me. She will be cursing me.

As the hands on the clock in the kitchen move towards

five o'clock, I go into the hallway and switch on the outside light. Then to the dining room, where I stand, watching. Looking out into the darkness. The outside light is not a strong one, but it illuminates the path down to the gate. Everything beyond is pitch black.

There is silence in the cottage. No noise from Fluffy lying on the sofa in the living room. Nothing from the nookery. The cottage is hushed, too. It often seems to me to be a living thing. The cottage. Forever creaking in the cold and groaning in the wind. But now it is still and waiting for something to happen.

The Lump is about to appear in the narrow shaft of light. He will walk up the path. Knock on the front door. Expecting Rosie to answer it. Dressed up. Inviting him in. She will hear him at the door, but will not come and answer it. I will. And I will tell him to go away.

All I can hear is my breathing.

And the beating of my heart.

I am scared. Of confronting him. The Lump.

I watch the snow coming down. There is so much of it already. A thick blanket on the ground and on the fence and gate and on the trees. But it is slowing, this latest snowfall. Just a dusting, really. Maybe adding half an inch, perhaps an inch, this time.

There must be layer upon layer now. Snow. Then turning to ice. And more snow falling. And more ice forming. Another layer of snow. I wonder how long it will go on. I think, maybe, it will be like the first national COVID-19 lockdown, when everyone was shut away for weeks on end.

It has a mesmerising effect, this snow. I am in something of a trance, just waiting. It should be peaceful and relaxing standing here. But I know he will step out of the blackness and into the light at any moment, and I will jerk and twitch and snap into life.

I glance towards the gate, having been diverted by the snow falling from the heavens.

He is there.

He has his hand on the gate, ready to push it open. He looks at the cottage, through the haze of the snow and the outside light, and sees me. I pull back the net curtain in the living room. So that he can see me clearly, watching him, waiting. The net curtain is stuck to ice on the window, and it tears itself free, a ragged, dirty piece in my hand.

There is a long moment of quiet agony when I think he is going to slam the gate open, storm up the path and bang on the door, rattling the handle. *Rosie!* he will shout. *Rosie! Rosie! Rosie!* Over and again. And she will come running out of the nookery. I do not know what I would do at that point. The point that I lose her.

My mind flips and turns and rolls, deciding what to do, dredging up my courage to do it, knowing it will be the end of everything either way. One way or the other. I swallow and brace myself. Then, as suddenly as he appeared, he turns and is gone, walking back, one step, two steps, into the blackness. Back to his house.

I stagger back and sit down, realising that my neck and back and shirt are soaked with sweat.

And Rosie is suddenly out of the nookery and into the kitchen, banging about with pots and pans. Making the tea. Everything back to normal.

Fluffy barks and follows her in. Just in case there are scraps to be had. His paw up, the little beggar.

I think, maybe, just maybe, with her coming back in and him walking away, that I have won the day.

But, just in case, and because I am a clever fellow, I have come up with a sudden plan to make sure. As I move into the hallway to go upstairs to change, whilst she fiddles about in the kitchen, I will detour into the nookery. I will turn off the heating. And then the water at the stopcock.

We will have our tea of hot mushroom soup and brown bread rolls warmed through in the oven, followed by a butter-scotch Angel Delight, made with blue-topped milk (a little more than necessary, to give it that extra whippy texture). And we will play cards or read a book and draw or whatever until it is time for bed.

Then she will hurry back in and say the bedroom is *so-oo* cold and that the toilet does not flush, and look at me to fix things. And I will go in and *um* and *ah* and pull a long face and express disappointment and sadness and say that it will need a plumber and that I will call one just as soon as the weather improves.

Meantime, she will have to come and sleep upstairs in my daughter's bedroom.

Next to mine. Safe from him.

And that, I think, will be a very nice and simple solution to the problem of the Lump.

THE SING-SONG VOICE HAS GONE.
I have not heard it for ages now.
It will not come back.
I feared the sing-song voice.
Yet I wanted to hear it.
Loved it in a way.
And now it has gone.
And I am still in my cell.
I cannot stretch out fully.
Nor stand up straight.
And I will die here.
And there are shouts and screams all around me.

But no sing-song voice.

SOME PEOPLE SAY that alcoholics have to hit rock bottom before they can possibly come back up.

That the desire to recover – to live – has to come from them. Not from their loved ones, cajoling, bullying, threatening.

I think this is all true. My live-or-die moment came after the death of my wife. But not straightaway.

My wife was cremated. Given the circumstances of her death, the cremation was not held locally at the Seven Hills Crematorium. There were only a handful of us there – including her parents, who spoke to me in the most cursory way; her sister, who looked at me coldly but never spoke; and two of her closest friends, who ignored me. I felt like a stranger. I think they all thought I was drunk. It might have made it easier if I had been. But I was not. I lived every second of it.

The night Laura committed suicide, I went back to the cottage in the early hours. In this time of utter clarity, I could see all that had happened came from my drinking. I did think about taking my own life then; I do not, now, know how I did not, nor why. Bizarrely, I remember thinking I had work at nine o'clock the next day. And that I needed to stop drinking for that. After what seemed like hours looking at it, I finally screwed the lid back on the whiskey bottle and placed it on the kitchen windowsill. I swore to myself I would never drink again. I went to work the next day as if nothing had happened. But I had still not hit rock bottom. That came later, after I was made redundant. The disciplinary procedures that I had been facing – those more formal meetings – were put on hold after my wife's death. But with various departments already merging, my job soon became redundant. I walked away with little more than a smile and a wave goodbye to colleagues one Friday afternoon. Then what? I had nothing left at all. Not even a routine to my day.

I tidied and cleaned the cottage when it stank.

I walked into town to get shopping when I had run out of toilet roll and newspaper.

I sat and stared into space, working out how to do it.

I tried to take my own life. I lined up bottle after bottle of vodka and packets of tablets I bought from different supermarkets around town. I took a handful of tablets with each mouthful of alcohol until I passed out. I thought, as I lay back on the bed to die, that my mind would flash back over happy moments of my life, but all I recall was being sick over myself and a thin stream of hot chunks running inside my shirt and down my neck. I think that must have been what saved me, getting most of the tablets out of my body. I woke up some time later, the next day, and just lay there for hours, beyond crying.

I tried again a day or two later. A high-backed chair in the cellar. I put a length of rope around the strip of light in the ceiling. Stood on the chair. Put the rope around my neck. Kicked the back of the chair with my right foot and tumbled forward. The light strip came away from the ceiling, and I lay on the floor with it and plaster and debris all around me. The rope had come loose, too. I had never been very good with knots.

I lay on the sofa in the living room day after day. Night after night. Ignoring the outside world. The neighbours' noise. Letters falling through onto the doormat. The odd knock at the door. The refuse collection van driving down and round and back out again.

Just waiting to die.

My wife and daughter. The shame. The grief. The drink.

My failed suicide attempts. It is hard to explain now. But I seemed to have gone beyond all of that. And was going to somehow die. Just by lying there. And giving up the will to live. I think I would have done had it not been for a local vicar who, tipped off by the vicar who handled my wife's cremation, had come knocking. Time and again, with no response.

I have a recollection of the noise of splintering wood. The breaking in of my front door.

Of people swarming round me. Paramedics. A vicar, eyes shut and hands clasped together tightly in prayer.

Being lifted, groaning with pain, to be taken away. Waking up in a darkened ward full of old men shouting and farting uncontrollably.

I spent five or six days or so in hospital. Weak. Incoherent. Rambling. I remember my arm being strapped. And in pain. Fed by drip. In and out of sleep. Vague conversations. Doctors and students. Falling in and out of consciousness. At some point, I seemed to be awake more than I was not. A talk from a young nurse. Slapping her arm instinctively as she tried to inject me. Crying my apology.

Then sitting up. Looking around at other hopeless cases in the beds opposite me. Not meeting their eyes. The shame and embarrassment of having fallen so far. I wanted to look at myself in a mirror but dared not ask for one. I would have looked old and unkempt. And thin, in some sort of NHS nightshirt with my bare arse showing. Going to the toilet seemed to be a big deal, pissing in some sort of container and being taken to the toilet in a wheelchair. Messing myself.

I was moved about as they needed different beds. Was visited by doctors and women with clipboards who asked all sorts of questions. I got quite angry with one or two of them going on and on at me. Exhausted, I started crying with another. I was completely and utterly fed up. Strangely, I did not seem to want to drink. Whether they had given me some-thing to stop the urge, I don't know.

Eventually, they gave me a haircut and a shave, and I felt a little better about myself, although I did not look in a mirror.

We're going to transfer you ... for two weeks," they said. "To the Priory ... on the NHS ... to get you better."

I do not know if they would have sectioned me if I had refused. I would have asked, but I found it hard to speak through my sobbing.

I spent four months in the Priory in Essex. At the begin-ning, when I thought I would be out in a fortnight, I treated it as a kind of a "pick me up" break. A week or two in a Travel Lodge-type place with breakfast, lunch and an evening meal, all there ready for you. In-between, there were talks with nurses and a doctor, and I knew, instinctively, the right things to say so that they ticked rather than put a cross in the boxes. There were various leisure and exercise classes, too. I made an effort with those. Yoga and drawing and the like. I learned how to draw the Beatles' Yellow Submarine quite well.

I was angry when I found out I was going to be there longer than two weeks. I caused some damage to my room and the corridor; it took four of them to bring me down as I was making my way to the exit. It became a prison. I did not calm down for ages. And I lost my privileges. It set me back a good while. Someone looked in on me every fifteen minutes for ever such a long time.

But I came good. Slowly but surely, over the four months. I learned to accept and deal with my alcoholism. I admitted it in group meetings. "My name is Philip Adams ... and I am an alcoholic." Dealing with the shame and the sorrow of what happened to my wife and daughter. Laura Jane Adams. Lucy Anne Adams. Learning to live with that. Accepting the past. Changing the present. Loving the future. Learning to handle the depression that overwhelmed me every day. A mix of medication and structure and routine, little goals and small rewards. A hand of solitaire. A game of chess. Watching a robin in the garden.

One gloriously sunny day, they let me out.

As I left my room for the last time, I looked in the mirror and accepted what I saw. A flawed and damaged middle-aged man.

Who was going to stay alive and devote my time to saving young and troubled girls. And, by doing that, saving myself, too. And maybe, just maybe, finding some kind of love.

———

I AWAKE SUDDENLY, disoriented for a moment or two. It is dark other than a shaft of moonlight shining through a crack in the curtains. My mind clears.

I turn my head towards the bedside table. The illuminated numbers on the clock show 1.20 a.m. precisely. Something's woken me. Fluffy lies still by my feet. Rosie is now in my daughter's room and is not very happy about that.

There is movement on the landing outside my room. A door closing. Heavy footsteps. It is the Lump. He is here. This monstrous being.

I am up and out of my bed, slippers on and heading for the door. I grab my heavy bedside lamp, wrenching its lead and plug out of the wall in my urgency. For my defence. And Rosie's protection.

He has come here. The Lump. Broken in through the back door of the nookery. Searched there. And come out and into the living room, making his way up the stairs to find Rosie. He is now on the landing. Ready to take her by force.

I have a moment to think as he arrives. He will not know which way to turn. To the left, my room. To the right, where

Rosie is sleeping in my daughter's room. I have to save her from him.

I pull open my bedroom door. He is there in the darkness, his back half-turned towards me. He jumps as he senses my presence, then turns. He is pulling his coat around himself. Now reaches for something in his pocket. A knife.

It happens so fast. I hit him on the head as hard as I can with the base of the lamp.

He stumbles back to the wall. Somehow staggers forward as I pull him round desperately, so his body is facing me, lined up at the top of the stairs.

I hit him again hard on the head. Once. Twice. The third blow missing him by inches, as he is already falling backwards and tumbling downstairs and hitting his head on the cold stone floor. I hear his skull crack. It seems to echo.

There is silence, and I stand there in shock at what I have done. What I had to do. I had no choice. But it paralyses me. I cannot seem to move. I know I need to do something. Then there is the sound of movement from my daughter's bedroom. Rosie is up. I hear the pit-pat of her bare feet on the wooden floorboards.

She turns on the light in the bedroom. I see it shining at the bottom of the door. She opens the door. Her little face. A long tee shirt. Bare legs. She looks at me standing there in my old-man pyjamas. A heavy blood-smeared bedside lamp in my hand. I drop it, and it lands on the top stair, and we both watch it roll and fall down the stairs in the half-light towards the body at the bottom. Her mouth drops open in horror at what I have done.

She takes charge. Pushing by me.

Moving down the stairs. Stopping to stand the lamp carefully up at the side of a stair halfway down. As if that matters.

She crouches over him.

He is all of a jumble on the floor. A big solid mass of bent arms and broken legs. She cannot move him, but I see her put her hand towards his head. His mouth. Checking for breath. Then rummaging by his arm. To take his pulse. Then inside his dressing gown. Feeling for his beating heart.

She looks up at me. Organised and sensible in the middle of this hell.

"Do you have a mirror?" she asks.

I don't reply. My brain is working. But it is somehow slower than usual. My brain does not seem to connect with my mouth.

"A mirror," she repeats. Then she adds, in a raised voice to get my attention, "Go into the bedroom for the make-up box on the bedside table. Fetch me the mirror from that. Go on." Suddenly, she is in charge.

I turn automatically and make my way into the bedroom. The room is messy, clothes spread out in piles on the floor-boards. The duvet has been thrown back, and I see an odd, wet mark in the middle of the sheet. I move closer. It is not blood. I reach out and touch it and lift my fingers to the light, and I realise what it is. It is from him. He has been here. With her. He was leaving. Not arriving.

"Hurry!" I hear her calling as I wipe my fingers on the duvet and reach for the make-up box, rummaging inside. I am then back out and down the stairs, handing the tiny mirror to Rosie.

She leans forward, the mirror pressed close to his mouth.

She sits back and brings the mirror up to her face, peering at it. She turns and looks at me.

"He's dead," she says in her matter-of-fact way. This man who was in her bed, inside her, only a few minutes ago. "You've murdered him."

PART IV

THE COTTAGE

14

FRIDAY, 29 NOVEMBER, 1.25 AM

I walk down the stairs one slow step at a time. Holding the handrail. Feeling sick.

I am done for now. Finished by this split-second fatal decision. The wrong one. A decision that was forced on me.

I will now be going to prison. I don't know what will become of Fluffy. Or me. I cannot face being locked away again. I would rather die.

I touch the light switch at the bottom of the stairs. The 40-watt bulb illuminates the stairs and hallway slightly, but not by much. It's a dirty half-light, and the cottage is still so cold. It really is a morgue now. She grimaces slightly in the light and crouches back. I see she has nothing on beneath her tee shirt, between her legs. I cannot seem to look away. Even now.

She notices my gaze and moves her knees together. Brings her head down. Kind of crouches over. She has the palm of her hand resting on the side of his – Andrew Lumb's – head. I cannot see the expression on her face. Warmth. Affection. Love. I cannot think there would be any of those from this alley cat, having sex with this man-child she barely knew. I do not know what possessed her. What to think of her. Too soon to tell.

But she is not who I thought she was. This girl with the tragic childhood. Locked away for so many years. Out at last into what should be normality. Ending up on the streets, beaten and abused by men. I wanted to save her. Nurture her. I would have been a mentor to her.

She stands up, her tee shirt somehow catching round her midriff, exposing her lower half to me again. She tugs it down and looks at me. Her face is blank; I cannot read it.

I look back, not sure whether she is going to take charge. Or wait for me. I do not know what to do. I feel I will be physically sick.

I look down at Andrew Lumb, one arm and one leg bent at unnatural angles. Like a swastika. His face is turned to the side and squashed as if he is gurning. He is ugly.

"He's dead?" I say, half-statement, half-question.

"Yes," she answers simply. "He's not breathing."

I bend over and repeat, almost without thinking, what she did. Checking his mouth for breath, his wrist for a pulse, his chest for a heartbeat.

I don't know why. He is clearly dead. His eyes are open and glazed. There is stuff hanging out of his nose. Some sort of froth on his lips. But I don't know what else to do.

A silence as I wipe my hand on the trousers of my pyjamas.

She waits for me to speak.

"He had a knife," I say. "In his pocket. He was reaching for it. I was defending myself."

She leans forward and slides a hand carefully inside the pocket closest to her. It comes out with a small Yale key. She opens her palm to show me.

"The other pocket," I say. "It was the other side."

She pulls and tugs unceremoniously at the dressing gown that's partly under the body to expose the other pocket.

She puts her hand in again and pulls out his hat. She holds it up. He was reaching for his stupid bobble hat, not a knife.

I am in anguish.

She folds the hat over and puts it back in the pocket.

She sighs. I am not sure why.

"Should I call the police?" I ask finally, not knowing what else to say.

She shrugs as if to say, *I don't know.* Then thinks and speaks.

"I'll have to go if you do ... I can't be found here. It's not my fault, this. I'd go back inside." She stops for a moment. Before I have time to think of my reply. She then adds, "You'll go to prison. You won't survive. You're soft."

She looks at me, and I look back. She is right. On all three counts. I know it.

"What else can I do?" I ask, my brain starting to formulate an idea. The one I think she already has. Being a step or two ahead of me.

"If you call the police," she says, "you'll go to prison. And I'll leave now." She repeats herself as if preoccupied; she is thinking out loud.

"If you take him to his house and leave him at the bottom of his stairs ... same as this ... no one will ever know what you did."

I am shocked. I should not be. It was the thought I had just had too. Was formulating. I think I am stunned at how impassive she is about it. I look at her and suddenly see her differently. This girl with years of brutality behind her. I see them all in her hard face.

"I hit him on the head ... back and front. There will be

DNA from me ... and from you ... and his DNA all over the lamp ... and in your bedroom ... in ... your bed."

She looks down at him as if she has not heard my comment, or at least does not want to address it. Then starts asking questions.

"Does he live alone?"

"Yes."

"He doesn't have a job?"

"No."

"Does he get benefits? Sign on?"

"I think ... no ... he wouldn't know what to do ... he probably lives off his parents' savings ... inheritance."

"And he has no family or friends, you said?"

"Yes. No. I don't think so. He used to go out once a week with a group of ... people like him ... on a minibus ... but I'm not sure he does any more."

"No one will miss him, then."

Statement or question, I'm not sure.

"And not many people come down this far ... down this lane?"

"Not really, no. Dog walkers. The postman. We've had kids on motorbikes in the summer, but nothing lately. A police car sometimes. But not in this weather." I go to mention the helicopter, but stop myself.

"Any letters sticking out the letterbox could be pushed through. You could watch for parcels." She says, thinking it through step by step.

"Move him and put him at the bottom of the stairs like he is here. Then leave him. Watch to see if anyone calls. If anyone asks, you say he is on holiday. If you see post, you push it inside. You get rid of parcels. Burn them on the fire."

I nod and swallow. For some reason, I can't answer. My throat is dry.

"He won't be found for ages. After the snow. After winter ... the spring."

"DNA," I repeat. "Fingerprints too. All sorts. There will be signs of us on him. Him on us. There and here."

She pulls a face as if to say, *so what?* "They'll not check. When he's found. They'll see him at the bottom of the stairs and will think he fell. You could loosen the carpet at the top of the stairs. Why would they think anything else?"

I look at her. She has this all worked out. This street urchin. So innocent in some ways. But not in others.

"Don't clean him up or anything ... don't try to be clever ... don't overthink things ... make it natural." She thinks a bit more, and she is close to smiling, as if this is some sort of game. "You could find himself yourself in the spring if you wanted. Then call the police. Anything of yours on him won't be suspicious."

"Move him now. I will open the kitchen door ... and the back gate ... and his gate." She picks up the Yale key on the floor. "You can then drag him through, unlock his back door and leave him by the staircase. I'll clean up here while you do that."

She looks at me. "Okay?" She repeats it. "Okay?"

I nod my agreement.

She hands me the key. I turn to go.

Wondering if this is the biggest mistake of my life.

I STOP for a moment to get my breath by the step up to the Lumbs' back door.

My hot breath against the cold moonlight air. A thin zigzag of blood in the snow, leading back to his gate and beyond to my cottage.

The heavy and cumbersome body lies by my feet in the snow, blood dripping onto my slippers.

I turn, exhausted by my efforts dragging him here by the shoulders, his head rolling back and forth against my thighs as I drag, stop, drag, stop, drag, stop my way from my cottage to his house. I am not used to this. It's hard work. There is blood all over my thighs. So much blood everywhere. I would not have thought it was possible. It as if his body is emptying itself of all of it.

I leave him on the ground as I open the back door of his house. Move in and wait, letting my eyes become accustomed to the dark. Checking the way is clear to the foot of his stairs. Through the kitchen into a small hallway. The size and layout are different to mine, although it all still feels just as cramped. And it seems so old, so out of time; untouched since the 1970s, I'd say. His grandmother's house originally, I think.

I flick the kitchen light on, for there is no one anywhere about to see it, to be suspicious, to remember the moment. The kitchen is a mass of orange and chocolate-brown colours: swirly wallpaper, tea, coffee and sugar jars, Formica surfaces, wood-effect linoleum floor. The house that time forgot. A full and wide-open bin bag of rubbish, leftover food and packets and wrappings rests besides the kitchen door.

The hallway has long-since-faded, striped cream wall-paper and a dark swirly carpet. An old-fashioned mustard-coloured door and a glass shelf with a cream-coloured rotary dial telephone on it. It all smells stale and dirty. I turn and look up the stairs, which has the same swirly carpet and dulled brass bars across each step. I wonder whether one of those might loosen easily near the top.

I go down onto my hands and knees and crawl up the stairs, feeling each bar as I get closer to the landing, pulling them in turn to see if one might come away. They are all tight, and so is the carpet on the landing. I can do nothing now. I will come back in the morning with a screwdriver and see if I can loosen one enough to rumple the carpet near the top of the stairs.

I edge my way back down, using a corner of my dressing gown to wipe each bar where I touched it with my fingers. A corner of my dressing gown catches on one bar halfway, and a thread is tugged out. I pull it loose and slip it into my pocket. I have to be careful.

Then I am at the bottom of the stairs and hurrying back outside for the body. I cannot stop and dwell on what I have done. I have to focus on what I am doing. One task at a time.

As I stand there looking down at his body, I see a dark pool of blood by the back doorstep. I doubt that will ever come out. I am suddenly sorry for what I have done to him. I made a spur-of-the-moment mistake, and he has paid for it with his life. But I thought he was a monster and a danger to the girl, that he was going to rape her. I was sure of it. And it all happened so fast. I thought he had a knife and that he would kill me with it. I acted in self-defence. Those are the facts.

But I do not know what the police would say about it if I called them. To confess. I killed him, after all. Hit him not just once – self-defence – but two or three times, spun him round, pushed him down the stairs to the cold stone floor below. He did not fight back. I could have stopped at any moment after the first blow. I did not. I lost my temper.

Manslaughter?

Murder?

A long sentence, I know that.

I do not know what she would say if I telephoned the police after she had gone back to bed and was asleep when they arrived. I remember her words: "You've murdered him." I wonder if that is what she will say to them. Feeling cornered.

That Andrew Lumb was in the cottage at her invitation. That I was jealous. Angry. A dirty, leering, possessive old man. She could put words, threats – maybe even death threats – into my mouth.

And whether, in her fury at being recaptured, she will go further and say I forced myself on her. "Look, he hit my face and twisted my arm so hard he almost broke it." And rage, "He raped me repeatedly." And that I have somehow held her here captive, maybe threatening to hunt her down and kill her if she left. "And," she'd add, "he killed Andrew when Andrew tried to stop him raping me, hitting him so hard he broke his skull. He pushed Andrew down the stairs and left him to die. I was too scared to do anything."

And it *was* me who moved the body, dragging it from the cottage to his house, blood dripping and smearing all the way. And I wonder how I would talk my way out of that. They will ask, if it had been an accident, why would I move the body?

The fact is, I will go to prison if I call the police. But if I do what I am doing now, moving Andrew and getting on with my life, I may just get away with it. So I lift him up by his shoulders again and drag-stop-drag, drag-stop-drag him through into his house.

She and I may still have a future together, starting over from this.

But somehow, I have my doubts.

I do not think this will have a happy ending. Not now.

———

I AM BACK at the cottage, having left him in the same swastika shape at the bottom of his stairs.

I will go back in the morning, in daylight, to loosen the carpet, double-check everything, and cover my tracks.

I suddenly realise how cold and wet I am. And covered in blood. Adrenaline, fear too, has kept me going on automatic this far.

I move through the hallway and into the living room. Stoke the fire back into life, watching the flames flicker and flash. I take off most of my clothes and put them on to burn. I stand there in just my boxer shorts, as close to the fire as I can get for warmth, thinking things over.

I then reach for a blanket and wrap it across my shoulders. I sit in front of the fire, facing forward, on my knees as I use the fireside poker to push the pyjamas back and forth in the flames. The trousers are soaked in blood, across the thighs and knees, and I can smell the bloodied cloth burning. Like a barbecue. It might be my imagination. I have always been a sensitive man, oversensitive, even.

I wait for Rosie to come to me. To see me sitting there. To maybe join me. Console me in some way. At least to talk through what has happened. What we have agreed. What we have done. Together. But there is no sign of her; I believe she has gone back to bed. I am not sure if that angers or disappoints me. Both, I think. And Fluffy will not have moved, lying there on top of my bed, maybe even burrowing under the duvet to keep warm. I am on my own.

I have much to do in the morning. I run through everything in my mind. To make sure I remember every little thing.

The trail of blood from the cottage to the house. The pool of congealed blood on the back doorstep of the house. A trail of more blood as I dragged him through.

I think I need to do something to the carpets, the walls on the stairs, and at the floor. He would not have fallen cleanly from top to bottom. He would have hit his head on the wall on the way down. Maybe once or twice. There would be more blood at the bottom. I do not know what to do about that.

The pyjamas blacken and smoke. They eventually turn to

charred remains, and then, as I press them repeatedly with the poker, to black and grey dust as the fire cools and finally goes out. I do not know how long I have been sitting here, thinking and prodding and poking and destroying the evidence. It feels like hours.

I get to my feet and move to the hallway where I last saw Rosie. I wonder for a moment whether she may have already left. A sense of panic as I consider she may have phoned the police, shouting down the phone, *There's been a murder. 3 Bluebell Lane, Felixstowe, hurry!* Then packing everything useful she could find into a carrier bag from under the sink and fleeing into the night, never to be seen again.

Leaving me to it. Abandoning me to my fate.

To my trial. And prison.

I would rather take my own life.

I move quickly to the nookery door, which is shut but not locked. I go in, moving through, flicking lights on and off. It is so cold. She is not here. Nor in the kitchenette or bathroom. Back and to the stairs and up to my daughter's bedroom door. Shut. I put my ear to it and listen. I cannot hear anything. I turn on the light on the landing, my feet in the same place where I killed Andrew Lumb. I turn the door handle and go in, standing in the doorway.

"What do you want?" she says in a neutral voice, lying there underneath the duvet, just her head showing. It is turned away from me, so I cannot see her face in the half-light.

"I've moved him. Andrew. Like you said to do."

She turns her head slowly. Her face now part-visible as she looks up at the ceiling. I see her arms move under the duvet.

"What are you going to do?" she asks. I sense her tensing, awaiting my reply.

"I'm going to have a bath, wash myself down. I have a bath brush. I'm going to scrub myself clean."

She seems to breathe out, and her hands drop back down to her side. I believe she has something under the duvet next to her. I wonder what it might be.

"I've cleaned the landing and the stairs and the hallway. I used bleach," she says. "From under the kitchen sink."

I nod, although she is not looking at me. "Thank you."

"Do you want me to leave?" She hesitates a second or two. "In the morning?"

A moment's silence. I want things back the way they were. I am not sure they can be. But I don't want her to leave. I would be forever looking over my shoulder. Thing is, she cannot go. Not now. But I cannot tell her that.

"No," I reply. "I want you to stay."

Another silence. And I think that somehow our relationship is changing. That we are both re-evaluating, working things out, weighing and balancing.

"Good night," she says simply, turning to look at me with that blank face of hers. No smile. Nor pained face. I can only guess at what she is thinking.

"Good night." My echoed response. I turn and pull the door to behind me. To go for a bath before bed and another restless sleep.

Andrew Lumb's death has changed everything between us. I sense it. And I wonder what that means for us.

15

FRIDAY, 29 NOVEMBER, 7.35 AM

We are having breakfast. Usual time. Usual place. The usual mix of cereals and drinks.

Her. Fluffy. And me.

But there is nothing else usual about it. After the sudden death of Andrew Lumb. We are both polite and mannered, but the whole thing just feels false. And forced.

The radio is turned up a little louder as we work our way through the meal. I reach out to turn it down a touch, to say something, to have a gentle conversation, to somehow return us to some sense of normality. Otherwise, we will have sat down together for fifteen to twenty minutes and barely said a word. I don't know how long we could go on doing that. Without one of us cracking.

I turn to look out of the window to the lane. It is still a picture-postcard white on the path and across the gate and up and down the lane as far as I can see. We have not had fresh snow overnight, and although it is still bitterly cold, there is only a 50 per cent chance of further snow today according to the BBC. The snow on the ground will harden into ice before melting. But not yet. And, of course, there may be more of it on the way.

If I say something, it has to be something and nothing, inconsequential, of no importance. A comment about the weather and snow still being here. Andrew Lumb's death looms large. As if he is standing on the other side of the dining room door. Waiting to come in. And we are both too nervous to speak of him. If we do, I fear we will go round and round. Making sense of it in our minds. Rearranging it. Explaining it. Rewriting it. The reality is I killed him, and I did not have to. And nothing will bring him back. We just have to live with that. And the consequences. Whatever they may be.

"I need to go into town this morning," she says as she finishes her cereal and places the spoon next to her bowl. She sees me watching and seems to think twice, lifting it up and placing it in her bowl.

I nod. Not sure how to reply. I cannot refuse her. The alternative would be to say no. But I do not know what I should then do. What I would then have to do. If she persisted.

She thinks for a moment, then asks politely, "Do you have any money? Not much. A tenner." Then adds, as if a *quid pro quo,* "If there's anything you want, I can get it for you." She looks at me, a straight and steady gaze.

I clear my throat, reach for my cup of tea. Bring it across, sip at it. All the time thinking I don't want her to go, to leave this house. To be seen. To run away. To tell the police. If she stays here, I am safe. If she goes out and is picked up by the police, anything could happen. She could reveal everything.

I shake my head a little. Non-committal.

"I don't think so; I can't think of anything. I've got some bread in the fridge-freezer. And some soya milk in the cupboard. I think we're okay for a few days." I look out the window. "If you wait, I think it will have started to thaw by then. We can drive out of town. To one of the big supermarkets. You can choose what you want. We can stock up."

She fiddles with the spoon in the bowl, clinking it back and forth: *clink, clink, clink, clink, clink, clink, clink.* She does it seven or eight times. It is an irritating noise, but I do not show my annoyance.

"I need to go to a supermarket ... or a chemist today." She says this plainly, but with each word emphasised.

I know why. And I know she is telling the truth.

She only had a few tampons left the other day.

At least it means she is not pregnant.

"Okay," I reply, for I cannot deny her. "If you go up to my bedroom, my wallet is on the bedside table. You can take what you need from that. Take a bit more, just in case you see anything else we could do with. Maybe some fruit. Bananas."

I catch her smiling to herself, almost as if she has scored a point over me.

I had intended to go back to Andrew Lumb's house straight after breakfast. Sort it all out. Get it just so.

But that strange little smile unsettles me. Worries me. Makes me feel sick inside. And suspicious.

SHE IS HALFWAY up the lane, head down, hood up, walking slowly towards the town. Stomping step by careful step through the snow.

I fear she will turn round at any moment.

I am following her, keeping my distance, but if she even glances back, she will see me for certain. I don't know what she would do. Nor I.

Watching her getting ready to go up the town, the top of an old hoodie of my daughter's pulled up over her head, filled me with an increasing sense of dread. As I stood there in the hallway, seeing her off, acting as normally as possible, I could not help but think this might be the last time I would see her. I could now live with that – my mind somehow seeing things more clearly since Andrew Lumb's death – but not with what she might do to me. As revenge for killing him. Her lover. She could tell the police what I had done and quietly disappear. The train to Ipswich, and away forever. The thought of her telling the police sickens me.

My common sense suggests my emotions are getting the better of me. She cannot simply walk into the police station in the town, up by the petrol station, and announce there's been a murder. Despite her hair dye and make-up, they might recognise her if her details have been circulated around the country. If not, there would be questions and details taken, even if they believed her.

Scorn and ridicule would be more likely responses, however well disguised they might be in this world of rules and regulations and political correctness. They would want to know who she was anyway – and want proof, a driving licence or something – and she cannot reveal herself to them. So she would not go to the police face to face. I am sure of that.

She could put a note through the door of the police station, though. She has her drawing pad and pencils, but I am not certain how seriously the police would take a scrawled note in a childlike hand. She could telephone, but she does not have a mobile phone, and mine sits in a kitchen drawer, long since unused. And there are no public telephones up the town these days.

Even if she told the police somehow, where would she go? Off back into the cold and wet and dangerous nights, sleeping in shelters or behind bins, waiting to be discovered by thuggish young men spoiling for trouble? Some wanting and demanding sex? No, I think she has to come back. I am sure of it. And yet ... I am sick with worry.

And being foolish. I think she will just go up the town. Buy what she needs from the supermarket. And return. Simple as that.

But I am not completely sure. I am scared. I may be mistaken.

That is why I am following her at a distance. If she goes anywhere else, somewhere unexpected, I will be forewarned. I will have a chance to do something. Either to stop her, or to flee before the police arrive.

I have gone by the perfect family's house, set back a little way from the lane. And I wonder what is happening inside. His car is there. Parked up from when he came back. The wife's car with its booster cushion and baby seat in the back has gone. He is alone there. Better than them all there, him screaming at her in this wintery lockdown and the children cowering in the corner of their bedroom.

I imagine the Man in the Suit inside the house, now alone, stewing things over. He is a dangerous man, full of anger and suppressed violence. He scares me. I do not want to see him or engage with him in any way. He is a fight waiting to happen, maybe something worse.

I am walking by Widow Woman's bungalow. I glance across, but there are no signs of anyone there. I think the grandchildren are staying, so they will be keeping her occupied. Running about and hiding. Leaping out from behind curtains to make her jump and scream. The windows are shut and the curtains all drawn. Her silly little car is parked outside by the front window, so I know she is inside.

As I move by the bungalow, I notice that a curtain at one of the bedroom windows twitches back a little. Someone is watching me, seeing what I am doing. I ignore it and stride through the snow a little quicker. If it is Widow Woman, she will be at her door in a minute, calling after me, inviting me in for a cup of tea. I hear noise, perhaps the unlocking of the door, as I move on. But the wind is chill in my face and in my ears, and I stride beyond hearing and out of sight as the lane curves slightly to the left.

Rosie is now out of view. Some way ahead. Younger and stronger than me, when all is said and done. It is a struggle to keep up.

I do not worry. There is really only one way she can go to town. And I need to keep my distance.

The air is cold and still; even the slightest noise is magnified many times. Each crunch of a boot in the snow seems to echo.

Three, four, five minutes on, and the lane curves back. I see her again in the distance as she heads up towards the main road that will take her into town. Hunched over, walking slowly but steadily, and, I think, always that little bit faster than me. I increase my stride again. These are surreal days, with the white sky and the snow on the ground giving everything an unworldly feel. There is no one about. All the houses to either side are shut down and closed off, with curtains pulled and no signs of life. I see nobody else in the lane. Just her and me.

I do not know how I feel about her now. To begin with, because she looked something like my daughter, I was drawn to her. As I have been with other girls. But I felt this one was different. That she was one whom I could grow to love and to look after. I admit it. I am, at least was, in love with her. Or wanted to be, anyway. In some kind of way.

She is not what she seemed. I think I expected her, or wanted her, to be sweet and innocent and loving. With all that has happened to her, the death of a child, the years being locked away, now hiding from the authorities on the streets, having sex with the man-boy from next door, she cannot be.

The truth is – and I see it clearly now – we cannot be what I had hoped we would be. And the thing is, I do not know what we can now be.

I go over it all in my mind time and again. The reality is that the death of Andrew Lumb has changed everything. If I had called the police immediately, I might have had a lesser sentence, but I am sure I would still have gone to prison. Now, that, and a longer sentence – one I could not cope with – would be a certainty. I cannot let her go. The thought of what that actually means in practice is starting to grow inside me. I do not wish to think about it.

In a way, I hope that she runs away and disappears, that she forgets me and what I have done. I would have to be ready to run if I ever I saw a police car coming down the lane, but I might, over time, begin to relax and realise she had not told the police. That would be the best.

But I think she will stay, for she has nowhere to go. And, if or when she is caught, she will go back inside for breaking the terms of her release. And she might then, to barter for a deal, tell them all about me. So she will stay here, in an uneasy truce, as she will eventually realise that no one knows where she is, and that if she were to go the same way as Andrew Lumb, no one would ever miss her.

I look up from striding through the snow.

She is at the junction with the main road, where she is about to turn left towards town. She then stops, turns slightly, and seems to be looking back at me.

She suddenly turns right and disappears from sight.

———————

I AM IN MY BEDROOM, an old leather holdall on the bed.

Back and forth, I am filling it as quickly as I can with whatever I need to go on the run.

In case she has told the police and a patrol car is already on its way.

When she disappeared from sight at the top of the lane, I panicked and tried to run after her, to catch up, to stop her going wherever she was going. Not up the town, that was for sure. The opposite way. By the garden centre. On a bus, if they are running in this weather. My money, however much she took, getting her at least as far as Ipswich. To the police station there. Or the railway station. I couldn't take that fifty-fifty chance.

But I stumbled on an icy patch, fell backwards, my feet going from beneath me, my head hitting the ground. I lay there, dazed and embarrassed, for a minute or two, then struggled up and carried on my way, my head and back hurting. By the time I got to the top of the lane, at the junction with the main road, she was nowhere to be seen. I dry heaved by the side of the road.

Growing ever more fearful, I hurried home as quickly as I could, taking longer and faster strides through the snow and ice. By Widow Woman's silent bungalow and the Man in the Suit's grand-designed house. To my home – my chocolate-box cottage – which I am going to have to leave forever.

Fluffy was in his basket by the fireplace.

He lifted his head up and turned to look at me as I came into the hallway. Then dipped his head back down into his sleepy state. Nothing to worry about in Fluffy's little world.

I do not know what to do about Fluffy. I cannot take him. Nor bear to leave him to his fate.

I have packed clothes: rolled-up tee shirts, two changes of trousers, pants and socks, and a sturdy pair of shoes for walking through snow. A shaver, with different attachments, so I can shave my head if I have to. A form of disguise. Hair dye, a packet from one of my wife's chests of drawers. A radio, to keep up to date with the local news on Felixstowe Radio and Radio Suffolk

£65 left in cash, in notes, that I had around the cottage in various wallets and drawers. I think she took £20, or maybe £40. A debit card so I can withdraw more cash. £250, £500, I guess. Maybe once this afternoon, if I can find a cash machine, and again after midnight, another day, one last £250 or £500 withdrawal. Perhaps £1,000, to see me on to the streets before the police start contacting banks, shutting down the supply.

I am looking at the paperback books in the bottom half of my bedside cabinet. Choosing one or two old favourites to read during quiet moments. An Alistair MacLean perhaps. Then it hits me. The stupidity of it all. The idea that I am going to run away with my radio and a paperback book or two to read when I am wherever I am going to be. Sheltering beneath a tree by the river. Rendlesham Forest, if I could somehow get that far. Underneath Southwold Pier. Some sort of fantasy: a Robinson Crusoe life. Some childish adventure. It cannot happen. Especially with snow and sub-zero temperatures.

There is nowhere for me to go. I would walk off as the police car arrived. Striding as fast as I could across the fields .

I doubt I would get more than half a mile with young policemen pursuing me on foot. Even if, by some good fortune, I got away, all this snow and ice and the overnight drop in temperature would mean I would not survive out there.

Even with some sort of shelter until the weather improved – a barn, a bus shelter – I could not live on the streets for long, just hiding until I ran out of cash, became ill, was forced to give myself up. Back to a longer sentence.

Then there is Fluffy, who is limping his way up the stairs towards me. *Clump. Clump. Clump.* I hear his careful step and the snuffly breath of his exertions. He is old now and struggles with the stairs. I forget sometimes that he is thirteen years old. An elderly man, in human terms. He gets to the doorway and hesitates before sitting down as if asking to be taken for a walk.

It is Fluffy that seals my fate. I cannot take him with me, nor leave him behind. And so I must stay here and wait to see what happens. I cross to the doorway and pick him up carefully in my arms. He has some sort of tender spot – a lump, maybe a growth – to the side of his stomach, and he whimpers a little if I pick him up and cradle his stomach with my hand. I have been meaning to take him to the vet for a while, to see what it is. But I have been scared to visit with Fluffy, as he is too old for an operation, so I nurse him along as best I can for as long as I can.

We sit together, two old men, two old *pals* – at the edge of my bed, looking out over the lane and the snow and the frost and the ice and this magical world that I will soon be saying farewell to. I put my arm around him as he stares into space with thoughts of chasing rabbits, and I feel suddenly full of sorrow that this life, what I thought was a sad and lonely one, is about to end. Me to prison. Him to the local Blue Cross, where everyone who sees him will love him to bits, but then sigh and say, *Sorry, thirteen is just too old.*

I put my head down and cry. It all comes out of me. I cannot stop myself. On and on I go.

Sobbing now. For this moment and for everything else. My wife. My daughter. What I have become. What I have done. And for her. And Andrew Lumb and everything else. It has all been such a mess of my own making.

I sit up as I hear the fateful click of the garden gate.

SHE STANDS there in the hallway, looking at me as I come down the stairs.

She is holding something up towards me in her hands. I cannot see what it is. A dark mass of some kind.

She half-smiles. I cannot read a meaning into it.

I get to the bottom of the stairs, Fluffy sitting and watching from the landing. And I see what she is holding. A little black pot with soil filling it to the top. I am bewildered. I do not know what it is. Nor do I understand why she is showing it to me.

"Did you go up the town?" I ask neutrally, knowing that she did not, could not have done. That she is back far too soon. So soon that I thought the gate clicking open was a sign that the police had arrived by car to arrest me.

"No," she answers simply, then adds, "I can manage for a day or two. Until we can go to the big supermarket." She pauses and goes on: "I went to the garden centre and bought this for Andy. We could place it here for him and plant it in the garden in the spring."

With that, she bends over and puts the little pot at the bottom of the stairs, in or very close to the spot where Andrew Lumb landed and his skull cracked open.

I stand there, not sure what to think, let alone say to her.

This little pot of soil, this tiny shrine, tucked in at the bottom of the staircase.

She turns and walks towards the kitchen. I follow her, wondering if we are now going to carry on just as we were. As if nothing has happened. As if the death of Andrew Lumb means nothing. I am not sure we can do that. I would like to try.

She goes to the fridge, opens it and rummages in the freezer section. She takes out two ice lollies. An orange one and a lemon one. I am puzzled by her behaviour. She offers them both to me; I choose the orange one. She then leads the way to the kitchen table, and we sit down opposite each other.

I am nonplussed by this sudden return to normality. I do not know what to say. She is licking and sucking the top of her ice lolly, head down, not looking at me. I am distracted, watching her, by my thoughts. I focus on eating my ice lolly, assuming that, as we finish, we will have a conversation that will somehow clear the air. I don't know how that can be.

She finishes eating her lolly first, laying the stick out in front of her on the table.

She waits for me. Head down in thought. She says nothing.

As I finish my lolly, she takes the stick I lay next to hers on the table.

She is then up and at the drawer by the kitchen sink. Takes out a ball of string. Scissors from the bottom of the block of knives on the side. A felt-tipped pen from the tub of pens and pencils on the window ledge. Back at the table.

She fashions, from the lolly sticks and string, a small, slightly lopsided cross. Snips the ends of the string to tidy it up. Takes the felt-tipped pen and, her tongue sticking out in concentration, draws an *a* on one side of the cross and an *l* on the other.

I follow her out of the kitchen and back into the hallway. She bends and puts the cross into the back of the soil in the pot and pushes it down carefully. Straightens it. She stands there, with me a step or two behind her, with her head bowed as if she is saying a few words of prayer.

Then she is done. The moment has passed. She asks if she can make lunch. On her own. As if everything is just as it was.

I agree, but say I have to sort next door first. As though I am doing no more than emptying rubbish into the big grey bin and dragging it out onto the driveway.

I will meet her back in the kitchen in an hour, to start her off. She goes to fetch a change of clothes and heads to the bathroom.

I STAND on the landing and push open my daughter's bedroom door. Where it all started with Andrew Lumb. In her bed. I strip the bed of its pillowcases, sheet and duvet cover.

Go downstairs and push them into the washing machine. I turn it on to the hottest setting. To wash away the evidence of Andrew Lumb.

After I have put fresh bedding back on the bed and settled Fluffy in his basket, I start my careful checks from my cottage to his house.

I look at every part of my daughter's bedroom in turn. There is nothing obvious to see. But I don't doubt that if police forensics were here, they would discover Andrew Lumb's DNA and more. No matter how well she has bleached the surfaces and hoovered the floor, there will be something somewhere. I have to hope the police never get this far.

I move to the landing, walk down and stand at the bottom of the cottage stairs, looking up, scanning to see any signs of Andrew Lumb's fall. There is nothing so far as I can see. No dent in the wall or bloodstains on the stone floor. There may be invisible-to-the-eye evidence, a telltale sign under a microscope. There is nothing more I can do than to go over it all every day with bleach as thoroughly as I can, just in case.

Then slowly, step by step, I go through into the kitchen and to the back door, looking for signs of his blood or anything else anywhere. Again, I see nothing at all. Police forensics might well turn something up though. There may be a hair or a flake of dandruff or an invisible pinprick of his blood. She has cleaned thoroughly from the bedroom to the back door, but something will have slipped through.

If the police come this far, I am done for.

No point pretending, nor fooling myself. They will uncover something. A microbe.

I have to make sure they have no reason to ever look here.

I go out onto my patio and look towards the gate. The snow is inches deep in places, flattened in others. I can see the trail of his dragged body and a haphazard mess of my footsteps. There is a dark thread of something – blood – in the flattest part of the snow where I dragged the body.

I fetch a shovel from the garage and scoop up the worst of it, dropping the first shovelful of snow into the drain that's below the kitchen window. It sits there with its zigzag of blood close to the surface. I turn the tap on, but it is stiff; I cannot turn it far enough for water to splutter out and wash the bloody snow away.

So I am in and out of the kitchen, heating up kettles and pouring the boiling water onto shovelful after shovelful of snow, until all the blood has disappeared down the drain. I then kick and spread and level out the remaining snow so that it looks as even as I can make it across the patio.

Killing someone is not an easy thing to do, nor live with.

I am haunted by what I have done.

And, on a practical level, I have left a trail of evidence waiting to be uncovered.

I go into the alleyway between the two properties and walk to Andrew Lumb's gate. As I glance back, I see the imprints of the soles of my boots, here, there and all over, to and from my own gate. Overwhelming evidence that I have been in and out. And, again, more trails of blood. Spatters, really.

I had hoped, against all forecasts, that there would have been fresh snow overnight, and that this would have covered any evidence between the two properties. There are reports of possible further snowfall tonight, but these are likely to be patchy showers rather than snow falling everywhere. And not this far east.

I go back and forth again, taking a shovelful of bloody snow across to the kitchen drain and pouring boiling water onto it from a kettle. I do this three, four, five times. Absorbed in what I am doing. Being careful. When I am done, I fetch a broom from my garden shed and sweep the remaining snow and ice across and around, to make it look as natural as possible.

I stop, satisfied. It does not look too bad. And if we have snowfall soon, it will leave everything just perfect.

I look back over what I have done in the alleyway. Down towards the fields. Up to the lane.

And I see a boy, Widow Woman's grandson, standing there watching me. He has her dog on a lead.

LOOKING up and at the boy seems to encourage him. That I am friendly and wish to talk. I am not, and I do not want to.

He tugs the dog's lead, and they walk down the alleyway towards me. This boy who does not seem to know he should not talk to strangers.

I stand up straight and tall and look at him, not sure whether to smile or not. I do not feel like smiling. I am worried about what he has seen. How long he has been standing there.

"Good morning," he says politely, this precocious little child.

"Hello," I answer, nodding at him. The fat Labrador waits patiently.

"What were you doing?" he asks, a touch of curiosity in his high-pitched voice.

I look at the boy, his innocent face, a touch of blond hair sticking out from underneath his woolly hat. Wrapped up nice and warm in his matching clothes. This loved and cared-for child.

If I am short with him, he will go home and tell his grandmother, and it might become an issue. So I will be polite, and he will go away. He will leave me alone and not think anything more of what he has seen.

"I was ... getting rid of some ... dog ... my dog ..." I gesture towards the path.

"My granny gives me bags." The boy takes a handful of black bags from his pockets and shows them to me. As if I would never have heard of such things.

There is a moment's pause. Not an awkward one.

Just that neither of us know what to say.

I hope he will be on his way. Children are not meant to talk to strangers these days.

"He's my granny's dog," the boy says. "Barry." He laughs, a little embarrassed. It is a happy sound. "My grandad was Barry," he adds, to explain it for me.

"I'm Conor," he says. "With one *n,* not two."

I hesitate, about to say *I'm Mr Adams*, but the world is less formal these days, so I say, "I'm Philip." I don't think he is going to go away as quickly as I had hoped.

He puts out his elbow, this well-taught child. Still mindful of COVID-19.

I smile and put out my elbow, too.

We do a clumsy elbow bump.

"You know my granny," he says. "She lives –"

"Yes, I know her," I interrupt. "She's nice, your granny." I'm not sure what else to say.

"She lets me walk Barry on my own if I walk down here ...

through the alley. I then go round the fields and come back in a circle." He draws the route in the air with his finger.

I smile and nod, wanting him to be on his way, but without wanting to be rude to him. He seems a nice and polite boy.

"My granny says to say hello to you if I see you. I saw you yesterday with a girl and your dog. I don't think you saw me. I was playing hide-and-seek with my sister." He hesitates, then adds quietly, "We were allowed out for some fresh air. We are not supposed to come down this end. Because of Andrew."

His voice tails off, as if he realises he shouldn't have spoken of Andrew Lumb. He pulls the lead, and the dog gets to its feet.

The revelation that he has seen Rosie with me is a shock. I wonder what that might mean for me. And what else he might have seen without me noticing him.

And the reference to "Andrew" alarms me. I had assumed Andrew Lumb was alone and unnoticed by the world around him.

"Andrew ...?" I ask.

The boy glances around, as if his granny might be standing just behind him.

"My granny says not to talk to him," the boy answers. "He comes out and says hello when he sees me."

The boy now seems a little nervous.

"What does he talk to you about?" I ask conversationally.

"Football. We both support Ipswich."

I nod and smile. Letting him talk on.

"He said he has a signed football shirt he's going to show me when he next sees me. From 1978. When they won the FA Cup. It's on his wall. Signed by Kevin Beattie. I'm not supposed to go in. But I'd like to see it."

He looks pensive and unsure.

This sudden sharing of information with me, almost in confidence, as if I were his grandfather. His grandpa.

"I think he's away at the moment," I reply. "Andrew. He's gone to visit his grandparents ... in Colchester." I nod. Yes, that's the best thing to say.

The boy looks confused. I can't help but think he was expecting to see the football shirt today.

He ponders that for a moment. Then he says goodbye, and he and the fat Labrador are on their way.

I hope that's the last I see of him. But something about the encounter unsettles me and makes me feel uneasy. That I have somehow made a mistake.

I am not sure what that mistake is.

16

FRIDAY, 29 NOVEMBER, 1.01 PM

I decide to do Andrew Lumb's house and patio later. After lunch. I am preoccupied with thoughts of the boy. And I do not want to leave Rosie alone in the cottage for longer than I have to.

I had assumed she wanted to make sandwiches. Or something equally simple. That these might be ready on the table with glasses of squash on my return.

But no. She wants to have a go at bolognese again. On her own this time. And she has been waiting for me to return.

We go through the whole rigmarole. Turning on the computer. Reaching for my notebook. She taps each letter and number of the password into the computer. Oh so slowly. She then clicks Google on the home screen, and I tell her to put *Bolognese* ... *B-o-l-o-g-n-e-s-e* ... space ... *recipe* ... *r-e-c-i-p-e* into the search. She stumbles over some of the letters – stopping, bewildered, when I say *space* – and by the time we have found a recipe with pictures, I have just about had enough.

I then have to point to each ingredient in turn and say what it is. Some are obvious. Others less so. Most of the ingredients I have, but not all of them. I tell her where they are and why the ones I don't have are not that important. She looks uncertain. She then asks if I can print off the recipe. I don't know why, since she cannot read properly. But I agree to it. My colour ink cartridge is low, and the print-off is rather faint. She looks at it for a moment without speaking as if she is thinking, *This isn't very good.* It is all I can do to stay calm and polite.

I go to the fridge and the larder, and in and out of various cupboards, back and forth, putting the ingredients in a pile on the table. All I want to do is to go and leave her to it, but I know I will need to explain what needs to be done, and in what order, and that I shall scream inside with frustration at every stage. As if any of this nonsense matters when Andrew Lumb lies dead next door and may be discovered at any moment. If the boy knocks to see the football shirt sometime soon and peers through the glass of the front door. My nerves are all on edge.

I explain to her what to do. She then shoos me away. Wants to be left alone to do it.

A sense of something close to delight. Excitement, at least.

As though we have moved on from what happened. She has. I haven't. I don't think I ever will. Killing someone is not something you forget.

I sit by the fireplace in the living room. Fluffy comes across, and I help him up onto the sofa. He lies beside me, the length of his body against my right thigh. For warmth, not affection. I am not naïve when it comes to dogs. But I love him nonetheless. I suspect it is one-sided, really. I stroke his soft right ear. I read somewhere once that dogs find that soothing. It soothes me a little. I can barely sit still.

It has occurred to me that, when I go back to the house and loosen the carpet and rearrange the body, I must be very careful. When he fell down the cottage stairs, he hit his head hard on the right wall and then landed on his forehead on the stone floor in the hallway. Two blows. Two marks. One on the right wall. One on the stone floor. There is blood on the floor of the Lumb house, but not on the wall.

Another thing: My staircase has walls both sides. The Lumbs' has a wall one side and a wooden handrail and balusters to the other. The wall is to the left. The handrail and balusters to the right. Andrew Lumb hit the side of his head to the right, and I wonder whether, had he fallen in his own house, he might have just broken balusters and survived.

The Lumbs' hallway, at the bottom of the stairs, is carpeted. It is, I think, quite thick, and again, that sets me thinking. If he had landed on his forehead on thick carpet rather than stone, he might have lived. And if he were bleeding, as he was at the bottom of my cottage stairs, would that blood not, in the Lumbs' house, have soaked through the carpet into the underlay beneath? Maybe I think too much. But a sharp-eyed, keen young policeman will notice all of these things, for sure.

She calls out. Says I forgot the carrots.

I'm sure I didn't.

I go into the kitchen to speak to her.

I hate the smell of burning meat. Rosie stands there, at the oven, pushing the mince backwards and forwards. Turning it over. Pushing it back again. She looks up at me. "I've got everything," she says, "but carrots. You forgot the carrots." I check the table. They are not there. I go into the larder. There is half a bagful on a shelf. I thought there were more. I suspect I did get some, but then put them down somewhere. No doubt I will discover them later.

I take a few out and put them on the kitchen table. "Here they are," I tell her and then ask, "Do you want me to chop them up?" She shakes her head and turns away, still cooking the mince. I hope she does it properly. I want to talk to her about Andrew Lumb and what I have been thinking. But she is so engrossed in what she is doing, so focused, that I leave her be.

My mind goes over everything. I do not know if the trail of blood and hair and flakes of skin from him and me from my cottage and across his patio and through the kitchen to the staircase can be completely removed or whether, on careful scrutiny, traces – traces of evidence – will remain.

I do not think it matters. I do not know whether the carpet could be loosened without seeming odd. Anyway, I think, given the straightness of his staircase compared to my twisty one, he would have fallen straight down. And survived the fall onto soft carpet. Obvious to anyone, really.

I slump back down next to Fluffy, who jumps, sits up and looks towards me.

I am in torment.

Everything I did is lying there next door. Clue after clue after clue, all of them pointing to me.

I USUALLY CUT up a plateful of spaghetti and eat a forkful of small pieces under some bolognese, one careful mouthful at a time.

But she rolls the spaghetti round and round her fork and tips her head back theatrically. Some of it goes in. Much of it doesn't.

I join in reluctantly. Inside, I am torturing myself. She has put it all behind her. I am not sure how I feel about that. I don't understand how she can do it.

"I've been thinking," I say as I reach across the table to unwrap a kitchen roll. I tear off the cellophane and take a sheet from the roll to dab at my chin.

She points her knife towards the wrapper, taps on the letters of the name, wanting me to read it out to her.

"Regina Blitz," I say. "Re ... gi ... na. Blitz. B ... litz. L-I-T-Z."

"Vagina tits," she replies, laughing.

I smile. But it is more of a rictus grin, really. I am so worried. And I don't think she's cooked this meat properly. It tastes funny.

"I've been thinking about Andrew Lumb," I say and look at her suddenly serious face. She does not want to talk about it, I can tell.

She puts her head down and focuses on her plate, mixing the bolognese and spaghetti together and continuing to eat. It's as if she is ignoring me.

So much to say, so many points, so many mistakes that I want to talk through with her. For her to consider. And reassure me. But I don't think she wants to know.

"I don't think he would have died from a fall downstairs next door. The staircase is mostly wood, and there's carpet at the bottom."

She sits for a moment as she sucks up a single strand of spaghetti through pursed lips. The last bit whips into her mouth, and she laughs. Then shrugs in a *so what?* kind of way.

I sit back, silent for a moment.

I am frightened, if I am honest. And angry, maybe more frustrated, with her.

For her, everything is as it was. For me, everything has changed.

"No one will find him for ages," she replies finally, through a mouthful of food. As if that explains everything. Then adds, "Not until spring. Or the summer ... if it's really hot." She laughs. It sounds raucous.

I take in the comment, the implication that the heat of

summer and a decomposing corpse will create an unmistakable stench when someone knocks on the door. The postman, whoever. I note the callous laugh. I find it disturbing.

"He's dead at the bottom of the stairs. They will just think he fell. That's all." Her simple summary.

She glances at me and looks away. And I notice, at least realise, for the first time, that she never looks directly at me for more than a second or two. Her eyes are forever here, there and everywhere. They never really linger. I wonder if she might be autistic.

I nod, as if I agree with what she is saying. And take a mouthful of food. She may be correct. If a postman sees the body through the glass of the front door any time soon. Breaks in, tramples over everything, moves the body to see if Andrew Lumb is still alive. Calls 999, and the ambulance men trample some more.

Then a doctor. And an undertaker. A whole queue of so-called professionals, who won't give a second thought about what they see. What is in front of them is a dead body. A loose carpet on the landing. A long staircase. That's it. But the police would know. A half-decent detective would see things as they really are.

I nod again. I have a thought, but I do not share it with her. It's something I don't want her to know. This little chick who's turning into a cuckoo in the nest.

Instead, I just say I'll go back this afternoon and sort out the patio and the kitchen and the staircase. And Andrew Lumb. As she says. As we have agreed.

And I think my thought. And what I will do. And what it might mean moving forward.

I CHECK the alleyway between the cottage and the house is all clear. That the boy is not around. Nor anyone else. Who might see me. And remember. Wait two, three, four minutes to be sure.

I take my spade and bucket and bleach and cloths and other cleaning equipment across with me. Hurry. Look back. Nobody to be seen out there in the snow.

See more trails and spatters of blood across the snow covering his patio. I shovel it up. Use my bucket. Back and forth to the tap by the kitchen window of the cottage. Then level the snow on his patio.

And into his kitchen, where there is more blood. So much of it. I would not have thought it was possible. It looks as though someone has tipped a stream of gravy from a saucepan from the back door, right across the linoleum, and out onto the hallway carpet. I scrub it away with bleach on a cloth and use water from the taps at the sink, again and again, to wash the whole floor. It is filthy, each long swipe of my arm blackening the cloth in my hand.

I dab, with a fresh cloth and squirts of washing-up liquid from a bottle by the sink, the carpet from the kitchen to the hallway and the bottom of the stairs. I cannot look at Andrew Lumb. His face. His body. His long and awkward arms and legs. I hold my breath as I rub time and again at the blood-stains on the carpet. I rinse the cloth and wring it out at the sink and flush everything away with the hot tap turned on fully. I do this five, six, seven times until the blood seems to have gone. But the places I have rubbed seem cleaner than the carpet around them.

I stand, finally, at the bottom of the stairs, my hands wet and soaked with water and bleach. I think, once everything has dried, it will pass a cursory glance, but not an examination. It does not matter. I look up the stairs and at the carpet and the wall and the balustrade and the body at the bottom.

And I know in my heart that this death simply does not look right. It will not stand up to close scrutiny. I stand there, thinking. What I have to do.

And I suddenly hear the sounds of footsteps outside, trudging up the snow-covered, gravel driveway to the house.

I freeze. Dare not turn round. The movement of my body will be seen through the frosted glass of the front door.

I wait. Not sure what to expect. There is a clattering through the letterbox. Something falls through. There is a loud and cheery "Thank you."

I wait. Do not move. A moment's silence. Then another. And one more. I am tense. Holding my breath. The thought, the expectation, that I am meant to shout back *Thank you!* That they, whoever they are, are standing and waiting for my reply. Andrew Lumb's reply. "Thanks," I croak, the word sticking in my throat.

I hear the footsteps again, trudging back across the driveway. I stand there, drenched in sweat, waiting for the sound of footsteps to disappear, off the driveway and back onto the path of Bluebell Lane and away. I turn and see the letters on the doormat. The postman. He must have seen me. My back, anyway. A shape through the frosted glass. That's why he called out.

That decides it for me. As I cross to pick up the letters from the doormat. Something from the NHS. A circular from a local wine merchant. I pocket them to put on the fire in my living room at the cottage. I have to move Andrew Lumb's body. Putting it here was a mistake. Someone, sometime soon, maybe the postman tomorrow, will look through and see the body. Things will then start to unravel fast.

I will come back tonight and move him. Clean the bottom of the stairs. Drag him out and through and down to the cellar in the cottage.

When she is asleep and will not know. For some reason, I want this to be a secret. I do not know why.

And I will move him and bury him deep in the heart of Rendlesham Forest once the snow has cleared. Somewhere he will never be found.

I AM BACK at the cottage, have packed my spade and bucket and cleaning equipment away, and washed my face and hands. And have knocked on my daughter's bedroom door.

She wants to play games this afternoon rather than reading and writing. "Boring!" she says emphatically. She seems full of childish silliness.

I follow her down to the dining room, where she rummages through the pile of board games in the dining room cupboard. Fluffy is by my feet, hoping for a titbit to eat.

She chooses Ker-Plunk. A game I have not played for many years. I remember playing it with Lucy on Sunday afternoons when she was small. Taking it in turns to pull out the plastic rods that held all the marbles at the top of the tube. Lucy's squeals of delight when she took out a rod and no marbles fell through the mass of rods that remained. Louder squeals when I pulled out a rod and one or two marbles trickled through into my tray below.

I remember the excitement on her little face when I "accidentally" tugged at a rod that held most of the remaining marbles in place, and they all tumbled into my tray. She would lift her hands up in triumph. Most often, we did not need to count the number of marbles we each had at the end of the game. I would have most or all of them. When we did have similar numbers, I would count so that she would win. On the odd occasion she obviously lost, she would want to have another game immediately until she won. And we could pack the game away until next time.

My wife would never join in. She did not like "loud games", as she called them, and would retreat to another room to read a magazine. In fact, thinking about it, I do not recall my wife ever playing games, loud or quiet, with Lucy and me. Of course, these Sunday afternoons of games were early on, when she was oh so small, before the drink had me in its grip. I do not remember when nor how we stopped playing. Nor whether my wife took over from me or if Lucy never played board games at home ever again.

I put my hand on the lid that she takes off the box. Staring into space.

Thoughts of Lucy and how her little hands would have been on this once.

But she is already putting everything together. I rally from my thoughts.

"You have to push all these rods through these holes in the middle of the tube," I say. "And pour those marbles through that hole in the top, so they sit on the rods."

"Duh," she says under her breath, but loud enough for me to hear. She stands the tube upright and pushes the rods through the hole in the middle.

"We take it in turns to pull out one rod each. Until all the marbles have fallen through. The winner is the one with the fewest marbles in their tray."

"I know," she says, and there is a flash of irritation in her voice. "I'm not stupid. I used to play it with my dad all the time."

There is a sudden sullenness in the way she speaks. I do not know why, but it angers me. More than I would have thought. The ungratefulness of it all.

"Your dad will be long dead. You do know that, don't you?" I say it suddenly, instinctively, really. My voice is hard and cutting. I know it. I am saying it in retaliation for the way she is speaking, and to hurt her. My quick temper again.

A moment's pause, and I wonder whether she is going to sweep the game from the table and storm off. In a way, I would like that. To see she has normal feelings and reactions.

Then she shrugs, says, "Maybe," and carries on putting the rods into the Ker-Plunk tube. Quite calmly. It is as if she does not want to talk about him nor recognise the reality of the situation.

She picks up a handful of marbles and tips them into the top of the tube, so that they settle on the criss-cross of rods. Then another. One more handful and all the marbles are in place; we are ready to play.

She is quiet now, subdued. I can feel the tension between us. She has come out of her shell since Andrew Lumb died, and I have had a sense of what she is really like. My statement about her father has knocked her back. I am on edge.

We play in silence. She takes a rod. No marbles fall. I take a rod. No marbles fall. She takes another. I do, too. The marbles stay in place. She is not playing properly, looking at each rod, checking it from different angles, to see if marbles will slip and fall if she pulls it out. Instead, she just pulls one at random in a couldn't-care-less kind of way. No marbles fall.

I pull out a rod at random, and three marbles roll into my tray.

"Ha, ha," she says mirthlessly. Then tugs at a rod that is clearly holding half a dozen marbles in place. They tumble into her tray. "Oh dear," she adds, but does not mean it.

I jerk a rod out at random. No marbles fall. I somehow wish they had.

"Loser," she says. I think it is meant to be jokey. But it does not sound like it. This time, she looks at the rods carefully. Puts her hand on a rod that seems to be holding most of the remaining rods in place.

"Don't be stu–" I start to say, but she has yanked at it, and all the marbles but one fall down with a clatter into her tray.

I lean forward and shake the tube so the last one falls out, too.

She stands up and walks off.

I sit there and am not sure how I feel. I reach out and stroke Fluffy. His eyes flicker towards me; then he sinks back into sleep, indifferent to it all.

SHE HAS SPENT the rest of the afternoon in my daughter's bedroom. Radio 1 blaring out louder than it should be. Various knocks and loud bangs now and then, possibly to gain my attention. I ignored them.

I pottered about, cleaning and tidying, but mostly thinking about Andrew Lumb.

What I am going to do. And when. And how. So that she does not see nor hear anything.

I walked Fluffy over the fields and back and round, a longer route than usual. Thinking things over. Playing devil's advocate. I looked at No. 1 as I passed by both ways, and all seemed just as it was.

When I got back, she was in the kitchen. Busying about. A sense of cheerfulness again. She swings back and forth.

Cooking a curry. Chicken from the fridge. A jar of curry sauce from the back of a cupboard. Simple as that.

She looked at me standing there watching her, and smiled. A placatory smile. I smiled back. I am not sure either smile was genuine.

Now we are sitting at the kitchen table, eating the curry. I wonder whether I should say something about what I said. Her dead father. To clarify and soften the way I said it, which was far too sharp. But her head is down, and she is eating as she always has, arm curled protectively around the plate and as quickly as she can. I think perhaps the moment has passed. She has moved on.

"I like your curry," I say. "You've put other things in it?"

More than just chicken and a jar of sauce, I think. I don't like the taste, to be honest. Almonds, possibly, which I have never liked. But I do not want to upset her again. This uneasy truce.

She looks at me and maintains eye contact and laughs. Almost to herself. "This and that," she replies.

She keeps glancing up at me between mouthfuls. She is about to say something. Ask me a question. I can tell. She wants something from me.

"Um," she says. Thinking of what to say. How to put it. Rehearsing it in her head. *Get on with it, for God's sake.*

"I'd like to go to college and do a cookery course." She gushes her words. Then laughs, flushes a little, but seems pleased that she has said it.

"Okay," I reply, nodding. Whatever. Not sure what else to say. My thoughts are elsewhere.

"Um," she says again, obviously wanting to say more about this cookery course.

I look at her. Distracted. On edge, too.

"Thing is," she says, "if I'm found, I'll go back inside. For ages. I've broken my parole."

I look at her. Not sure how to respond.

She goes on: "I was wondering ..." She looks up at me as if she does not want to complete the sentence, or maybe she expects me to finish it for her.

And I realise suddenly what she is going to say, to ask for. Lucy's driving licence and passport. A similar age. An appearance that's close enough to pass for Lucy at a glance. She could use my daughter's ID to do just about anything other than go through passport controls.

But the thought appals me. She's touched a raw nerve. A gaping wound, more like.

"No!" I laugh, more in shock than in humour. Disbelief, really.

"You don't know what I was going to ask."

I shrug. "If it's to borrow Lucy's driving licence or passport, then it's no. You'll get found out. You'll have the police at the door."

She does not say anything, so I go on. I can feel my anger rising.

"It's not like using it for ID to get into a pub or a club, where someone just glances at the photo and date of birth," I say. "And there would be forms to fill in at college. National insurance numbers and things. And it will be on record with all sorts of government bodies that ... Lucy died." I sound like I am ranting, but I cannot seem to stop myself. On I go.

"You can't just pretend to be her. It's ... madness." I laugh again, but I'm angry, really. "I mean, seriously ... People knew Lucy. She had friends here and in Ipswich. What would you do if you said to someone you were Lucy Anne Adams, and they used to be her best fr ... that's so stupid."

I sit back. Knowing my last comment was again too strong. Too loud. I have always overreacted when I am angry.

We finish our meal in an increasingly strained silence. I would really like to leave half of the curry and walk away. But I don't. It would make things worse.

We wash and dry in silence, and she is gone again. And I know I will spend the evening alone.

I HAVE BEEN HERE all evening, sitting quietly on the sofa by the fire in the living room, reading my Agatha Christie novel, *And Then There Were None.* The judge has just been pronounced dead. There is snowfall again. Unexpectedly. Enough to cover everything with an inch, maybe more.

Fluffy is by my feet. He makes whimpering noises at odd intervals. As if dreaming bad thoughts. I push him awake with my right foot. She is upstairs in my daughter's bedroom, and I have not heard a sound from her for ages.

I am waiting for her to go to bed and to sleep. I will then get up and move Andrew Lumb's body back from the hallway of his house to the cellar of the cottage. Everything is being covered with fresh snow, removing traces of my movements there and back. His body will be safe downstairs until the snow has gone, and I can move it to the forest under the cover of darkness.

Even so, I am tense and troubled and deeply unhappy. This terrible shift in the relationship. Between her and me.

Since he died, the relationship has turned completely.

She and I cannot go on together. I know it. I think she does, too.

If she stays here, she has a hold on me. She knows the truth of Andrew Lumb's death. She will forever have that over me. Whatever she asks for – using my daughter's ID, money, anything else – I will, eventually, have to relent and give to her. If I do not, I risk everything – her walking away and revealing my secrets to the police.

I do not think she would walk away by choice. Back into hiding on the streets in the cold and the snow and the winter that lies ahead. The worst winter in living memory, someone predicted on Radio 4 a day or two ago. And she knows, at least believes, she is on a good thing here, perhaps for life. And I cannot ask her to leave. The risk of revelation is too great. I could not live like that every day, waiting for the knock on the door.

But the relationship has turned, soured, changed totally. I was her benefactor, her mentor, her inspiration. I would have guided her, loved her, given her a happy life. She was grateful at first for my kindness, and thankful for all that I was offering her. Eliza Doolittle. This is not how it is now. I feel, somehow, that she has the upper hand.

I hear movement above. Her footsteps in my daughter's bedroom. Back and forth.

I hear her coming downstairs. Onto the stone floor of the hallway. And into the living room behind me.

I turn and see her walking, with some of my daughter's clothes over her arm, towards the door to the nookery.

"You're moving back?" I ask, a stupid, instinctive question. I do not know what else to say. It will be cold, and she cannot use the bathroom. She knows that.

"Yes." She stops and answers, but does not look at me. Her eyes are all over the place. It makes her look shifty and untrustworthy.

"Why?" I ask as neutrally as I can, although I know the reason. She is doing it to upset me, that's why.

"It's ..." She hesitates, and I wonder what she will say next. *Further away from you. Apart from you.* "I'm just moving some things across."

I nod. I am not sure what else to say or do.

So I sit there without speaking as she comes back and forth, two, then three times. I am not sure how I feel. It's another opening skirmish in what will become a war of attrition.

"Good night," she says on her final walk through. I am formulating my reply, but she shuts the door behind her before I can speak.

And so, I think, our course is set. I had hoped that things might return to what they were after Andrew Lumb's death. But it changed me. And her. And what was between us. What might have been can no longer be.

There is only one thing it can be from now on. Hell.

Complete and utter hell. For as long as it lasts. She believes she has the upper hand. That the knowledge she has about Andrew Lumb gives her power and control over me.

What she does not seem to recognise, let alone understand, is how vulnerable she actually is. No one knows she came to Felixstowe. The authorities do not know she is in this town. Let alone this lane. This cottage. She believes I cannot go to the police because of Andrew Lumb. That she is safe. She is right about one belief, but not the other.

No one will know if she simply disappears. Is never seen again. Just vanishes off the face of the earth.

I think perhaps she should be told that. To know. That our relationship, such as it is, is not as one-sided as she thinks. That things are, shall we say, finely balanced. On a knife edge.

I get up, whistling for Fluffy. It's time to get ready and go to bed for an hour or two before I get up to move Andrew Lumb. All sorts of thoughts are swirling round my head. They are not pleasant ones.

I STAND BY THE GRAVE.

And watch the ground.

That shakes.

And moves.

And shudders.

I want to run.

To hide.

To leave it all behind.

But I have to stand.

And wait.

And see.

What will happen.

When the ground breaks open.

I SET the alarm on my bedside clock for 2.00 a.m. But, with my nightmares that come most nights to torment me, I am already awake.

Pushing the button down three minutes before the clock starts to *brrng-brrng, brrng-brrng* its noise through the cottage.

And I am dressed and downstairs, creeping by Fluffy asleep in his bed in the living room, to the nookery door, where I listen to the silence before heading to the kitchen door and away.

A dark night, as chill as ever. A silent night.

The snow lying crisp and white after a further light fall.

The world is asleep as I walk slowly, carefully, towards his house.

Every step seems to echo, to ricochet, between the buildings. The sound of my boots crunching into the snow and ice seems to be magnified so many times in the utter silence. The *click* and *clunk* of my gate. My footsteps in the alleyway. The *click* and *clunk* of his gate. My footsteps on the patio. And to the door of the kitchen. The deafening silence. My deafening noise.

I take out the pocket torch that I slipped into my coat from my bedside table drawer. Its beam shoots up into the sky. I lower it and watch it shake and shimmer in the darkness as I aim it towards the lock of the kitchen door. And, at last, I am inside the house. I can relax for a moment. Safe from being seen or heard outside.

I walk through the kitchen, illuminated by my torch, and into the hallway, where Andrew Lumb's body lies in its twisted shape at the bottom of the stairs. I do not hesitate. For I fear, if I did, I would not be able to do this. I turn off the torch and slip it back into my pocket. Then turn him over. Struggling this way with him. Then that. Until I have him by the shoulders and drag him, stop-start, stop-start, stop-start, to the back door in the kitchen. Where I leave him.

Take a cloth from my coat pocket. Rinse it in water from the cold tap.

Double back to the bottom of the stairs. Torch on. Wiping away at the blood in the carpet.

To and fro five, six times. I doubt it is enough. But it will have to do. I will check it again in the morning.

I open the back door of the kitchen. Step outside. All is still and quiet and peaceful, and everything I do, each bump and knock, every footstep, the long dragging of his body, will be a cacophony of noise. To be heard by her. And by anyone else who is awake. The Man in the Suit. Someone walking a dog. Widow Woman. To be heard and remembered. Recalled when interviewed by the police later on.

And I pull Andrew Lumb's body, drag-stop, drag-stop, drag-stop, to his back gate. Lay him down. Retrace my foot-steps. Lock the door. Sweep the snow on the patio with my left boot so that it looks even. Open the back gate. Check the alleyway. It is dark, but I do not want to shine a torch up and down to make sure there is no one there. All is clear. So far as I can see.

I drag him through into the alleyway. Lift the latch and push open my gate. Drag him inside. Lay him down again. I go back and shut his gate. Kick the snow this way and that in the alleyway, evening it out. Pull my gate to, waiting for the click as the latch falls back into place. But I am distracted as I step back inside my garden. My eyes are suddenly on the nookery. A noise, possibly. I wait to see a movement at the window. A light going on. Her face appearing at the window. Rubbing the pane with the side of her fist. Looking out. Seeing me.

I walk quickly to the back of the nookery. Lean my head towards the window. Listening in. Ready to duck down if I hear her coming towards the door.

And then I hear it. High up above. Clear and unmistakable. The sound of the helicopter. Back again.

I cannot see lights. It must be too high. But I panic as I imagine the pilots looking down. Using some sort of equipment. To see me in the garden. Andrew Lumb by my back door.

I have no choice but to act fast. I open the back door into my kitchen. Turn round and drag Andrew Lumb's body up and over the ledge and onto the kitchen floor. I stop and listen. The helicopter sounds as though it is coming in closer. I wonder if it has seen me. It is flying lower to take a look.

I drag Andrew Lumb into the hallway. Stop to gather my breath. No noise from within the cottage. Fluffy will be lying in his bed by the fireplace. She will be fast asleep in the nookery. Wrapped up deep beneath a warm duvet.

I open the cellar door. Walk backwards down the steps, dragging him along with me. There is a moment when I think I may lose my balance with the weight of the body. Tumbling back with his body falling onto me, both of us landing with a loud thud at the bottom. But I take an extra step back to keep Andrew Lumb's body at a distance, and we are finally in the cellar. I cover him with a tarpaulin and put him in the corner. I hurry back upstairs and lock the cellar door behind me, slipping the key into my pocket. Then I hear a sudden noise, something like a click.

I stand in the hallway and listen. And wait, my nerves on edge. But all is quiet inside the cottage.

I step quickly into the kitchen to see if I can hear the helicopter. I cannot. It has gone.

I smile to myself and laugh. A sudden sense of release. I have got away with it. It is time for bed.

17

SATURDAY, 30 NOVEMBER, 7.33 AM

J ust gone half-past seven. I have been sitting quietly by the kitchen window, nursing a mug of tea for forty minutes or so. I have my binoculars by my side, hoping to see the robin in my garden. I have forgotten to watch for it for a while, what with one thing and another. I do so now, as I am struggling to keep calm.

I do not know what today will bring for what is becoming an increasingly strained relationship. I cannot walk away from it. I wish I could. Neither can she walk away. At least, I cannot let her do so. We are locked together – and we are doomed.

I am waiting to hear the creaking of the nookery door and for Fluffy to come clippety-clopping out, ready for his walk. Even in the deep snow and the cold wind, I enjoy walking. It gives me the chance to think things through. To try to settle myself.

7.38 a.m. 7.42 a.m. I am starting to get edgier. I can feel it. The medications I have stopped taking work both ways, of course. I know that. When I was taking them, they kept me balanced and in check. They dulled my senses so that I could cope with things, life, really.

I came off medication so that I could feel the highs more. Meeting her. Being with her. Creating a new and happy life together. I would not want to have had that joy muted by medication. Off tablets, I seem to have less patience. I can also sense my anger down below. It bubbles away. Never far from the surface.

I am angry now. I have a schedule. Through the day. Things I do at certain times. I have relaxed my breakfast routine since she arrived. We eat forty-five minutes to an hour later. But I still like to have a structure to my day. I have a need to keep busy.

Fluffy is still wrapped up beneath Rosie's duvet, no doubt making that snuffling, snorty noise he does when he is asleep. He has put my schedule and everything else out.

Gone 7.50 a.m. now. Almost 7.55 a.m. I finish my mug of cold tea. Put it in the sink. I am dressed and ready to go. Warm hat and coat. Gloves. Wellington boots. I pick up the lead and poo bags on the side. And his little tartan coat. My little McFluffy.

I am at the nookery door. I listen. All silent. No sound of movement. I tap on the door. And again. A little louder. I bang on it. Much louder than I need to.

I hear an "uh" as my banging wakens her. I imagine her sitting up in bed, confused for a moment. I bang again to get her attention. I know it sounds urgent, more important than it really is, as I bang once more. Then stop as I hear her footsteps pit-patting on the floor.

She opens the door. Hair astray. Eyes sticky. Tee shirt. She has the duvet wrapped tight around her. It is as cold in there as it is out here. She looks at me with her blank face.

"Fluffy," I say in a raised voice. I know I sound angry. I lower my voice and slow my words. "I just want to get him walked. It's almost eight." It sounds accusing. The last sentence. I smile. More of a grimace.

She yawns, not taking it in. Then turns back towards the bedroom. "He's not here," she says. "I thought he was with you."

Her nonchalance panics me. I had assumed he had scratched at the nookery door some time in the night to be let into her bedroom. I shout at her to check for Fluffy in her room. Bathroom. Kitchenette. "Now!" She jumps, startled.

I turn and hurry towards the kitchen and the back door, trying to remember what I did after I left Andrew Lumb's body covered by a tarpaulin in the cellar. I had assumed Fluffy was still lying in the living room. But I did not check. Instead, I listened for the helicopter at the back door of the kitchen and went straight to bed. A sense of relief overwhelming me.

When I came down this morning, I glanced into the living room. Fluffy was not there, and I assumed he was with her. Never gave it a thought. I then went into the kitchen and noted the back door was slightly open. I just pushed it shut without thinking. The latch is loose. If it is not locked, the door sometimes blows open in a strong wind.

I think Fluffy must have followed me out when I went to the Lumbs' house. I pull the door open, expecting to see Fluffy out there dead by the step. But he is nowhere to be seen. The snow around the step and into the garden has been brushed even, but I can still see my trodden-in footprints to and from the gate. The back gate is slightly open. Enough for Fluffy to have gone off in search of shelter and warmth.

I lurch desperately into the garden.

A sudden intake of breath as my body chills, and I feel the wind on my face. And something else.

An utterly overwhelming sense of distress.

I SET off across the fields as fast as I can. Our regular walk.

Desperately scanning the white landscape for any sign of Fluffy. Hoping he's somehow followed our usual route and perhaps got lost. That I will find him sheltering somewhere.

I know, deep down, this is a forlorn hope. That I will not find him alive.

Fluffy did run off once before, just after I got him from the Blue Cross. He would have been ten years old then; he'd been in the Blue Cross centre for no more than two days when I came along. I liked the look of him immediately. He sat there in his cage all straight-backed and dignified whilst the dogs around him whined and barked and pawed at the bars of their cages.

The staff let me take him out, and he walked to heel straightaway, and when we got back and I sat on a bench talking to the young girl who worked there, he rested his head on my knee and looked up at me with his chocolate brown eyes. I fell in love with him then and have loved him ever since.

One weekend, early on, I drove to Rendlesham Forest with him. We parked by the side of the road and headed off along a path in amongst the trees. He was on a long lead, and I noticed that he liked to pull ahead, sniffing and searching, darting one way and the other, as we went along. I don't think he'd been to a forest before. So many new smells. How excited he was, tugging at the lead.

It got to a point where, as he seemed such a well-behaved dog, I unhooked the lead from his collar. He ran straight off after something, a rabbit most likely, and disappeared from sight into the undergrowth. For hours. Literally, two and a half hours. Close to three. I was beside myself. As I finally gave up the search and went back to my car, I saw him sitting straight-backed and dignified by my car. I cried when I saw him.

As I am crying now, walking, almost running, along the side of the path.

I am calling for him. Over and again. And whistling. I have a little *peep-peep-peep* ... *peep-peep-peep* whistle I do just for him.

But there is nothing, no sound, no movement ... just a long stretch of white as far as I can see.

There is a ditch on the far side of this field, running parallel to a path that leads to another lane and beyond. It has struck me that, in the snow and ice, Fluffy may have chased a rabbit across the field and, in his excitement, fallen into the ditch. My old boy, seeing the white tail of a baby rabbit, suddenly becoming a young and eager pup again.

I reach the ditch and walk its length, looking down, fearing what I might see. I do not think that Fluffy, at his age and perhaps with a broken leg, could have made it through the night with the temperature at minus two or three degrees. But I have to hope and, no matter what, I have to bring him home. I could not bear to leave him out here, abandoned and alone, to the vermin and the elements.

I see, at the far end of the ditch, something there, a darkness, a shape half covered by the snow, partly exposed. I move towards it, stumbling in the deep snow where it has not been walked in and remains all white and frosty. The thought of Fluffy dying here, struggling to get out of the ditch, breaks my heart. How could I have been so stupid, so careless, as to let him outside to wander off into the night.

It is not him, thank God.

Just a Waitrose carrier bag with what looks like a large black oil tub in it – used for topping up car engines.

I do not know what it is doing there.

I move towards the path that leads to the lane and,

beyond, the next field. The snow is crushed into a frosty ice in places; I can see the footsteps that have trodden here. I would never have believed there would be so many. I thought this was a barely trodden path. I look to see if I can see paw prints, Fluffy's paw prints, but the ground is just a mishmash of imprints of heavy shoes and boots. I cannot tell them apart.

The field is a blanket of white, and I can see the prints of animal feet that have criss-crossed it; I am no expert, but I think I can see a fox's paw prints and the prints of birds, maybe even seagulls, here and there, where they have landed, searching for food. I strain my eyes to see a pattern of Fluffy's paw prints as he made his way across the field. Going out. Or on his way back home. But there is nothing.

I stand here, turning slowly 360 degrees, and I can see all across the fields and the lanes in all directions. I see no paw prints anywhere close to me. No odd shapes in the snow further out. Nor dark masses. I whistle. *Peep. Peep. Peep.* Our secret code. *Peep. Peep. Peep.* Just Fluffy and I know it is me calling for him, calling him back to his breakfast, fresh chicken and biscuits at the weekend, and his nice warm bed by the fire.

Peep, peep, peep, I go. *Peep. Peep. Peep.*

But there is no response. He is not here. This side of the cottage.

I turn and trudge back. Any sense of hope was fading. Now it's almost gone.

BACK AT THE COTTAGE, it strikes me to check the CCTV. To see if it shows Fluffy leaving, and whether he went left or right.

But the hard drive on my age-old system is full; it has stopped recording. I drop my head in despair. And frustration at my inattentiveness.

I will spend all day searching for Fluffy. Until it is dark. I owe him that. My best pal. I am in torment. Flooded with grief.

In the morning, I go up and down the lane, looking side to side as I go. I *peep-peep-peep* a whistle every few yards. Then stop and listen. There is no response. I know in my heart that Fluffy has gone. *Peep. Peep. Peep.* But I have to keep going. Check every possibility.

I knock on almost every door in the lane, staying there, banging ever more loudly, until someone answers. "Have you seen my dog?" I ask. "A Jack Russell," frantic at first, then more subdued and finally in a despondent tone. I cannot bring myself to knock on the Man in the Suit's door nor Widow Woman's. Instead, I stand and scan the land around their properties. Hoping to see something, my old friend walking on shaky, arthritic legs towards me. With no success.

There are no houses to the right of the lane, just a long line of conifers, beyond which there is an endless ditch full of snow and ice and fields rolling away forever into the distance. Fluffy may have gone through the trees somehow, after a rabbit, and fallen into the ditch. Or somehow made it across to the fields. I walk and walk and walk. There are no signs of Fluffy anywhere. On and on I go, never giving up.

Wet and close to exhaustion, I force myself to go back to the cottage at one o'clock. To get a hot drink and warm myself through. To start over. Have another go in the afternoon. To keep searching until I have looked everywhere he might have gone.

She puts a bowl of mince in front of me. "I invented this," she says. "With stuff from the cupboards." I spoon it down, trying not to gag on the spices. I do not like food like this.

She is not sympathetic about Fluffy, telling me how gangs from London roam the countryside for small dogs to act as bait in dog fights in the cities. I leave as soon as I can. It is not what I want to hear. Everything she says and does sets me on edge.

Angry now, I knock on the door of 5 Bluebell Lane. The Man in the Suit's house. As I stand on the front doorstep, faced with this futuristic mix of oak and steel, I feel fury surging in me. A mix of so many negative emotions. *Clunk. Clunk. Clunk.* He slides back bolts. Opens the door. I show him my favourite photo of Fluffy, from our first Christmas together. Fluffy has a party hat on. "Have you seen my dog?" I say in a neutral voice.

He glances, disinterested, almost disdainful, at the photo. "No," he replies bluntly. I turn and go before he can add, "Fuck off."

And I am walking up to Widow Woman's house. I have to try everywhere. "I've lost my dog," I blurt out as she opens the door. "Fluffy ... he got out the back gate ... has gone off. He's not here." And it is all I can do not to cry. I see the boy, Conor, standing behind her at the end of the hallway. He waves at me. I put my hand up, acknowledging his presence. The small girl is there, too, but she ducks back out of sight just as soon as she sees me.

Widow Woman reaches out and rests her hand on my arm. I want to pull it back, but do not. "We will look across the fields on our walk," she says in a gentle, put-on voice. "This afternoon. If he's out there, we'll find him. Don't you worry."

I nod and smile my thanks. And then I am turning to disguise my tears and am gone, off to the main road at the top of the lane, to walk its length and breadth before going home. The hours drag out to the point of exhaustion.

I return to the cottage when it is dark. I know now that Fluffy must be dead. Wherever he is. He could not have survived out there so long on his own. I sit, my head hanging, at the kitchen table.

"Has anyone called ... has the phone gone at all?" I say to her as she comes in the kitchen a half hour later. I suddenly recall that the Blue Cross had microchipped Fluffy. Had he been found and taken to the police or a vet or the Blue Cross, someone may have been trying to get in touch.

"No," she answers as she moves towards the oven to dole out her latest meal into bowls. As I look down into the bowl of mince with red and green peppers, this guts and innards slop, it is all I can do to swallow it down between mouthfuls of water. I'd rather lie down and die.

We eat in silence. Going through the motions of basic civility.

Things have turned even further between us now. Unmistakably.

As we finish, she gets up. Goes to the nookery. Leaves the washing up and drying to me.

I sit there at the kitchen table for ages.

My head down, beyond tears now. The hopelessness of my life. My utter gloom.

There is a sudden knocking at the front door.

I would normally ignore it. The knocking. It is dark and late; there can be no one there whom I would want to speak to. But I have Fluffy on my mind. And the knocking triggers a surge of hope within me. That maybe he has somehow been found somewhere.

That someone from the Blue Cross is standing there now, outside my door, holding Fluffy in his arms. And I will open the door and see Fluffy there, looking at me, his mouth open, his tongue out, panting. Exhaustion, possibly. But excitement, seeing me, as likely.

And I am up and moving out of the kitchen and into the

hallway and to the front door. Where I pause. Leaning forward. My head against the wood. Trying to suppress, to quell, the hope that is rising in me, overwhelming me. The complete and utter joy.

It is the boy. Widow Woman's grandson. But no Fluffy.

Just the boy and his earnest, eager little face.

I hesitate. But I invite him inside. Out of the cold.

We stand there awkwardly in the hallway for a moment or two. And I wonder whether I should have asked him in at all. What Widow Woman would have said to him. About not talking to strangers. Let alone going into a stranger's house. Then again, maybe I am not seen as a stranger by her. And I think she must have sent him here. To say something to me.

He bends down to take off his wellington boots. As if it is rude not to, in someone's home. First one, then the other. He stumbles slightly, pulling at the second boot, and tips back against the front door. I steady him by taking his arm. I then go down onto my knees to help him take off his boot.

He stands there, still dressed in his coat and hat and gloves, but with his boots now off. I gesture towards the living room, inviting him in. Then lead the way. He follows me. There is a sense of embarrassment somehow, of not being sure what to say or do, in this strange situation. Or perhaps that's just me. Knowing it's not a good idea for an adult to be alone with a child these days.

He flushes suddenly, all excited, and swallows, about to speak his prepared words. The words Widow Woman will have told him to say. Probably on the doorstep, not indoors, but no matter now.

"We saw paw prints going over towards the farm ... your dog may be in one of the barns." He looks at me and grins.

"Granny says ..." He stumbles over the words he is meant to say. "It was getting too dark to search, but we can all search tomorrow morning. My granny knows the farmer." There, he got it out just so.

I smile back at him, touched by the eager excitement on his face. But I know this is futile. To get to the farm, you have to cross three fields and two lanes, and even then, the farm is some way down the third lane on the right. Somewhere you get to with a stout, fifteen-to-twenty-minute walk through snow. Fluffy won't be there.

I thank him, though, and it seems somehow right and proper, with this well-mannered little boy, to acknowledge his help. I decide to shake his hand rather than go for another elbow bump. I put my right hand out towards him. He grins and pulls the glove off his left hand. Then the right. Confused. Laughing. We shake hands. I shake it up and down theatrically, and he joins in and laughs again. This delightful little fellow.

And we are back in the hallway, and he sits on the step at the bottom of the stairs. Where Andrew Lumb's skull cracked open. Pulling on his boots. He does not seem to notice the small plant pot that's there. I am reminded suddenly of when I was a small boy, visiting my maternal grandmother occasionally, and she would always give me something to go home with. A fifty-pence piece for some sweets. Or a banana, if she were short of money that week. I tell the boy to wait there as I go to the kitchen.

I rummage in the cupboards, trying to find a chocolate bar to give to him. But I do not have a Mars Bar or a Milky Way or anything like that. There is nothing there he would like. Only cereal bars with rolled oats and honey. Old people's treats. But I want to give something to him.

So I hand him a cereal bar in the hallway, and he takes it cheerfully enough, thanks me, and says goodbye ever so politely. He adds that he'll see me in the morning. I am rather taken with this little chap. I don't know why. I think it is because he reminds me a little of myself at that age.

I turn to go back into the kitchen, and as I go through the hallway, I notice the door of the nookery clicking shut. She has been listening in to our conversation. I am not sure what to make of that. Nor why it bothers me.

SHE STAYS in the nookery all evening. I cannot hear anything. Even with my ear pressed against the door at regular intervals.

It must be so cold in there. And uncomfortable. With the heating and water turned off. I wonder how she manages. I suppose it has been worse for her. When she was on the streets.

I wonder what she is thinking. How she must feel about me to shut herself away like this. We cannot go on this way.

Fluffy weighs heavily on my mind. The grim reality is that, as an old dog in sub-zero temperatures, he will be gone, long gone, by now if he has been out in the snow and the wind and the cold for more than twelve hours.

If he is inside somewhere, a barn over at the farm, unlikely though that seems, he could maybe still be alive. If he is huddled away under straw, safe from the snow and the wind and protected a little from the falling temperature. Even that is an unlikely hope.

But he may have been found wandering somewhere. His best chance. And mine. He has a collar on, but no tag with "Fluffy" and my phone number or address on it. I don't know why. I never seemed to get around to buying one.

But he has been microchipped. By the Blue Cross. So they told me. At the back of his neck. Between his shoulder blades.

And there is some sort of database for chipped dogs on

the internet. And I have a little pamphlet somewhere. With Fluffy's microchip number written in it.

If I can go online, I can maybe see if he has been registered as being found. If not, I could at least email the local Blue Cross to tell them Fluffy is missing.

A sudden surge of hope. I get up quickly from my chair at the kitchen table to fetch the pamphlet. Too quickly, I think. A moment's dizziness. Nothing to worry about. I get it from time to time. It's just an age thing. And I have a stomach ache. That doesn't help. I don't want to move too quickly if I have a stomach upset. I once had an accident when I was locked away; it was not very pleasant. The staff thought it was some sort of dirty protest. It wasn't. I just got myself in a bit of a muddle.

I make my way upstairs to my room. There is an old-fashioned bureau, an inherited heirloom from my maternal grandmother, by the back window. It's where I keep my key documents: passport, driving licence, insurance papers and more. All filed in their own little spaces.

I look at the different compartments inside the bureau. They are filled with documents, some neatly put away, others pulled half-out haphazardly. I cannot remember when I last searched the bureau, nor what I was looking for. I have left it messier than I would normally do. I must have been in a hurry. I know Fluffy's documents are in the compartment to the far right, my miscellaneous section.

I used to look at them regularly in the days and weeks after I had adopted him. As if, by reading them time and again, I would somehow discover something about his past. The Blue Cross could not, perhaps would not, tell me anything other than his name was Harold, that he was about ten years old and that the "old boy" who'd had him had died. None of the old boy's children wanted to take on Fluffy.

I was so pleased and happy to have him. I had always wanted a dog.

We became friends. Dearest pals.

And now he has gone; I have failed him.

I sit there with the Blue Cross documents in my hands, unfolding and reading them again as if this is the first time I have seen them. I remember how pleased as punch I was the evening I got Fluffy. He settled down by my feet in the living room. In his new basket that I had bought from the Blue Cross, along with all sorts of other bits and bobs: two bowls, tins of food, different brushes, two types of shampoo and glossy grooming pads and no end of various squeaky toys, which he always ignored.

Those first few mornings, I'd nudge Fluffy out into the garden to do his business. When he was about halfway down the garden, before or after, I would whistle to catch his attention. As he looked up at me, standing on the doorstep by the kitchen door, I would squeak one of the toys over and over again. I would then throw it as far as I could. Most times, it would land just in front of him, and he would look at it as if he did not know what to do.

The only time he did react in any way was when I threw the squeaky toy as hard as I could and it hit him on the head. At that, he turned and walked away in a disdainful manner to the bottom of the garden, where he crouched and did his business. To start with, I did not pick any of it up, assuming that it would somehow decompose into the ground. After several weeks, I realised the error of my ways and spent an afternoon out there with my rubber gloves, a spatula and a Tesco carrier bag, which I filled up. We went for walks after that.

389476092376891. Fluffy's number. I reach for a pen in a pot on the top of the bureau. Scribble the number on a Post-it note. Check it's correct.

Then tidy everything away. Go downstairs with my sticky note. Sit in front of the computer. Turn it on, waiting for it to warm up and come to life.

Take my notebook with my various passwords in it on the side. Tap Q1W2E3R4 into the computer to gain access.

It won't let me in. I delete the password. Enter it again. One letter and number at a time. Q. 1. W. 2. E.

The E on the keyboard feels different. Sticky and stuck. I hit it two, three, four times with a finger, to loosen it. It seems to have a smear of jam on it. I wonder whether it is typing out as an *e* in lower case rather than an *E* in upper case.

I try again. Q. 1. W. 2. E. 3. R. 4. One at a time. Still, it does not allow me to enter. I had this once before when I could not get in. When I did the letters in upper case but kept my finger down on Shift when I did the numbers 1, 2, 3, 4 which came out as !, ", £, $. I now know to keep Caps Lock on, and I can just do the whole password in one go.

I try again and again. Without success. And growing increasingly frustrated. I need a new keyboard. And I do not know how I am going to get it. I cannot order it online. And there is nowhere to buy one in Felixstowe. And the roads out of town to Ipswich are too dangerous to drive on at the moment. I sit back and decide instead to telephone the Blue Cross in the morning.

I switch everything off. It's time to go to the bathroom and then to bed.

I feel down and despairing, and I have a stomach upset, which just makes me feel ten times worse.

The sooner I am in bed, wrapped up under my duvet, the better. I doubt that I will sleep, what with everything.

18

SUNDAY, 1 DECEMBER, 2.23 AM

I wake up and look at the bedside clock. 2.23 a.m.

I think for a second that I have heard a door open or close somewhere. But I've woken because I have stomach cramps.

Strong and intense. Doubling me over in pain.

I fear I have a stomach ulcer. These things are hereditary. My father suffered with his stomach all through my childhood and teenage years. I remember he had to be very careful about what he ate. So as not to exacerbate it.

My mother would sometimes feed him bananas and yoghurts and milky rice puddings instead of proper meals. I once called them "baby food" as we sat around the dinner table. It was a joke.

He shouted at me to be quiet and sat back and gurned with pain. As if even the effort of speaking was too much for him. It was hard not to laugh. But now I have the same excruciating, twisting pain.

I get myself up and sit on the edge of the bed.

I am sweating profusely despite the cold night air.

I need to make my way downstairs to take some sort of medication.

It occurs to me that her cooking may be the cause of my sudden pain. Bolognese and curry. These spicy bowls of meat and peppers. My body is not used to such exotic fare.

Truth is, she is keen and enthusiastic, but has little or no idea what she is doing. The meat is probably undercooked. And she cannot read properly. A teaspoon is likely to be read as a tablespoon. Or a bloody shovel.

But it is worse than that. The pain. This is more than an upset stomach. I have some sort of fever, too. I am scared of what that might mean.

I am at the staircase. Holding the handrail tightly.

Edging my way down.

Step by agonising step.

It could be cancer. In my blood. Coursing its way round my body. Into my vital organs. Into my brain. Rotting me away from inside.

I have always had a fear of a long, drawn-out cancer. Father's lung cancer. Eighteen months from decline to death. I am frightened of wasting away in a ward and a hospice where no one visits me. Breathing in the sickly sweet smell of my own death towards the end.

Or pancreatic cancer. My mother died of pancreatic cancer. From having a bad back to dying was little more than six weeks. I think the pain was intense. She cried a lot. She died alone. In the hospital. In the early hours. A doctor left a message on my telephone answering machine. I could barely understand what he was saying.

I am at the bottom of the stairs.

I do not know how I made it.

I am close to collapse now.

I have no idea what to do. I do not want to call to her. To wake her. To tell her that I am sick. More than that. Ill. Dying.

I have never known pain like this before. Crippling. Deep down inside. As if something is ripped, torn, blood vessels leaking into my stomach. I wonder if I will pass blood. Coughing it up into a spray.

I cannot call an ambulance. I do not think it could get down the lane. And I do not want to draw attention to myself anyway. Nor leave her here alone. I do not know what to do.

I sink to the stone cold floor. Make my way slowly towards the kitchen. On my hands and knees. I have an old bottle of kaolin and morphine somewhere under the sink. From God knows when.

I shake the bottle. Unscrew the cap. Drink mouthful after mouthful. I finish it. Two-thirds of the bottle.

Then lie down on my side on the kitchen floor. Curled up. Waiting for the agony to pass. Or the end to come.

I think this might be the end of me. What an ignominious way to go.

In the forest.

By the moonlight.

Shining through the trees.

I see the graves.

Not one.

Nor two.

But three.

All fresh dug.

And filled with corpses.

They all move.

And the soil.

It shakes and shudders.

And I wait for them to come for me.

I am awake. I do not know how I could have been asleep. I would have thought the pain would make it impossible. Maybe I am just slipping in and out of consciousness.

I do not seem to be able to move, curled up as I am on the

kitchen floor. If I stay in this foetal position, I can live with the pain in my stomach and back.

When I move, the pain shoots from my stomach, so intense that I can barely breathe. If I stay like this, quiet and still and on my side, I can at least breathe in and out.

In and out. In and out. In and out. I focus on my breathing. That this will keep me conscious. Keep me alive. It is so cold. And I am in agony. I just have to stay awake, alive, until the morning.

Until she comes out of the nookery. Into the living room. Through the hallway. Into the kitchen, where she will see me lying on the floor. Unmoving. Alive or dead. I wonder what her reaction will be.

There are three graves.

In the forest.

Always three.

I know who is buried in them.

I see their faces.

But I do not know their names.

I was told them.

But I cannot remember.

If I could just recall the names.

They would let me go.

And I would be free.

And I awake.

Freya. Nicole. Emily.

I am still in pain. But not agony. It is painful. But not agonising. I remain curled up in my foetal position, moving as little as I can. But it is more of a deep, dull ache now, less a sharp and stabbing pain. When I move. I try not to.

I am awake more than I am asleep. Unconscious. I try to ignore the dreams that crowd into my mind when I am not awake. The nightmares. They come at me repeatedly tonight.

I am bathed in sweat. The nightmares seem so real. It takes me a moment or two to realise I am conscious.

She. Her. Whatever. I have been thinking about *her*.

I cannot think of *her* by her chosen name any more.

I have worked it all out. What has been going on. I believe she has been trying to drive me mad. That she let Fluffy out and drove him away. That she has been poisoning me. With something she bought from the garden centre. I wonder what her reaction will be when she sees me here in the kitchen. I think she expects to find me dead. But she will find me still alive.

Shock.

Disappointment.

Fury.

I am going to stay awake now. Not let myself fall back into another nightmare. I am going to stay strong and alive. She will not find me dead on the floor. She will see me sitting up at the kitchen table. My feet on a chair. Drinking a cup of tea. And smiling. I will watch her face closely as she enters the kitchen. That split second when her thoughts and feelings are revealed before the bland and neutral mask she wears falls into place.

But I need to lie here a little longer. I am in pain when I move. An arm or a leg. My head on the cold linoleum floor. I think that if I were to try to stand up, even to sit, the pain would overwhelm me. And I would pass out. I just need to lie here and work things through in my head. And I must build up my strength.

Freya.

Nicole.

Emily.

They came here, and then they left.

To die.

In the forest.
In these graves.
That move. And shake. And shudder.
They are coming for me.
And I wait for them.
Freya.
Nicole.
Emily.

I am stronger now. The pain and the agony have subsided. There is still an ache in my stomach. But I can live with it. I stay in the foetal position but move my hands regularly. Followed by my feet. Arms and legs. And I lift my head up from the cold linoleum floor. I could get up now, but I do not. I lie here. As the sun rises and shines through the kitchen window. Thinking things through.

I have known, in my heart, that she could not leave. Not after what happened with Andrew Lumb. Had she gone, she would always have been out there somewhere. With that knowledge. And I would have lived the rest of my life in fear. Waiting for that knock on the door by the police. Two at the front. Two at the back.

I think she decided to stay anyway. To live here. She may have wanted Andrew Lumb. But she did not want me. And after his death, things soured between us. My refusal to let her use my daughter's ID. She has tried to kill me once. With whatever she put in the food she gave me. I do not doubt she will try again. Given the chance. She will not get it.

She sees me as a benign old fool. A weak man. A loser. Someone who is stupid. Despite what happened with Andrew Lumb, and the words she said – "you've murdered him" – she does not see me as a killer. But she is wrong. I have no choice. She has tried once. She will try again. It is her or me. As simple as that. I am going to have to kill her this morning.

GONE NINE A.M., and I am sitting on a chair in the kitchen by the table. Have been for a while now. Just waiting. Restlessly. I rather suspect she thinks I am dead and is having a lie-in. She'd normally have been up an hour and a half ago.

There is a hammer from under the sink on the chair beside me. I have tucked the chair out of sight below the table. I can reach and pick up the hammer in a moment. The kitchen door is pushed to. So I can see her face the instant she nudges the door open, expecting to see me dead on the floor. I want to see that face. To confirm my suspicions. To be certain. Before I kill her.

I am still in pain, and my clothes have dried in sweat and stick to my shoulders and back. I have not changed. All I have done is unlock the cellar door. Ready for her. After that, I will have a bath, a good and proper long soak, and be about my day. Searching for Fluffy over at the farm. Later, when the snow has cleared, I will pack up the boot of my car under cover of darkness, take my spade, and drive over to Rendlesham Forest.

I hear her. At long last. She is up. I listen to her humming as she comes through the living room. Her feet on the stone floor in the hallway.

She stops for a moment. There is silence. She is listening, I think. I wonder whether I will hear the creaking of the stairs as she creeps up to see if I am lying dead on my bed. I wonder, idly, what she intends to do with the body she expects to see.

I have a wheelbarrow in the garden shed.

That is where she would take me.

Before continuing her life here .

She is coming towards the kitchen. The door swings open. Like she owns the place. She looks at me, startled for a

split second, then carries on as if nothing is out of the ordinary at all. "Morning," she says simply as she goes to the
fridge. As if it is just another morning.

But I saw her face.

I know the truth.

She tried to kill me.

"I overslept," she adds as she brings out a carton of orange
juice, goes to the cupboard for a glass, and pours herself
some of the orange juice. "I'd have made breakfast."

"What would you have made? For breakfast? For me?" I
reply, trying to keep the sourness out of my voice.

She shrugs and kind of laughs. "I don't know. What would
you have liked?" As if we are playing some sort of cat and
mouse game. She thinks she is the cat. She isn't.

"I imagine it would be something spicy, wouldn't it?"

"For breakfast?" She laughs again and pours herself some
more juice. Then moves toward the bread bin and toaster.
Her back to me.

Enough of this charade. I could pick up the hammer now.
Walk across. Hit her as hard as I can on the back of her head
as she turns towards me.

Once and once only. To do it. To be done with it.

But there is something I want to do first. Something I
need to say.

"You are not the first girl who has come to stay here when
they have been down on their luck," I say as steadily as I can,
in an even voice.

She turns and glances at me. A half-smile. She reaches for
a bowl and a packet of Weetabix as she waits for the toast.

"The first was a Dutch girl called Fenna. She was a
backpacker who missed the last train to London. I gave her
a bed for a night. In the nookery. Where you are now. Same
bed."

She turns and glances at me again. Another vague smile.

A sense of uncertainty. She goes to the fridge for milk for her Weetabix.

"She could have stayed here. If she wanted. Lived with me. I thought she was a nice girl. But when I woke up the next morning, she had gone. I don't know when she left. But she took my wallet and my cards and cash. I'd left it on the side over there." I point to the tea, coffee and sugar jars close to her.

She looks at them as if she expects to see my wallet there. I think she is playing games with me. Again. It angers me, this insouciance. I have always hated stupid people who think they are clever. Cleverer than me. Few people are.

"Then there was Elsa," I explain. "The second girl. I met her by the railway station in Ipswich one night. Brought her back here. Hid my wallet and most of my valuables. Put them up in my bedroom. I came down in the morning, and there was no sign of her. Other than a wet patch in the corner of the nookery. Nice, that was."

She turns away to sprinkle sugar on her Weetabix. I cannot tell what her reaction to my comments is. A look of horror. A smirk. I do not know. She angers me so much.

"There have been other girls stay since then," I say. "I have always tried to help them ... although ... three of them are dead now."

The toaster makes a pinging noise as the toast pops up halfway through my final sentence. I do not think she heard me properly. Nor my voice cracking.

She has her back to me, putting toast on a plate from a cupboard. She is about to turn again to get a buttery spread from the fridge. Then stops and opens the cupboard where I keep the jam and the marmalade and my favourite lemon curd.

I reach for the hammer. It's on the chair under the table next to me.

I get up out of my chair and move towards her.

I will make this as quick and as painless as I can. God help me.

PART V

THE FARM

19

SUNDAY, 1 DECEMBER, 9.36 AM

As I get to my feet, there is a sudden hammering at the front door. A woman's voice calling out incongruously: "Oo-ee." Children's chatter and laughter. Someone bangs excitedly on the living room window.

Widow Woman. The two grandchildren. The boy and the girl. To look for Fluffy. As if it is all a game. I had not expected them until at least eleven o'clock or later. I don't know why. But they should not be here now nor for ages. It's far too early for a Sunday morning.

I drop the hammer on the chair. Step back. Gulp in breath. She turns and looks at me. Up and down. It is a peculiar look. Something almost sympathetic. I cannot make it out. I think I must look hot and ill. I certainly feel it. I may also stink of soaked-in sweat.

"Who's that?" she asks.

Of course, she does not know they are here to search for Fluffy. She was in the nookery last night. Waiting for me to die. I still feel ill. But she will die before me. Be sure of it.

"The woman from the top of the lane. Widow Woman. Angela Willis," I answer. "With her grandson and granddaughter. Conor and ... ah, Bella, I think. They saw Fluffy's paw prints last night. They know where he is. They're going to show me."

She swallows. I know why. Because she let Fluffy out. Maybe took him over the fields whilst I slept the previous night. Dumped him in a ditch. Left him to die.

There is more banging at the door. This huge sense of excitement. And adventure. And, before I can say anything to her or her to me – that I will go and she will stay – there is a commotion at the back gate. The boy and the girl come through and up to the kitchen door. They stand there, grinning. The girl presses her face against the pane. Nostrils splayed. Teeth bared.

She swallows again. Knows that she has been seen. Has to play along. She looks at the happy girl. Then the cheerful boy. And smiles back. There is nothing else she can do but go with it. As must I. For now.

I gesture to her to let them in. As I go to the front door to greet Widow Woman and her wretched dog, who puts his nose straight into my crotch as if we are long-lost friends.

And we are all then in the hallway. Introductions. Smiles. Laughter. False bonhomie. Hats and coats and gloves and boots on for her and me. She is coming, too.

And off we go down the path. The five of us and the dog. The Famous Five on an utterly pointless Enid fucking Blyton adventure. I just hope nothing out of the ordinary happens. That we get back to the cottage as soon as possible. And I can finish what I was about to do.

IT IS a dull and overcast morning, with black clouds in the distant sky. It is still cold. Snow and ice lie on the ground as we head towards the first field.

The boy leads the way. Head down. Determined. As if he is in charge. He knows where he is going. The girl keeps up with him, anxious to be by his side, if not in front. She follows close behind the two children. But on her own.

I am at the back, a little way behind, with Widow Woman next to me when she can. We take it in turns to go in front when we cannot walk side by side. I would rather walk alone. Her dog gets in the way as often as not.

Widow Woman asks who the young woman is.

Rosie, I reply simply.

And who is Rosie, she asks.

My niece, I answer nicely.

I do not want to say much. If Widow Woman questions her later, there is a chance she will give different answers.

What does she do? Widow Woman persists.

I pretend I cannot hear. With the wind and all.

I add that she has been staying with me since the snow fell. So I sound friendly.

Where does she live? Widow Woman goes on.

I pull a face. As if I cannot hear her clearly. But I want to be polite.

I then say she will be leaving shortly.

When she disappears, nothing will seem strange about it.

I turn and move in front of Widow Woman. I walk ever so slightly faster. Closing the gap with her in front. And the children who are pulling ahead in their enthusiasm. Widow Woman slips back, the fat Labrador by her feet, as she walks along as fast as she can to keep up.

We march now in line.

Single file along the path by the side of the first field.

Heads dipped in the wind on our way to the farm.

As I walk, the storm clouds gathering ever closer, my mind turns to Freya, the stray from the East End of London. I picked Freya up by the amusements at the seamier end of the seafront. I handed her a plastic bracelet I won on a penny cascade machine. She was standing next to me. She laughed and took it. I searched for and found her several times in the days and weeks after that. One arcade or another. Struck up conversations. Gave her money. Bought her blankets.

I invited her back. She accepted. I thought I was a clever man who picked well. I think, with hindsight, she picked me. I told her whatever I had was hers. Said she could spend her life here. I gave her money. And little surprise gifts.

One day, I came back from Tesco, with my bags full of goodies, to find she had gone. She had not taken anything from me, nor left anything behind. I searched far and wide for her without success. Six weeks later, I read of her death, almost in passing, in the local newspaper. An accidental drug overdose. A paragraph, that's all.

The boy stops as he gets to the edge of the first field. The girl stands by him, holding his hand.

They wait for the rest of us to catch up.

We stand there all together, the children full of breathless excitement. I glance at her face. She seems caught up in the moment, too.

Somehow, as we regroup and the children lead on again, Widow Woman and her dog are ahead of me, walking next to her. I am at the back, now stomping through the snow on my own.

And I can hear Widow Woman starting a conversation with her.

Rosie's a nice name, Widow Woman says.

I think she inclines her head, but does not reply.

Your uncle says you are staying until the snow clears?

Widow Woman's attempt to start a conversation.

She nods her head, but does not seem to add a comment to that.

I wish Widow Woman would shut up.

Are you at college? Widow Woman persists, desperate to find out all she can.

This busybody of a woman. Who gets on my nerves.

She says something in reply. I do not catch it. Widow Woman doesn't seem to either.

Widow Woman moves in closer. And, for a few minutes, their heads together, the fat Labrador between their feet, the two of them have some sort of prolonged conversation.

I cannot hear what they are saying. But it looks as though they are sharing confidences. Their heads almost touching as they pick their way carefully through the snow and ice.

They are pulling away slightly, quite naturally, as they continue walking. And she moves ahead, and Widow Woman and the dog fall behind. And Widow Woman turns towards me. She gives me a strange, triumphant look. And I wonder what has been said between them. And what it might mean for us all.

WE MOVE SLOWLY, step by careful step, to the side of the second of the three snow-covered fields we are crossing. The two children at the front. Then her. Widow Woman and the dog. Me at the back.

This farce. This nonsense. This pretence. That we will find Fluffy. And live happily forever.

We won't. She will be dead soon after our return to the cottage. Not immediately. I need to know what was said between her and Widow Woman first.

Widow Woman has her head ducked downwards, concentrating on her footsteps on the path.

Pulling the dog along. Its paw prints pattering out in the untouched snow of the field beside her.

I wonder what Widow Woman now knows. And what she is thinking about me. I know what I am thinking about her.

Nicole was a former drug addict from Norwich. She had been with me at the cottage for five, almost six weeks. We had become good pals. I was happy. And I thought she was, too.

But she kept disappearing. Weekend nights. I confronted her. I knew what she was up to. With men. I could almost smell them on her. She would not talk of it. We had words, strong words.

In the morning, she was gone. I did not try to track her down, I was so angry. And I stopped getting out and about for a while. Later, much later, someone in an amusement arcade told me she had died, choked to death on her own vomit. That didn't even get a mention in the newspapers.

We move towards the far side of the second field, to cross the lane that takes us over to the third field and the last lane and then the farm.

Widow Woman turns and looks at me again. A smug and self-satisfied look this time. I cannot make it out. It does not bode well. No, not at all.

I am not a man who makes excuses. I killed Andrew Lumb in anger. When I lost my temper. And I will kill her because I have to. It is her or me. But I do not know if I can kill in cold blood. To keep my secrets.

Widow Woman.

The boy.

And the girl.

WE STOP AGAIN after we have crossed the lane and stand looking across the third and final field before the farm.

We group ourselves around the boy, who is jigging about

with excitement. The girl is jumping up and down. I'm not sure she knows why.

There are glances between her and Widow Woman and smiles. Knowing looks. I let them pass. For now, anyway.

"We saw the paw prints all across this field," the boy says proudly, pointing ahead. Somehow, this Little Lord Fauntleroy charms rather than irritates me. I think it is his gleeful innocence.

"We all saw them," he adds. "Didn't we, Bella? Granny?"

The girl waves her hands in the air. Then spins round like a ballerina before falling over.

"We did," Widow Woman replies, and leads the way across the side of the field.

One long line this time.

Widow Woman. The dog. The little boy. The small girl. Her. Then me. On this endless march to nowhere.

Freya and Nicole have haunted me ever since. Both of them came from the streets. Had long since disappeared from society. And, with or without my intervention, were almost certainly on an endless downward spiral that could only ever end one way. Even so, I still blamed myself.

Emily from Bury St Edmunds was a posh girl from a private school. She had a falling-out with her parents. Then her boyfriend from nearby Stowmarket. Turned up at the pier. Needing a bed for the night. I obliged. We became close over the following days. Just good friends, as they say. But then she bumped into the boyfriend, who was searching for her on the prom one afternoon, and decided to go back to him.

I tried to persuade her not to. I should have tried harder. A few months later, in the local newspapers, I learned about her death at the hands of that boyfriend. The local press featured stories for simply ages. It even made the national newspapers for a while. And the television. I felt I failed her, too. She haunts me still. The three of them, really. In my dreams. My nightmares.

Widow Woman has her head down, just plodding on and on, occasionally pushing the dog out of the way with her right boot. Labradors are such stupid animals.

The boy and the girl are walking along hand in hand. The little boy is gazing across the field for signs of paw prints. The small girl is ambling along as best she can. She asks the little boy questions. He bows his head to answer them.

She walks comfortably enough, that strange stride in boots that look too big for her feet.

I am tiring now. I would really rather like to stop and turn back to the cottage. Be done with this stupidity. This childish adventure. But I cannot risk leaving them all together without me. I have to go on to the farm and back again.

She and I will then stand face to face in the kitchen.

I will ask her what was said between Widow Woman and her. Why the smiles? The sniggering? The looks?

I will make sure that she tells me before I strike the blow.

20

SUNDAY, 1 DECEMBER, 10.04 AM

"Here!" The boy shouts excitedly, pointing and moving towards the middle of the field as quickly as he can. He looks, with his gawky, awkward strides, like he is walking on the moon. "Paw prints!"

The girl tries to go after him, but her left boot gets stuck in the snow, and she stumbles over. Widow Woman and she go to help the girl up. Like a proper happy family, they are.

I stride by them and make my way over to the little boy. I rest my arm on his shoulder as if to balance myself. In truth, I am drawn to him and his eager cheerfulness. I then pat him on the back.

"There!" He grins and points.

"And there ... there ... there ... there ... all the way over there!"

He points across the field towards the next lane.

I look down and can scarcely believe what I see. There are paw prints, lots of them, just like the boy says. They are of a small dog that could so easily be Fluffy.

I know in my heart that these could be the paw prints of any small dog. And that Fluffy would be unlikely to have come this way. Nor this far. But there is hope. And hope is the best feeling of all.

The worst, too, if it is not fulfilled.

The little boy looks up at me as I struggle to speak, my words choked by tears. And the others then come towards us, and they start chattering away, as if this is the greatest adventure they have ever had.

"It's a dog that's lost," Widow Woman announces loudly over the top of everyone else. "And it is not a dog that was being walked. Look ... there are no boot prints anywhere nearby. This dog was walking on its own."

This is true. I had not really noticed. In my emotional state.

"And," she goes on, pointing to her Labrador, "these are the paw prints of a little dog, like a terrier. Like your dog. Look at Barry's paw prints."

I look at where the Labrador has just walked. The paw prints are clearly larger.

"And," she adds, as if she is Sherlock Holmes concluding a case, and all of us are hanging on her every word, "the lights from that farmhouse there would have been like a beacon to a lost dog in the snow."

I glance up and to my right, to the lane and along, and I can see the tall old building of the farmhouse. There are four or five windows on the upper floor. They may well all have been lit up when Fluffy got out in the early hours of the morning.

This is the farm where I buy my meats – where I bought two halves of a pig and other joints that filled my freezer before we first went into COVID-19 lockdown, and I was expecting Armageddon. That I have pretty much left untouched since then.

I have a thing about sawing bones. I don't know why. I

don't mind the squelch of cutting meat, but the sound of a saw on bone sets me on edge. So it's all just sat there.

This is also the farm where I bought sausages up to being snowed in, great long strings of home-made sausages, which I would cut up and fry and feed to Fluffy at teatimes. I wonder if, somehow, some happy memory has led my lost little Fluffy to this place.

There are looks of delight on everyone's faces. Even hers.

And Widow Woman speaks, pointing to telegraph poles in the lane that leads to the main road to the left and to the farmhouse to the right.

"I should have said ... there are posters up over there, too."

I rummage in my pockets for my binoculars. The ones I use to search for robins. I look through them, adjusting the focus until I can see the poster that is nearest to us.

And I see Fluffy's happy little face.

It is all I can do not to break down completely.

Instead, I hurry on, leading everyone towards the poster on the telegraph pole in the lane.

FOUND! is written in big black capitals across the top, although the black ink has run in jagged streaks down the poster. The damp in the night air turning into water, I assume.

There is a photo of Fluffy in the middle. He is being held by a teenage boy with bleached hair. It is what's called a selfie. Fluffy's tongue is lolling out. He is panting. I think it must have been taken just after he had been found.

There is a telephone number at the bottom, although the last two numbers are blurred and hard to read. "Fuller's

Farm" is clear enough though. The farm that is a minute or two's walk up the lane.

"He must have got out overnight ... gone exploring," I say, slightly choking on my words. I stop and gather myself together. "This is where we come to buy sausages ... he must have had a fancy for sausages for breakfast."

I wink at the little boy.

He gets the joke and smiles. Then thinks for a second or two, as if daring himself to respond in kind. He winks back at me. A big, over-the-top, theatrical wink. It's hard not to laugh.

I do an equally exaggerated wink at the small girl, who is looking at me with her ever-so-serious face.

Then she does a big clumsy wink with both eyes, more of an eye twitch, over and over again, than a plain and simple wink.

Widow Woman and she both see what we are doing, and they smile and laugh.

We stand there, the five of us with the Labrador on the lead, and I can sense the complete and utter joy in the whole group. I feel very emotional.

The little boy is now holding the small girl's hand. They are both jigging about. Full of happiness.

She grins at me and looks embarrassed. To show such emotion. I think suddenly that maybe she likes Fluffy. I had thought she had led him away. Maybe hurt him. Now, I am not so sure. This is not the reaction of a horrible person.

Widow Woman steps forward and pats me on the back. There is a brief moment where I believe she is going to lunge in and hug me. I hold my nerve. Keep still. And she does not. Instead, she speaks, taking charge.

"Well," she says emphatically, "let's go and get him!" And we do.

I lead us all on to the farm.

To be reunited with Fluffy.

My dear old pal.

WE WALK UP THE LONG, wide drive to the farm. Snow and ice have been swept clear from the middle of it to the sides. I have been here with Fluffy many times. He would always stop about halfway and sniff the air. That farmyard mix of animals and manure. Maybe the anticipation of sausages for tea.

The farmhouse is to the left. The farm shop to the right. It usually opens 10 a.m. to 4 p.m. on a Sunday, but what with the snow and the cold and the difficulty of driving in and out, it is shut today.

Other buildings and fields, with pigs and cows and chickens and more, are behind the farmhouse and farm shop, stretching into the distance. The reality of a working farm. I have never been further than the shop; the smells and the thought of some sort of abattoir are enough to keep me away.

We stand there for a moment. The five of us and the dog, who seems to have picked up the scent of animals in barns somewhere close by. Head up and slobbering. This fat and greedy Labrador, always wanting food.

We are waiting for something to happen.

Widow Woman takes charge again, taking us towards the farmhouse. The rest of us follow. The boy and the girl tuck in behind her, the little boy looking back over his shoulder and grinning and giving me a thumbs-up sign.

I respond the same way. A smile. A thumbs-up. A lovely moment.

If I had had a son, I would have wanted him to be like this little boy. Polite and friendly. All innocence and unconditional love.

The small girl is cute, too. Full of mischief. Loves her big brother to bits. I'd have been a good father to children like these. I know I would. Given the chance. Or a grandad. *Grandpa*. I like the name *Grandpa*. I love the idea of being *Grandpa*.

She drops in behind Widow Woman and the children to walk by my side for the first time since we set off. I glance at her. She is looking at me and smiling. It is a warm smile that unsettles me. She has not smiled at me like this before. With something close to genuine affection.

"I've really missed Fluffy," she says. "He was like a hot water bottle at night in my upstairs bedroom."

I look at her, not sure what to think. I wonder if she is indicating she wants to move back into the cottage itself. Maybe I think too much.

Did she let Fluffy out? Drag him across fields and abandon him to his fate? Or did I just leave the back door open, and the back gate, and Fluffy went off to explore like he did in Rendlesham Forest all those years ago? And got himself lost.

Thing is, I'm not certain. I think, maybe, I should give her the benefit of the doubt.

"Me too," I say finally. Not sure what else to add.

Widow Woman *rat-a-tat-tats* the knocker on the farm-house door. I can see through the window at the side of the door into a homely-looking, old-fashioned kitchen of pine and dried flowers. It might have been fashionable thirty years or so ago.

We stand there patiently. My heart feels as though it is rising towards my mouth. That it will choke the breath from me. The thought of seeing Fluffy is almost unbearable. And the hope that, when he sees us all, he will trot straight through to me in his excitement.

There is no response. Even though the lights are on and we can hear a television somewhere in the distance – a living room or a dining room, maybe, behind the kitchen we are now all peering into.

Silence. A long silence, other than the movements of the children's restless feet. And the whining Labrador, who wants some food.

And then, somewhere further up the driveway, behind the farmhouse and the farm shop, and beyond the barns and way back in the fields, I hear a whistling. Not my *peep-peep-peep, peep-peep-peep,* but something much like it.

I move back onto the main part of the driveway to see up into the distance. The others follow and gather around me. And I see a figure far away in the fields but heading in this direction.

A man.

With a dog.

My Fluffy.

We all wait as the man and Fluffy come closer. It is some way. The man looks young, but seems to be walking with what looks like a stick. A shepherd's crook might seem fanciful. Fluffy walks just behind in his footsteps, lifting one little leg at a time up and out of the snow and placing it carefully ahead of himself.

I think this might be the young man with the bleached hair in the photo on the poster. He does not seem to be wearing a hat despite the cold. Just, I can see as he comes into view, a scarf and gloves and a big heavy coat. I need one like that rather than this thin old thing that's seen better days.

He sees us and lifts his stick. The children wave at him. As does Widow Woman. And she does too. Rosie.

I do as well, caught up in the emotion of it all. Everyone, Widow Woman, the children and her, starts calling to Fluffy, encouraging him to run towards us. He remains as stoic as ever, walking step by careful step, as if concentrating hard, through the snow by the farmer's side.

The farmer hangs back and taps Fluffy lightly on the back with his stick, urging him forwards towards us.

There is a moment when I think they will all rush at him. That I will be left at the back, waiting for them to finish making a fuss. But the little boy suddenly steps back, taking his sister by the hand and pulling her gently away. And Widow Woman and Rosie, to either side, do the same. They are respectful, and I am touched by it.

And Fluffy walks stiffly through them all towards me – just as I had hoped – and I sink to my knees and fold my arms around him.

My old pal is safe and well. And back with me again.

I am filled suddenly with joy and happiness. And love.

And the overwhelming desire to put all that has happened behind me and just live happily ever after.

SUNDAY, 1 DECEMBER, 10.45 AM

I want to get away and go home as soon as I can.

But Widow Woman and Rosie are talking to the man with the bleached hair, and he is flush-faced by their attention.

Asking him about Fluffy and what happened.

And the man with the bleached hair, who is the youngest son of three sons of the couple who own the farm, is chatting away. I had always thought that farmers were dour and surly types. Not this one. He cannot stop himself. He tells Widow Woman about his older brothers, who are both at university, one just starting some farming course, the other soon to qualify as an accountant. He is doing his A Levels and does not know what he wants to do. He plays the guitar and would like to do something creative. He is, he says, artistic. He says he might like to be a tattoo artist.

Rosie hangs on his every word.

And he keeps glancing at her, more and more.

I just want to go back to the cottage.

Rosie, going all bashful, asks him how he found Fluffy. The boy with the bleached hair rolls off his well-prepared story. How he was coming back at 2 a.m. from a mate's house up near the roundabout. Saw Fluffy in the field by the lane. Lost and without a collar. How he took Fluffy in and warmed him by the fire and fed him scraps of chicken. Came out the next morning with home-made posters, which he stuck on poles, fences and posts up and down the lane and beyond. Had put copies, smaller leaflets, through every letterbox, wherever he thought Fluffy might have come from.

He swallows and looks at Rosie, and his face reddens at regular intervals.

She looks back at him, all wide-eyed innocence. Says she was thinking of getting a tattoo done. On her ankle. A lizard or something. She has not decided.

All I want to do is to turn around and go. To get back and make a proper fuss of Fluffy.

Trying to bring the conversation to a close, I thank him and say I must give him something for his trouble. I reach into my pockets before realising all I have in one are my keys and binoculars and in the other a dirty tissue and a half-eaten packet of Polos. But he is already telling me that it's no trouble, he's enjoyed having Fluffy and would love to come and see him again sometime.

At that, Rosie turns and smiles at me, as if to ask if it is okay to give him the address.

Before I can answer, she is saying, "Three Bluebell Lane," and starting to describe where it is and what the place looks like.

He nods and smiles at her and says he knows where Bluebell Lane is and which one it is.

And so we are leaving. Widow Woman and Rosie, with one final look at the boy with bleached hair, lead us away. Widow Woman dragging the fat old Labrador behind her. Then me, cuddling Fluffy in my arms, his head turned away from my face as if reproachful that I let him get lost. And finally, the children, all fidgeting and twitchy, either side of me and both reaching up to stroke Fluffy's legs as often as they can.

***

WE GET to the first field of the three we need to cross to get home. It is cold with a biting wind, but I seem to feel revived because of Fluffy's return.

Widow Woman and Rosie are again at the front, heads bowed close together, sharing thoughts and confidences. I think it will be stuff and nonsense about the bleached-hair boy.

The little boy and small girl walk beside me as and when they can, jostling for position to hold my arms and to stroke Fluffy as much as possible. He ignores it all, his head held high and aloof in the wind. My little prince.

I have to say I am rather taken with these children. Smitten, even. Their politeness and their manners (although he has sometimes had to move in to correct her). The way they stepped back so Fluffy could come to me. The fuss they are making of me now (even though it is as much about Fluffy as it is about me). I love their *joie de vivre*. They enthral me.

"I love Fluffy," the little boy says, taking hold of one of Fluffy's back legs. The excitement is clear in his raised voice.

"I love Fluffy," echoes the small girl, anxious not to be left out. She cannot reach Fluffy, so holds her brother's arm instead.

"He loves you, too." I smile down at them and waggle one of Fluffy's front paws. Fluffy takes no notice, as if he is far too grand for any of this silliness.

I put Fluffy down on the snowy path. He hesitates for a moment and then walks on after Widow Woman and Rosie. He is a well-trained dog and has never really needed a lead for as long as I have had him. He seems to know how far to go ahead or fall behind. The small girl darts forward, stumbles and regains her balance, and grabs at Fluffy, trying to lift him up. The little boy moves to help or admonish her, I'm not sure which, and the two children hold Fluffy together in a clumsy embrace.

"Let him down," I say as jovially as I can. "You can then walk beside him for this next bit."

The path to the side of the field is wider here, although, truth be told, the snow blurs the edges of it into the field.

Fluffy starts walking on slowly. As if he is rather put out at having to walk at all. The little boy and the small girl hurry to either side as though they are guarding him.

I have a sudden urge to walk closer to the children, and maybe even put my arms around their shoulders in a warm embrace. I think perhaps, sometime, I could become more to them than just the man down the road with the dog. A friendly uncle, at least. I like the idea of Grandpa, too. And so I do. Move forward. Put my arms gently around them as if steadying and protecting them from falling over. They both turn and smile up at me. And my battered old heart softens a little more.

We walk like this through the rest of the field, following in the footsteps of Widow Woman, the Labrador and Rosie.

It is a moment of almost perfect bliss. I feel like Father Christmas with two happy children about to get sackfuls of presents. And it strikes me suddenly that, for once and at long last, Christmas might be rather fun this year.

We all gather together at the end of the field and smile at each other. I can honestly say I haven't felt as happy as this for a long time. Maybe even ever.

FLUFFY TAKES us forward into the second of the three fields, seeming sure of the way home. The boy and the girl take turns to march with him, one to the side, one behind.

Widow Woman, after glances and smiles at me, tugs at the Labrador's lead, and they follow next. Her coquettishness no longer irritates, but now amuses me. She has a nice smiley face. And she is a good woman at heart, I think. Even though she has the biggest arse I have ever seen in my life. I think it is the arse that has put me off her most. I must try to ignore it as best I can.

Rosie walks beside me and, almost automatically, slips her arm into mine. I tense suddenly, at the unexpectedness of it, before relaxing. I am not sure if she has done it to stop herself slipping over or whether it is a gesture of affection. Either way, I do not mind so much.

"I really missed Fluffy," she says conversationally.

"Uh-huh," I reply neutrally.

"I went out and spent ages looking for him. Looked everywhere. I never thought of the farm," she adds, in a sad voice.

I am not sure if she really did go searching nor, if she did, exactly when that was. But I am happy now, so I let it go. Anyhow, it is not that easy to talk on the snowy path, where we are both concentrating on walking and not falling over. I nod, and not sure if she saw the gesture or not, I pat her arm with my hand. We walk on, trudging after Fluffy and the children and Widow Woman and the Labrador.

She says something or other about the farm and the boy with the bleached hair in a roundabout way. Like it's something and nothing. I know it's not. That it is a big deal to her.

I make various approving noises, suspecting that, at some point, she's going to ask if he can come round.

"I've decided not to do a cookery course," she then adds. "I'm not terribly good at it. I've had a tummy ache for ages."

And I realise that this – her not terribly good cooking –

may have been why I felt so ill overnight, and still do, in all honesty. My excitement at finding Fluffy – that burst of adrenaline – has kept me going so far and for so long. But my clothes are stiff and stuck to me with sweat. I think I probably smell really bad as well. And I need the toilet, too. At least she has acknowledged it. And I think perhaps I overreacted when I was first struck down. My mind playing tricks with me.

She says something else about the farmhouse and the boy with the bleached hair, as though she is just making polite conversation. I know it is more than that. Much more.

So I reply that he can come round and see Fluffy in a day or two. Maybe have his tea with us. They can take Fluffy for a walk together. She seems pleased as punch.

And I add that if she wants to sort out a course or something, we can have a talk about how she might do that.

And as we get towards the far side of the second field and everyone is waiting there for us, she turns towards me and smiles. I think for a moment that she might just lean forward and kiss me on the cheek. Like a daughter would do. And I will hug her. Like a dad would do. But instead she reaches into my pocket and takes out my front door key. "Bagsy the first bath!" she says, laughing.

And I laugh back.

We are at peace.

At last.

ROSIE HEADS across the third and final field towards Bluebell Lane and the cottage. To home. Our home.

Followed by the two children and Fluffy.

Leaving me to bring up the rear with Widow Woman and the Labrador.

"Rosie's taken a shine to Luke," Widow Woman says,

referring to the bleach-haired boy. I had not caught his name, in the excitement of the moment.

"Yes," I reply conversationally, trying hard to keep the breathlessness out of my voice. It has been a long walk through the snow and ice, and I have not felt that well. I am tiring now rather badly. I may have to stop. I feel dizzy.

We walk along slowly for a while in our companionable silence. Chuckling to ourselves at the way the two children keep pushing by each other to walk with Fluffy.

We seem to walk slower as they pull further and further ahead of us.

"I've said he ... Luke ... can come round and see Fluffy in a day or two," I tell her. "Maybe stay and have his tea." I stop for a minute to get my breath. I am out of puff. And my head is fuzzy.

"You're playing Cupid!" she says, stopping too. She gives me a funny look, and I wonder if I have something stuck on my face. Perhaps some dried vomit from the early hours. But it is an affectionate look, really. I've not had many of those over the years. If at all.

"Well," I reply, not sure what to add. "Anyway ... he seems a nice boy."

We start walking again. She takes my arm and holds it until we come towards the edge of the final field. We have fallen some way behind. And I wonder if she has engineered this moment so that we can be alone together for a while.

"I was talking to Rosie, and she said she would be happy to babysit for Conor and Bella one night."

There is a long pause.

"Oh yes?" I say.

"If we wanted to go out."

She looks at me again, and there is a kind of hopefulness in her face. As though she really wants me to say *Yes, I'd love to.*

"Yes," I reply with feeling. "I'd love to."

She smiles widely. And I wonder if she is expecting me to lean forward and kiss her. I feel I should do something. So I sort of untangle her arm and go to pat her on the back. She seems to think I am going to put my arms around her and draw her in for a passionate embrace, so she lurches forward.

We compromise and settle for an awkward hug. I keep my hand on her back for longer than I would have expected.

It has been a long and winding road, but I feel now that I am in a good place. And there are better times to come.

We walk into Bluebell Lane and head for home. And I wonder again what Christmas will be like this year. I think it might be really rather lovely. Just the happiest Christmas ever.

EPILOGUE

We hear the screaming at the same instant.

Widow Woman and I.

First one child. Then the other. I cannot tell which is which.

I am the faster of the two of us. Although, in wellington boots on snow and ice, it is more of a stomp than a run.

Widow Woman lags behind. I glance back and see her reaching inside her coat pocket for her mobile phone.

These are not screams of surprise, nor of childish drama. They are screams of fear and terror.

The screams come from the cottage.

I had assumed Rosie would return there. The little boy and the small girl carrying on to Widow Woman's bungalow.

But they have not.

They have all gone together into the cottage.

I push back the half-open front door, moving into the hallway.

The cellar door is open.

I move into the kitchen.

Rosie stands by the sink with Fluffy at her feet. Her left

arm is around the shoulders of the small girl. Her right arm is resting on the little boy's left shoulder. The children are both crying and shaking as they look at me.

I stand still and look back at them.

"What?" I say.

"They wanted to come in and play hide-and-seek with me," she says, with such anger in her voice. "They went to hide in the cellar. And found Andrew Lumb's body."

It happens so fast.

Widow Woman is behind me. She sees and hears and presses 999 on her mobile phone. Starts babbling away incoherently about a dead body.

I step forward and pick up the hammer that's hidden on the chair under the kitchen table. An instinctive reaction, that's all. No more, no less.

Rosie turns towards the block of knives on the side.

Pulls out the biggest knife of all.

Steps forward. One. Two. Three movements.

I look down at my tatty old coat.

The knife handle is sticking out of me, the blade inside.

I see the horror on the children's faces. I notice, for some reason, how much they look alike. It's the eyes.

I sink down to my knees.

Rosie kisses first the little boy and then the small girl on their heads. Kind of squeezes their shoulders.

There is blood all over my chest and stomach.

She bends to pick up Fluffy and walks by me to leave.

I am in such pain.

I imagine Rosie walking across the fields with Fluffy under her arm. Disappearing into the distance. Vanishing forever. I wonder whether she has some cash or my bank card tucked into her pocket. To keep her going for a while.

I slump suddenly onto my side.

Widow Woman crouches down and leans forward. Her

face is close to mine. She has a stunned expression. As if she cannot take it all in. I hear her jagged breath. Feel it on my face.

The pain is unbearable.

The little boy and the small girl stand there, still crying and shaking. He reaches for her hand. She takes it. She cannot take her eyes off me. Transfixed by the horror.

I roll onto my back.

"You have to hold on," Widow Woman says, "for as long as you can. Until the ambulance arrives. And the police. They won't be long. They're on their way."

I am holding my breath. Because I know, when I let it go, it will all be over.

I want to explain. To say I am sorry.

To Laura. And Lucy. I should have been there for you. Freya, Nicole and Emily. I should have saved you. And to Andrew and Rosie and Luke. For what I have ruined. And to Angela and Conor and Bella. For what might have been between us. A happy family. Please forgive me.

I open my mouth.

But it is too late. I am dying.

I let my last breath go.

THE END

ABOUT THE AUTHOR

Did you enjoy *The Girl Downstairs*? If you could spend a moment to write an honest review on Amazon, no matter how short, we would be extremely grateful. They really do help readers discover new authors.

Iain Maitland is the author of three previous psych thrillers, *The Scribbler* (2020), *Mr Todd's Reckoning* (2019) and *Sweet William* (2017), all published by Contraband, an imprint of Saraband. *Mr Todd's Reckoning* is coming to the big screen in 2023.

Iain is also the author of two memoirs, *Dear Michael, Love Dad* (Hodder, 2016), a book of letters written to his eldest son who experienced depression and anorexia, and (co-authored with Michael) *Out Of The Madhouse* (Jessica Kingsley, 2018).

He is also an Ambassador for Stem4, the teenage mental health charity. He talks regularly about mental health issues in schools and colleges and workplaces.

Find out more about Iain at www.iainmaitland.net

AUTHOR'S NOTES

The Girl Downstairs is my fourth psych thriller and, with the previous three, readers have often asked me similar questions – "Where did the story come from?" etc – via email and Twitter and at book launches and other events.

So I thought I'd write a few notes about how the book came to be.

I should probably state that if you've somehow come to these notes before you've finished the book, or even started it, you may wish to look away now. I'll not be too spoiler-ish though just in case you keep reading.

My best-known book, *Mr Todd's Reckoning*, which is coming out as a movie in 2023, features a sad and angry, middle-aged man, Malcolm Todd, living with his grown-up son, Adrian, in a cramped bungalow in Ipswich in Suffolk during the hottest summer since records began.

The basic story – two people trapped together with tensions rising and some terrible event seeming inevitable – really appealed to me and I wanted to do something similar to it again; albeit with a little twist and turn.

So I had the idea of Mr Adams, a kind of cousin to Mr

Todd, who lives alone in a house down a lonely lane in woodlands on the edge of Felixstowe in Suffolk. And he comes across a homeless young woman, Rosie, by Felixstowe Pier and, eventually, with the snow falling hard and endlessly, she makes her way to his home – her possible sanctuary - at 3 Bluebell Lane.

I live in Felixstowe in Suffolk and I set all my thrillers hereabouts.

Felixstowe is a good place for creepy goings-on. To some, with the pier and fun and games on the seafront, it's a jolly family resort. To others, with its woodlands and fields and the docks and that cold dark sea, it can be something more than that.

And I like to see the settings in my head – it just makes it all feel real.

So Mr Adams has Rosie in his house – his 'cosy cottage' – and it looks as though we are heading into a standard psych thriller with a creepy middle-aged man and a young woman in the cellar. You know the sort of thing. At the end, she stabs him and runs away to safety.

I wanted the book to subvert expectations especially for those who have read *Mr Todd's Reckoning* and would think 'Here we go again.' Mr Adams' past has brought him to where he is today and his motives are largely driven by his former experiences. So too is Rosie – Alice Beech – and, yes, there are shades of Mary Bell in here.

Those who have read my memoirs, *Dear Michael, Love Dad* and *Out Of The Madhouse* (with my eldest son Michael) will know much of my family background and related mental health issues. Mr Adams is not me but his back story and its consequences are very familiar to me from amongst wider family and friends.

I wanted the first part of the book to swing one way.

The middle part – with the Lump – puts the two main characters in a finely balanced equilibrium.

The third part of the book swings the other way.

And so, the ending - which will, I think, trigger the most questions. It would, I suspect, have been a nice poetic ending if I had stopped the book just before the epilogue with the prospect of a happy Christmas and a bright New Year ahead.

But I didn't. When I write books, and I really get into the writing and my mind is racing ahead of me and I cannot keep up on my keyboard, the story takes on a life of its own. And that's what happened here.

I had planned to end the story without the epilogue. But, as I came towards the ending, I saw all the characters in my head, felt I was in that setting and I suddenly heard all those noises ahead of me. And that's what took me into the cottage ... and the denouement.

Some readers will love it. Others will hate it. I like it. I hope you do too. Let me know...

Best Wishes

Iain

AUTHOR'S ACKNOWLEDGEMENTS

I'd like to thank ...

Brian and Garret at Inkubator Books for publishing *The Girl Downstairs*.

Dee Dee - I love your cover.

Barbara Nadel for the cover quote – thank you so much for your ongoing support.

My MS readers who double-checked various facts for me. Any errors, artistic licence aside, are mine and mine alone.

Mentioning artistic licence, I should state that Bluebell Lane does not exist – at least not in Felixstowe anyway. In my head, for those who know the town, it is Grimston Lane in Trimley St Martin but relocated beyond The Grove and Abbey Grove Woodland in Felixstowe.

All of the characters – Mr Adams, Rosie, the Lump, The Man in the Suit, Widow Woman etc – are figments of my imagination ... although Fluffy, to be fair, is the spit of my lovely old Jack Russell pal, Bernard (2004 - 2018).

Jodi Compton for copy-editing my MS – you made it a better read and I thank you for it.

Pauline Nolet for reading and correcting the proofs – thank you too.

And finally, my family – Tracey, children, partners and grandchildren. You are always in everything I do.

Printed in Great Britain
by Amazon